The Debs

Love, Lies, and Texas Dips

ALSO BY SUSAN McBRIDE

The Debs

The Debutante Dropout Mysteries

Blue Blood

The Good Girl's Guide to Murder

The Lone Star Lonely Hearts Club

Night of the Living Deb

Too Pretty to Die

Susan McBride

The Debs

Love, Lies, and Texas Dips

DELACORTE PRESS

Delacorte Press is a registered trademark and the colophon is a trademark of
Random House, Inc.

Visit us on the Web! www.randomhouse.com/teens
Educators and librarians, for a variety of teaching tools, visit us at
www.randomhouse.com/teachers

Library of Congress Cataloging-in-Publication Data
McBride, Susan.
The debs : love, lies, and Texas dips / Susan McBride. — 1st ed.
p. cm.
Summary: Houston debutantes, Laura, Mac, Ginger, and Jo Lynn, fall in love and
plot revenge amid their first round of etiquette classes.
ISBN 978-0-385-73520-9 (trade) — ISBN 978-0-375-89100-7 (e-book)
[1. Debutantes—Fiction. 2. Interpersonal relations—Fiction. 3. Wealth—Fiction.
4. Houston (Tex.)—Fiction.] I. Title
PZ7.M478276Dh 2009
[Fic]—dc22
2008024931

The text of this book is set in 11-point Berthold Garamond.
Book design by Trish Parcell
Printed in the United States of America
10 9 8 7 6 5 4 3 2 1
First Edition

To Ed, my one and only,
and living proof that sometimes
the geek does get the girl

THE GLASS SLIPPER CLUB
DEBUTANTE PROGRAM

Overview of Rules

- Ten qualified girls (Rosebuds) will be selected each year, the first week of Pine Forest Preparatory's fall semester, to comprise that season's Glass Slipper Club Debutante class.

- Debutantes must be in good standing academically and must demonstrate high morals.

- Regular meetings will be held the first Monday of each month from September through May. The season will culminate with the Rosebud Ball the last weekend of May.

- The debutante class will receive training in deportment and dance, and will attend specially arranged functions, such as teas, luncheons, and philanthropic events.

- All debutantes will be daughters or granddaughters of members of the Glass Slipper Club, or will be sponsored by an active GSC member.

- Parents, grandparents, or guardians of debutantes are required to make a $12,000 donation to the Glass Slipper Club Foundation.

- Each family of a selected debutante must purchase a table at the Rosebud Ball.

- Each debutante will select a young man of quality to be her peer escort to the ball. However, her father (or another male family member) will present her.

- Debutantes are responsible for purchasing their own ball gowns* and gloves and for the cost of professional photographs. (*In order to ensure that no two Rosebuds' gowns are alike, prior to the ball each gown will be cataloged for reference.)

- During their debutante year, all Rosebuds must dress appropriately, per GSC Selection Committee standards, with no visible tattoos or piercings (other than a single piercing in each ear) and no excessive use of makeup.

- Debutantes should exhibit proper etiquette and ladylike demeanor during all GSC events (for example, no chewing gum, eating with hands, etc.).

- Rosebuds must maintain a "clean" lifestyle and refrain from using drugs and alcohol.

- If a Rosebud demonstrates blatant disregard for GSC standards, an appointed member of the Selection Committee will speak with her. Should said member so recommend, the board will be notified, as will the girl's mother.

- Should the board deem it necessary, a debutante may be removed from the program, and eligible girls on the waiting list will be considered to fill the vacancy.

A Texas dip is quite literally
a to-the-floor curtsy in which
the debutante gets so far down
on her high heels that her dress flares out
around her like a marshmallow.
As the coup de grâce, she lays her left ear
on her lap for a moment. The reason she
turns her head is to prevent getting
a lipstick mark on her virginal white dress.
—*Girls on the Verge: Debutante Dips,
Drive-bys, and Other Initiations,*
by Vendela Vida

Don't let a man put anything over you
except an umbrella.
—Mae West

No one jerks me around.
and gets away with it.
—Jo Lynn Bidwell

One

Where is everyone?

Jo Lynn Bidwell entered the Houstonian's Grande Ballroom in a rustle of tulle petticoats and silk. She'd expected to hear music, to see the arch of raised military sabers that she was supposed to walk beneath on her daddy's arm when she was formally introduced, but the enormous room was dead silent.

"Hello?"

Despite her elbow-length white kidskin gloves, goose bumps rose on her arms, and she rubbed them as she wandered around, gazing up at chandeliers that dripped from the ceiling. The crystal-beaded lamps were bare, without the clouds of white dendrobium orchids Bootsie Bidwell had said would be flown in from Hawaii to decorate the room for the Rosebud Ball. Jo noticed too that the tables had no linens, and there were folding chairs parked around each. *Where are the gold Chiavari chairs and the enormous floral centerpieces that Bootsie had specially designed by Lyman Ratcliffe?* They were nowhere in sight.

"Hello?" she repeated, though her voice merely echoed in the huge space. "Is anyone here?"

She glanced around, catching her reflection in a mirror on the wall—then realized it wasn't *her* reflection at all. The girl in the silvered glass was at least twice her size, and she was smiling maliciously as she approached.

Oh, hell. It was Laura Bell, wearing the exact same Vera Wang gown as Jo Lynn: a silk satin underlay with a layer of English netting and a silk voile overlay with delicate hand-sewn flower appliqués and seed pearls. Except Laura's dress was much larger than Jo Lynn's. Forget her being a debu-tank. She was more like a debu-blimp, as in *Goodyear.*

"Surprise, surprise," Laura taunted her, the sparkle from the heavily jeweled tiara in her upswept blond hair so intense Jo felt blinded. "What's wrong, girlfriend?" Laura's square-jawed face leaned close enough for Jo to feel the girl's hot breath on her skin. "You look like you've seen a ghost. Or is it envy, since I look better in this gown than you? Or maybe it's because I've got the best-looking escort in the room, and you're all by your lonesome?"

Jo Lynn started to open her mouth to fight back, but all words caught in her throat when she saw the broad-shouldered guy in the tuxedo walking toward them. He ignored Jo completely as he took Laura's hand.

OMG. It was Dillon Masters.

Her Dillon.

"Noooooooo!" Jo Lynn screamed at the top of her lungs.

Hands gripped her, shaking her shoulders, and a gravelly voice said, "Jo, hey, calm down. It's all right."

But it isn't all right. Dillon is with that lard-ass Laura!

Jo struggled against the arms that wrapped tightly around her. A sob wedged in her throat, and she felt the rush of tears behind her eyelids.

"Babe, I'm here. It's okay."

She stopped fighting and forced her eyes open to see Dillon's chiseled features hovering above her. His wide brow wrinkled with concern. She wiped the dampness from her cheeks and touched his jaw, the unshaved skin like sandpaper, and she let out a huge sigh of relief.

"You're here," she whispered, and glanced around them at the familiar living room of the Bidwells' guesthouse. They lay on the L-shaped sofa, across from the plasma TV, its screen dark and empty. It had all been a dream, she realized, the crazy beat of her heart slowing down. *This* was real. How could she ever have believed someone like Dillon would escort a slob like Laura to the Rosebud Ball?

"Oh, God," she cried, burying her face in his chest. "It was awful."

"I knew we shouldn't have watched *Shaun of the Dead* again," he said as he stroked her hair. "All that salsa and chips probably didn't help either, and neither did falling asleep on the couch." He squinted at his wristwatch and groaned. "It's already eight o'clock."

"Eight?" Jo lifted up her head, panicking momentarily because it was a Monday morning, until she remembered it was Labor Day. She sighed and settled down again. "It's a holiday, Dill. We don't have to go anywhere for a while if we don't want to."

"Your mom's still gonna freak if she wakes up and sees my car here."

"Please." Jo laughed. "Bootsie adores you."

And it was true. Her mother *loved* Dillon. He could do no wrong in her eyes, so long as he was making Jo Lynn happy. Jo's mother would totally buy that they'd passed out in the guesthouse watching movies, which was mostly all they'd done. Bootsie thought Mr. Star Quarterback was the model gentleman and he was, more than Jo Lynn would've liked, although he *had* macked on her plenty last night. Jo's face heated up even now, thinking of Dillon's strong hands on her skin and the firm way he'd kissed her, like he had something to prove.

Which he does, she reminded herself, figuring it was the least she deserved after the romantic drought she'd endured the past month. Dillon always had a million excuses too, like the stress of football practice, training sessions, and pressure from his dad and college recruiters.

"Jo?" Dill's voice brought her back to the present as he settled against the deep cushions, his pale gaze glued on her. "So, what's with your nightmare?"

He obviously isn't in a hurry to disappear, she thought smugly, hoping that things were getting back to normal between them. She'd missed being close to him.

"It was more like a fright-mare," she said, shaking off the flashes of it that still lingered. She squeezed her eyes closed a couple times to clear the visions. "I was at the Houstonian, but no one else was there for the deb ball except that skank Laura Bell, and she was wearing *my* couture Vera Wang gown, although hers was *way* bigger than mine, of course. But that couldn't possibly happen because the Glass Slipper Club's historian records everyone's dresses so no two are alike—"

Dillon was staring at her like she was a lunatic so she stopped herself. "Never mind," she told him, because explaining it did make her sound totally obsessive. "I think I'm just feeling the pressure. The first Rosebud meeting's

10

tomorrow night, and *she'll* be there, acting like she's all that and getting in my face unless I—"

Jo Lynn didn't finish. Dillon didn't need to hear her scheme to get Laura ousted from the Rosebuds no matter what it took, no matter how important it was to her. He wouldn't understand. She gnawed on her lower lip, itching to ask him a question that nagged at her. Finally, she just blurted out, "So what do you think of her?"

"Who?"

"Laura Bell." She enunciated clearly, practically spelling out the name.

Dillon shrugged. "I don't know her that well, except from when Avery used to bring her around, but she seems okay."

That wasn't exactly what Jo Lynn was getting at, so she went right for the jugular: "You don't think she's attractive, do you?"

Her boyfriend drew back, giving her a "what the hell?" look. "Why would you even ask that?"

Because you were her deb ball escort in my damned dream, Jo nearly howled, but checked herself. "Like you said, Avery went out with her, and I thought he had better taste than that. She's . . . supersized."

"Do you hate her because he was your boyfriend first? That's what bugs you the most, isn't it? Avery went from dating *you* to seeing a girl who's definitely not your idea of a beauty queen." Dillon exhaled slowly, and the muscles in his jaw twitched. "Jesus, Jo, I'm surprised you let someone like Laura get under your skin so much that you're having nightmares about her."

"You don't get it," Jo Lynn snapped.

"No, I don't get it at all. You have everything any girl

could want, but instead of being happy you keep fixating on someone who can't hold a candle to you." Dillon sighed again, and there was something in his eyes that caused a chill to fall between them. "You need to give it a rest."

That got Jo's back up. "So I'm a bitch for not liking her, is that it?"

Dillon looked at her for a long time before he said quietly, "Sometimes I'm just not sure what I've gotten myself into."

What was that supposed to mean?

Is it because I brought up Avery? Is he jealous? she wondered. Or was it something else?

Don't push it, Jo, she told herself, and her mind quickly shifted gears. She hurried to fix things, before all the warm, fuzzy feelings from their evening together evaporated.

"Look, I'm sorry. I don't want to fight. Just the opposite," she assured him, playing with the collar of his shirt. "Seriously, thanks for staying with me last night. *All* night," she added, leaving out the rest of what she was thinking, namely, *even if we didn't actually* do *it.*

"I'm the one who should thank you," Dillon said, and squeezed her hand.

"Why thank me when it doesn't have to end yet?" she whispered and, in one smooth motion, she slipped a leg across his thigh and slid onto his lap. She pressed up against his chest, kissing him gently at first and then more roughly when she felt him kissing her back.

Slipping her tongue between his lips, Jo Lynn tasted his morning breath, but didn't care a bit. She unfastened the buttons on Dillon's shirt and ran her hand over the solid muscles of his chest, feeling his heartbeat quicken beneath her palm and his grip tighten around her waist.

"Jo," he moaned, and she couldn't tell if he wanted her to stop or go on. So she kept going.

She tasted his skin, kissing his jaw and then gently licking his throat as her fingers tugged at the waistband of his cargo shorts, which was when he caught her wrist.

"Didn't we agree to slow things down a little?" He peeled her hands away from his pants, setting them safely aside. Within seconds, he'd refastened the buttons on his shirt while Jo just tried to catch her breath. "Sometimes it feels like everything's moving so fast around me that I can't think straight."

"Yeah, right, slow down," Jo repeated, still feeling flushed all over, and thinking, *When did I agree to that?* It was more like *he'd* slowed down all on his own this past summer, after two years of going hot and heavy, and the only thing she could do to hold on to Dillon now was to go along with whatever he wanted. Something was up with him, but he obviously wasn't willing to share.

So far as she knew he hadn't been born again, and it was for damned sure *she* wasn't into reconstituted virginity. She'd heard of girls accepting some kind of creepy promise ring from their dads for pledging to swear off sex until marriage. Ugh. Besides, it was *way* too late for that. Avery had made sure of it their freshman year. Weren't guys the ones who always wanted to move faster? As much as she wanted to ignore it, Dillon's need to put the brakes on didn't make sense.

"I should take off," Dillon said, and wriggled out from beneath her. He jumped up from the sofa and ran a hand through his tousled blond curls. "I need to work out this morning before I help my folks get ready for the barbecue."

13

He looked around him as he hiked up his cargo shorts and smoothed his vintage bowling shirt. "You know where my shoes are?" he asked, getting down on his hands and knees as he poked beneath the couch for his missing Vans.

Jo Lynn got a nice view of his butt as he bent over and scrounged around for his kicks. It was almost too bad when he found them.

"I'll see you at one o'clock, yeah?" Dillon slipped on his shoes. "My dad would kill me if you didn't show. I think he's got a crush on you," he added, and wiggled his eyebrows.

"Stop it." Jo shook her head, grinning. He could be such a goof. "Of course I'll be there. I'm looking forward to it."

"Cool." He nodded as he slipped his wallet into his back pocket and picked up his cell from the coffee table without bothering to check it for messages. Then he grabbed his keys and headed for the door.

Jo Lynn shoved her feet into her floral-embroidered Christian Lacroix flats and snatched up her iPhone, which she'd turned off last night so nothing would interrupt them. Hopping off the sofa, she followed him to the door. She flipped tangled blond hair over her shoulders, coming up behind him as he paused before leaving.

"Bye, babe, I'll see you this afternoon," he said, kissing her lightly before he loped down the steps toward his black Mustang.

Jo closed the door and stood on the porch, listening to the sports car roar to life, the engine growling as it pulled away. She suddenly realized Dillon had never actually answered her question about whether or not he found Laura Bell attractive.

I'm surprised you let someone like Laura get under your skin, she heard him saying, and she hated the fact that he was right. She shook off her attack of insecurity, something she'd rarely felt since she'd had to give up pageants her sophomore year.

Of course Dillon doesn't think Laura is pretty, she told herself. The girl was as tall as an Amazon and had a body type Bootsie politely referred to as "sturdy." Not to mention the fact that she had no manners at all. Laura was known throughout Pine Forest Prep for saying precisely what she thought without thinking first, and often ended up with her hefty size-eleven foot in her mouth. They might both be trust fund babies, but that was *all* they had in common. Well, except that they were both blondes and their mothers were good pals . . . and, unfortunately, Laura had also been picked by the Glass Slipper Club to be one of ten Pine Forest Prep senior girls in this season's debutante class.

Though Jo Lynn was bound and determined to see Miss Ding-Dong Bell booted out of the Rosebuds on her "sturdy" ass. Jo had already played an ace—or what she'd assumed was an ace—when she'd anonymously messengered a photo of a drunk and disrobed Laura Bell to every woman on the GSC's debutante selection committee. Astoundingly, that trick had backfired, leaving Jo Lynn with no choice but to try something else—which reminded her that she had some work to do on her "Get Laura Drop-Kicked from the Rosebuds" project before Dillon's family barbecue this afternoon. It *was* Labor Day after all, wasn't it? Only this bit of labor would be fun.

She turned on her iPhone and found a new text message. She paused on the flagstone path that led around the pool to the main house, went to her SMS screen, and read Camie Lindell's note. Her friend was obviously curious about how things had gone with Jo and Dillon.

So??? Whassup with U and Big D?

Jo smiled and texted back: He just left.

Camie's reply bounced back like she'd been sitting on her cell, waiting for Jo to respond. No way!!!

Way! Jo tapped into the keypad. And I'll C him L8R at his BBQ. I so heart him!

You suck! I'll B hanging out with Trish while U have real fun. We're going 2 the country club 4 yoga, lunch & mani-pedis. Spill All when U get back!!!

Jo answered: U know I will.

My BFFs will have to do without me today, Jo mused as she slipped her phone into her back pocket and strode across the flagstone walkway through the manicured lawn. Though she was usually too preoccupied to admire the pretty acre in Houston's pricey Piney Point Village upon which sat the home her daddy had custom built before she was born, she took it in now. Tall pines soared heavenward and enclosed the property, hugging close to its borders like giant guardians, keeping the Bidwells safely separated from the rest of the world. Graceful cypresses dripped Spanish moss; fluffy asparagus ferns flourished; and the hibiscus, oleander, and Mexican honeysuckle still bloomed wildly in early September. Sago palms looked like verdant umbrellas, while velvet-leaved princess flower bushes still bore a few dark purple blooms.

Jo inhaled deeply, the sweet mix of scents so pervasive on the humid air that she could almost taste them.

Today, she decided then and there, *will be absolutely perfect. Nothing and no one can ruin it.*

Having the day off from school after two weeks back at good ol' all-girls Pine Forest Prep rocked, particularly since it meant she'd be spending the afternoon with Dillon. Even though she wished they were doing something alone and not having to play nice with Dillon's parents, plus most of the Caldwell Academy football team. Still, Jo Lynn kind of enjoyed being Dillon's arm candy, and he seemed to like showing her off to the other guys, as if he'd won a big prize that they'd never get.

Texas men were kind of possessive that way, even the well-bred ones who'd been reared in River Oaks or the Memorial Villages with silvers spoons in their mouths and Gucci saddles beneath their butts (if they rode at all). For sure, Dillon Masters was no redneck. He didn't like to hunt, for one, and he didn't do chaw, wear Lucchese boots day in and day out, or drive a pickup—with or without a gun rack—with that omnipresent bumper sticker that read: DON'T MESS WITH TEXAS.

Not that Jo Lynn didn't appreciate the motto, because she did. She kind of wished the whole world lived by the credo "Don't mess with Jo Lynn Bidwell," though it was pretty much unwritten law at PFP that most girls seemed inclined to obey. At least, the ones who knew what was good for them.

There was one woman, though, who intimidated Jo Lynn, and it wasn't a prep school rival or any competitor she'd ever encountered on the pageant scene, but rather Bootsie Bidwell, her mother, who just happened to be this year's chair of the GSC debutante selection committee. And Jo Lynn didn't want to cause an early-morning stink with her mother for strolling in at breakfast time, even if she'd spent the night only yards away in the family's guesthouse with the

17

Golden Boy of Caldwell Academy whom she had every intention of marrying one day.

Jo used her key to open the door to the main house and stepped into a rear hallway near the utility room, just past the butler's pantry, where kitchen deliveries were received.

She heard the familiar noises of pots and pans clanking in the granite and stainless steel kitchen as the Bidwells' long-time cook prepared brunch, always served promptly at eleven. Jo figured Cookie was getting double pay for sticking around and feeding the fam on a holiday when even the housekeeper, Nan, had been cut loose for Labor Day. But Jo liked having Cookie around, since it meant the house would smell like cinnamon and spices all day.

Deciding it best to slip in unnoticed, Jo removed her shoes, dangling them from her fingers as she tiptoed past the kitchen and scurried across the foyer, the marble floor cold beneath her feet. She briefly glanced up at the impossibly high painted ceiling—Bootsie's ode to Michelangelo's frescoes in the Sistine Chapel—and took the curving stairwell up to her bedroom as quietly as possible, avoiding the floorboards that creaked beneath the Oriental runner just outside her parents' bedroom. She had one hand on the knob of the door to her bedroom suite and was about to turn it when a voice from behind startled her.

"I believe you missed your curfew," Bootsie said, her honey-eyed drawl laced with sarcasm.

Please. Like I actually have a curfew.

Jo Lynn slowly turned to face her. "Good morning, Mother."

Her mom gave her a slow once-over, and Jo knew she looked a mess. Her makeup no doubt was smeared, and she wore the same pair of hip-hugging D&G jeans and pleated white shirt she'd had on last night when she'd gone out to eat with Dillon, only now she looked severely wrinkled. Her fabric flats were damp with dew. In stark contrast, Bootsie appeared her typical unruffled self, the model nouveau riche mummy, perfectly dressed in tailored pearl gray Chanel slacks and sage green silk side-wrap blouse. She'd always been the best-dressed mother on the pageant scene, and Jo rarely saw her with a hair out of place.

Jo Lynn shifted on her feet, uncomfortable beneath Bootsie's critical gaze.

"Good thing I'm not doing pageants anymore, huh? I wouldn't even win Miss Junior Oil Refinery looking like this," Jo cracked, then pressed her lips together, waiting out her mother's silence. Such a lengthy pause meant Bootsie's brain was making a list of Jo Lynn's imperfections, like she'd done back in Jo's pageant days.

"You do look a mess," Bootsie said finally, crossing her arms and tilting her head. "But I guess that's what happens when you don't sleep in your own bed."

Aw, hell, here it comes.

Jo Lynn squirmed but couldn't escape.

"Did Dillon stay over?" her mother asked, point-blank. "And don't lie, because I heard a noise a few minutes ago and I caught his car pulling out of the drive."

"It was no big deal really," Jo muttered, glancing down at her feet. "We fell asleep in the guesthouse watching movies." Well, it was the truth. She just left out the part about them mashing, because no mother alive wanted to think her daughter put out for anyone, even Mr. Perfect, Dillon Masters. "I've got some stuff to do before his parents' party this afternoon," she said, meeting her mother's eyes as she inched her bedroom door open. "So if you'll excuse me . . ."

"You be careful, baby girl," Bootsie warned, catching her by the shoulder. "The Glass Slipper Club takes their debutantes very seriously, and you know the rules. Any public indiscretion could cost you your position."

Public indiscretion?

"It's not like we were getting it on in the street, Mother, for God's sake," Jo Lynn groused. "If anyone spread any nasty gossip about me or Dillon, it'd just be because they're jealous."

But the warning look didn't leave Bootsie's narrowed eyes. "I'm serious, Jo Lynn. You need to watch yourself. All it takes is one unforgivable slip, and the GSC will review your Rosebud status. If that happens, I won't be able to do a thing about it. We've already had to terminate one girl, and it hasn't been pleasant."

"What?" Jo Lynn perked up. "Who?" she asked, hoping against all hopes it was that fat blob Laura Bell.

Bootsie gave a little shake of her head. "Now, Jo, you know I can't discuss that with you. You'll find out soon enough. Besides, it's not anyone else's daughter I'm worried about. It's you."

"You don't have to worry about me, I swear," Jo Lynn insisted, but her mother didn't look completely reassured.

Still, Bootsie nodded, giving her shoulder a squeeze before she released her. "Why don't you get cleaned up, and I'll see you at brunch? Cookie has a new stuffed French toast she's trying out on us this morning, and an egg soufflé with green peppers and caviar."

"Egg soufflé with caviar?" Jo Lynn made a face, and Bootsie laughed.

"You can stick to the French toast."

"I think I will," Jo said, watching her mother stride down the Oriental runner toward the stairs. Then she pushed into her room and shut the door, locking it behind her. She had something to take care of before she showered and made herself presentable for brunch.

She dumped her shoes on the floor and slid into her cane-backed desk chair.

Settling in front of her widescreen flat-panel monitor, she palmed her mouse, which was yellow and shaped like a VW Bug. When she clicked on it, tiny headlights lit up and it beeped. She pulled up a bookmarked page and prepared to place an order, her third in the past few weeks. Last time, it was for Godiva. This time, it was for two dozen brownies from the Fairytale Bakery. Just for the hell of it, she added a Caramel Endings dessert sauce and a bag of cashews. *How many calories are in those suckers?* she wondered. *Like, a million?*

Enough, she was sure, to lead the already oversized Laura Bell on a course to debutante destruction, if she wasn't already on the fast track to an early exit. *We'll see if big girls* do *cry,* Jo Lynn thought, pulling out her prepaid debit card (which she'd bought with cash, so there was no way to link the purchase back to her) and smiled as she clicked Order Now.

If I were well-behaved,
I'd die of boredom.
—Tallulah Bankhead

Is screwing with your enemy's head
considered a legit hobby?
—Laura Bell

Two

"If I have to drag you out from under the covers and haul you over to the country club in your underwear, believe me, I'll do it. C'mon, Laura! You're the one who made such a big deal about working out this morning since we don't have class." Mac Mackenzie sighed and stabbed her fists onto boyish hips. Her blue eyes narrowed behind her black-rimmed specs, and the way her usually wild dark hair was pulled back into such a tight ponytail made her square face look positively menacing. "Now are you gonna get up, or do I have to spray you with the hose to get you moving?"

"Maybe I changed my mind," Laura growled, her sleep-tangled blond hair spilling over her pillow, and she tugged the sheets over her head. "If you'd called first, I would've told you so," she added in a muffled voice. "Now go away."

Okay, so Laura *might* have complained about adding a pound or so since their Rosebud invitation dinner at the end of August, not long after school had resumed two weeks back (school in Texas always started *way* earlier than the rest of the civilized world). Her teensy weight gain could've had something to do with a mysterious admirer who'd been sending her chocolates (the last box contained to-die-for truffles from Godiva—oh, Lord, those were *good*!). And she *might* have whined a little about humiliating herself doing the Texas Dip and falling on her face in the Grande Ballroom.

Still, it was Labor Day, for God's sake. If Laura had nagged Mac about working out today, she must've been crazy drunk or at the very least crazy, which had to be the case since she hadn't gotten trashed since the summer before last when she'd passed out and Jo Lynn Bitchwell and her toadies had penned slurs on her body with laundry marker *and* snapped pics of the whole sordid thing—a memory she was still trying hard to blot out.

"I did call, you lazy bum," Mac insisted, "and I can prove it."

Laura heard a gentle clunk on the nightstand, which had to be Mac picking up her BlackBerry.

"Your last three incoming calls were from me, starting a half hour ago. When you didn't answer, I had no choice but to head straight over and kick your sleeping butt."

"Did I say 'go away' in Swahili or something?" Laura mumbled from beneath the covers, having no intention of crawling out any time soon. "Where's Ginger, anyway? I would've thought you'd bring backup."

"She's still grounded, remember? Now, for the last time, *get up!*"

Mac poked at Laura's backside through the covers, though Laura didn't budge an inch. Instead, she muttered, "I've got an idea. Why don't you go play with Ginger at *her* house?"

"She's stuck going to her grandmother's for tea this afternoon with Deena," Mac said, then cleared her throat before doing a bad impression of Rose Dupree's dry Southern drawl: "I do declare, isn't that what all properly bred Rosebuds do for fun?" When Laura didn't so much as chortle, she quickly dropped the accent and continued in her own voice, "Ginger thinks Rose is plotting something, so she's a little freaked out."

"I'd rather have tea with a sneaky old bird like Rose than sweat buckets on the club treadmill this early on a holiday," Laura whined, still refusing to get out of bed. "Please, just leave me in peace so I can get my beauty rest?"

If she was going to win back her one true love, Avery Dorman, she needed all the help she could get. Though Laura didn't say as much to Mac, considering how Mac felt about Avery. Hell, Mac called Caldwell's star running back "the Ratfink" because he was such a player, jerking girls around and never able to commit, as Laura could attest to.

"I'm counting to three and then I'm playing hardball." Laura felt a tug on her pale pink Ralph Lauren sheets and ruffled floral spread. "One . . ."

"It's my God-given right to sleep in," she protested into her pillow, steadfastly refusing to open her eyes.

". . . two . . ."

"*Maaaac.*" She breathed the name, exasperated. "*Pleeeeze.*"

". . . three!"

With a yank, the covers were gone and Laura felt the cool rush of air-conditioning on her exposed skin. She yelped, her eyes popping open as Mac pulled the sheets and down comforter below her ankles, leaving her bare legs and her Victoria's Secret nightshirt and undies with PINK printed across the butt in plain view.

"You brat!" she cried, and scrambled to grab the sheets

and blanket so she could enfold herself inside her warm cocoon again and go back to sleep.

But Mac kept pulling until all her bedding was in a pile on the floor at the foot of the four-poster bed.

Laura scowled at her pushy pal, who stood with arms smugly crossed. "What in the name of Gucci are you wearing?" she asked, gawking at Mac's striped green hoodie and clashing red sweatpants, which looked way too much like Christmas and didn't go at all with her black smart-girl glasses and the polka-dot headband and scrunchie that held unruly dark hair off her face.

Mac raised an eyebrow defiantly. "Let's see who's making cracks after I dig up something for *you* to wear."

Without waiting for Laura's approval, Mac headed straight for the mahogany chest of drawers, pawing through them until she unearthed a running bra, a faded Pine Forest Prep T-shirt, and a pair of cropped yoga pants.

"I hate those elliptical machines," Laura whined as Mac tossed the clothes onto the bare bed. "They make me feel so uncoordinated."

"Then you can walk on the treadmill," Mac replied. "And if you keep griping much longer, I'll whistle for Tincy. Your mom offered to help drag you out to my car if you tried to wimp out. I think she'd do it, too."

Though Tincy Bell was as tiny as Laura was tall and big-boned, Laura was sure her mother wouldn't hesitate to do just as she'd promised. Tincy was probably thrilled that Mac had taken Laura's vow to work out so seriously. After all, it was Ma Bell who'd packed up Laura and shipped her off to fat camp in the Hill Country of Austin this past summer for two months. If Tincy had her way, Laura would miraculously melt from her size-fourteen self to a size two overnight. Not that Laura could ever see that happening, even if she used an elliptical machine every day for the rest of her life.

Still, she had to watch her curvy figure in the months ahead, as Tincy constantly reminded her. Even though she was a legacy, the Glass Slipper Club wasn't keen on plus-sized debutantes, so she felt lucky they'd let her slide onto the list of ten. Of course, that didn't mean she couldn't slip right off it if she gave them any reason.

"All right, I'm coming." She swung her legs over the side of the bed, muttering, "And you call yourself my friend."

"I'm the best kind of friend," Mac assured her. "It's my duty to make you suffer."

"Well, better to suffer now than make a fool of myself doing the Dip," Laura muttered as she pulled on the yoga pants. "Even my sister had trouble with it, and Sami's, like, tiny and was a gymnast in junior high. Think about it—all eyes on you as your name is announced. You have to grace-fully bow to the floor with your flowers in one hand and your hundred-pound dress with all those petticoats and corset stays." Laura paused and swallowed hard. "I'll be hor-rified if I get stuck on the floor like a klutzy swan in front of everyone. You can't tell me you're not the least little bit afraid too?"

Mac let out a dry laugh. "Like I could give two craps. I might even refuse to curtsy in protest."

"Don't even joke about that!" Laura said gravely. "Sami's friend Leanne wouldn't Dip, and she got herself banned from every important social event for, like, five years!"

The true-life tale of poor Leanne was one Tincy brought up every now and then to remind Laura what happened when girls "act uppity," as she put it. She couldn't even imagine bucking the Glass Slipper Committee on purpose. Even thinking about it made her shudder.

"Swear that you won't refuse to curtsy," Laura begged her friend.

Mac crossed her arms over her chest as if to say, "Try me."

Scowling, Laura grumbled, "I wish you'd stop being such a Debbie Downer. Our debutante season is supposed to be *fun*, dammit."

"Fun?" Mac made a noise of disgust. "You've got to be kidding."

Laura wanted to grab Mac by the shoulders and shake away her cynicism. "One of these days, Ginger and I are gonna take you to the doctor and have your head examined."

"Whatev," Mac replied with an exaggerated eye roll.

Laura opened her mouth to further chastise her friend, but Mac threw a hand up in her face. "Not another word! Quit with the distractions and get changed."

With that, Mac stomped off, straight into Laura's walk-in closet, emerging with a pair of black and pink Nikes in hand. She tossed them across the room toward Laura. One smacked her squarely on her exposed shin.

"Ouch!" Laura rubbed the pink spot on her skin and glared at Mac, who merely smiled in return.

As soon as Laura had finished dressing, she made a bee-line for the bathroom, doing a five-minute version of her usual morning routine, sticking to the basics like teeth-brushing and face-washing. Forget the makeup. Who'd see her at the country club gym on a holiday morning anyway?

"What's taking you so long?" Mac yelled from the other room.

"I'm going as fast as I can!" Laura pulled her long blond hair into a ponytail, squinting at her naked face in the mirror. *Aw, hell,* she thought and snatched up her mascara, giving her lashes a quick two coats before she dabbed her lips with gloss. Well, she couldn't go out with her face *completely* bare, could she? Houston might be a huge city, but living in the Memorial Villages was like living in a small town in many ways. What if she ran into Avery? The last thing she wanted was for her on-again/off-again (and hopefully on-again) boyfriend to catch her looking less than spectacular.

"You ready to go?" Mac's bespectacled eyes peered into the bathroom. "And no need to bring supplies. They'll have Fiji and towels at the club."

"Bottled water?" Laura squawked in mock horror. "If Ginger heard you say that, she'd beat you with a hemp whip for not being earth-friendly."

"What Ginger doesn't know won't hurt her." Mac shrugged. "Besides, we'll recycle them."

"So much for our no-secrets rule," Laura joked, and slung an arm around Mac's shoulders. "Okay, I promise not to rat about drinking water from plastic bottles so long as you swear not to tell anyone how spastic I look on the elliptical, or, God forbid, doing the doggy pose in yoga class."

Mac held up her right hand with the thumb and pinky folded down. "Girl Scout's honor, I will never breathe a word about you being a spaz or doing the doggy pose," she said with a straight face.

And of course, she wouldn't, Laura knew, since Mac had actually been a Girl Scout and had earned, like, four hundred badges by the time she was a sophomore; at which point Laura had begged her to drop out because Mac was nerd

31

enough for being on the honor roll every frigging semester and in Mu Alpha Theta, the math honors club.

"I'm good to go. So let's boogie," Laura said, and brushed past Mac to lead the way out of her bedroom and through the marble-floored hallways of the Bell mansion. Before they blew out the front door, Laura yelled back to the empty foyer, "See you later, Mother! I'm going to the club with Mac!" which, she figured, sufficed as a news flash if either of her parents was within hearing distance. Although she had a good idea her dad wasn't even home—Labor Day meant nothing to a workaholic CEO like Harrington Bell—and God only knew what Tincy was up to, except that it probably involved a deep-tissue massage or some kind of age-defying skin treatment.

Without further ado, Laura hopped into Mac's Honda Civic, enduring her friend's reminder to put on her seat belt. Mac started the car and checked her mirrors. Then they took off, leaving the Bells' house on Hedwig Drive in Hunters Creek Village, cutting across Green Bay to Memorial Drive and enjoying a relative lack of traffic on the busy road all the way past the Voss intersection, where the Villages Country Club was located.

Mac pulled in at the pretty stone sign with a monogrammed VCC in its center, scooting around landscaped berms planted with neat rows of petunias. They veered left at the tennis complex, finally driving into the parking area near the whitewashed clubhouse and pool.

Parking spots abounded since, Laura figured, the majority of the country club's membership was taking the Labor Day holiday seriously and sleeping in or having a leisurely breakfast in their sunrooms. Though, as the morning progressed, the swimming area would doubtless swell with sun-worshippers enjoying themselves before the pool closed for good until Memorial Day next year. Like that mattered, Laura mused, when all the members of the VCC had pools in their own backyards.

But at five minutes to nine, the Olympic-sized pool was still deserted. Only fitness addicts or those with early spa appointments were out and about on this humid September morning. Laura noticed a handful of Maria Sharapova never-will-bes in pastel outfits, chasing balls around several of the two dozen tennis courts. She wondered how many exercise addicts would be working out in the humongous fitness room, eyes glued to the plasma TV screens, ignoring the wall of windows beyond, which offered a view of the bayou.

The Honda's brakes squealed as Mac brought the car to a stop as near to the clubhouse as they could get.

Laura swallowed the last few bites of a granola bar she'd dug out of her purse. "Can we stop in at the Grill for a quick breakfast?" she asked, her mouth tasting like grit. "I could use a glass of OJ."

Mac sighed. "Your delay tactics aren't gonna fly with me." She turned off the ignition and grabbed the door handle.

"Yes, sir, Sergeant Mac," Laura said, and gave a quick salute before she scrambled to exit the Honda and follow Mac's deliberate strides toward the club's front doors.

Once inside, soft music played from hidden speakers, something jazzy and instrumental. Laura glanced to the left at the pro shop, which wasn't even open yet, then at the frosted glass door to the day spa farther up on the right, thinking she'd rather spend the next hour getting a massage instead of working out. Laura had an aversion to sweat, which showed just how much she wanted to be the perfect Rosebud. Everyone knew the Texas Dip was what separated the real debs from the poseurs, and Laura wasn't about to get shown up by her archenemy, Jo Lynn Bidwell, or any member of Jo's Bimbo Cartel.

"Stop looking like you're going to your execution," Mac said over her shoulder. "You want to do a perfect Texas Dip or not?"

"I want to do it so insanely perfect that Jo Lynn Bidwell's pea green with envy," Laura retorted as she followed Mac down the hallway hung with photographs of golf and tennis champions, hoisting trophies or posing with local dignitaries.

The fitness center was at the far end, behind a pair of etched glass doors. Mac pushed her way in first, holding the door open for Laura. Mac even signed them both in before herding Laura toward the locker room so they could put away their bags.

"Leave the CrackBerry!" Mac commanded when she saw Laura palm her BlackBerry Pearl.

"But I need—"

"Oh no you don't." Mac grabbed her cell from her, set it firmly in the locker, and slammed the metal door. Then she gave the combo lock a spin for good measure.

"Out," Mac ordered next, pointing at the exit.

Laura snatched up a towel, Mac right behind her, emerging just as the nine o'clock yoga class began in an adjacent room.

She peered into the studio through a wall of windows and did a double take when she recognized two of the class's participants.

"You want to go in?" Mac asked, and looked relieved when Laura shook her head.

34

"Pass," Laura told her, gazing disdainfully at the pair of girls in trendy pastel yoga outfits. "I'd rather fall in a pit of fire ants than sit in the same room with any of the Bimbo Cartel." She turned her back on the window when she realized Camie and Trisha had spotted her and were staring back, heads bent together, whispering.

"Oh, yeah." Mac caught on fast enough. "Wow, I'm actually surprised that the Queen of Hos let those toadies out of her sight. I didn't think they went anywhere without her."

"I guess she gives them time off so they can attend their Yoga for Anorexic Chicks with Giant Fake Boobs Class," Laura got out with a straight face.

"Well, I'm surprised Jo Lynn's missing that one," Mac cracked back.

Even Laura couldn't resist smiling. "All right, let's sweat fast and then bounce before they're done with doggy poses. I don't want to run into either one in the locker room. I might hurl my granola bar."

"So long as you aim for their shoes and not mine," Mac said, pushing at the bridge of her black-rimmed glasses as she glanced down at her unsullied white Asics. "These suckers are brand-spankin'-new."

"Then it's time to break them in."

"Let's do the elliptical machines," Mac suggested.

"Fine," Laura agreed, busy glancing around the gym, relieved to find it relatively empty, except for a gray-haired woman in velour sweats on a recumbent bike, and a couple of guys using the weight bench, one spotting while the other lifted. She squinted harder at them.

Mac had already started walking toward an open machine, but Laura found herself frozen in place, stuck on the dudes pumping iron.

Isn't that Dillon Masters on the bench? And is that– Oh, God.

Laura's heart stopped for a split second until she realized the guy spotting Dillon wasn't Avery Dorman. Maybe it was the light brown hair (cut a little too short) or the broad shoulders (that weren't quite broad enough) . . . or just her wishful thinking.

Dillon's buddy *did* look familiar, somehow, like she'd seen him before at one of the Caldwell football games. Was he another player? Or a team trainer maybe? He did look a little older on second glance. Well, whoever he was, he stood hovering above Dillon as Jo Lynn's boy-toy grimaced, lifting the heavily weighted bar above his chest, holding it for a couple seconds, and then lowering it again.

So Jo Lynn's two BFFs and her man are at the club without the Chief Bimbo anywhere around to keep an eye on them?

If Jo Lynn had any idea that Laura was standing right across the fitness room from Dillon this very moment, it would totally freak her out.

Hmm, this could get interesting.

The thought of messing with Jo Lynn's head was way too tempting, Laura decided, making up her mind just as she caught the loud clank as Dillon finished his set and dropped the bar back into its cradle.

Why not?

She wiped her hands on her yoga pants and lifted her chin, then started walking across the gym toward the weight bench.

"Laura?" Mac called from the nearby elliptical machine. "Where're you going?"

"Be back in a sec," she promised, and kept on strolling through the neat rows of equipment, homing in on the

36

weight bench where Dillon resumed his presses; his biceps and triceps bulging impressively. His rock-hard pecs strained against his sweat-soaked Caldwell Mustangs T-shirt, which was damp enough to outline his abs, which looked more eight-pack than six-pack.

"... but if you go to Austin, that's just a couple hours' drive from here," Laura caught Dillon's pal saying to him.

"You're assuming I'll sign with the Longhorns," Dillon shot back. "But I don't want to be red-shirted, dude, and I don't want to play third string. I want to start as a freshman. I'm not playing by my dad's rules my whole senior year for nothing—"

He stopped talking abruptly when he realized Laura stood but a few feet away.

She was close enough to see the pale hair glisten on Dillon's arms and legs. She could even make out the flecks of gold in his sea blue eyes as he gave the weighted bar a rest and sat up on the bench, facing her. He picked up a water bottle from the floor, giving it a good swig before he rubbed the back of his hand against his mouth.

"Laura, hey," he said. "What's up?" He shot her a curious look. "Is there something I can help you with?"

"I don't know," she said, sounding totally lame. But she hadn't quite figured out just what she was going to say yet. She did know she didn't want an audience. "Um, do you mind?" she asked, and jerked her chin at Dillon's buddy.

"No problem," the guy said, and moseyed over to a pull-down machine across the way.

"So?" Dillon set the water bottle at his feet, near where his cell phone and a Zone bar lay. He leaned his arms on his knees and waited.

Laura scrambled to come up with something fast that Dillon would buy. He might've been a jock, but he wasn't a total him-bo. "It's the Rosebud Ball," she started babbling. "It's only eight months away and counting, and I'm panicking already."

He cocked his head. "Panicking about what? Getting to party like a princess?"

"I'm already walking a tightrope, Dillon, seeing as how I'm not exactly the cookie-cutter debutante." She waved her hands dismissively. "But that's only part of the problem. I have to be able to bow down in a ball gown while hundreds of my parents' friends watch to see if I'll eat it. I don't know anyone in better condition than you"—*Okay, except Avery,* she thought, but left that out—"so if anyone can help me out, it's you. Please, say you'll do it," she finished, and took a deep breath.

Beneath the damp curls of his hair, his forehead creased. "You want me to train you?"

"Yeah." She nodded. "Kick my ass, tone me up, make me buff, whatever it takes."

He squinted up at her. "You're joking, right? 'Cause you could hire a personal trainer and not even have to leave your house."

"But I don't want any old trainer." Laura shook her head. "I want you, Dillon."

His mouth tightened into a thin line. "I don't think that's such a good idea," he said quietly. "And we both know why."

"Because of Jo Lynn?" Laura saw his shoulders stiffen. "My God, Dillon, you're what? Six four and solid rock? You can't be scared of a skinny thing like her. Besides, she doesn't have to know what we're up to. She can't keep tabs on you every minute, can she? Or does she have you on that tight a leash?"

"No," he said brusquely, "she hasn't got me on a leash."

Right, Laura wanted to say, but wisely kept that to herself. "Well, I definitely won't be the one to tell her, and you'd be doing me the biggest favor." She dropped down on her knees in front of him, clasping her hands. "Look, I'm begging . . . no, I'm groveling. Pretty please, just give me a few minutes before or after your workouts. Show me what I need to do and supervise me, just so I don't hurt myself or anything. That's all I'm asking. Here, look—" Impulsively, she snatched his phone from the floor and flipped it open. Before he could even react, she was into his address book, adding her name and number to his list. Then she hit the Call button and lifted his cell to her ear, until she heard the voice mail on her BlackBerry, imprisoned in the locker room. "We're good," she said. "So call whenever, and I'll drop whatever I'm doing to meet you here."

"Jesus, Laura!" He grabbed his phone from her, flipping it shut and setting it beside him where she couldn't reach it again easily. "Let me think about it, okay?"

But Laura knew if he thought about it—or if he even mentioned the idea to Jo Lynn—he'd blow her off. She'd never have this chance again, and she wasn't about to let this golden opportunity slip through her hands.

"Did I ever tell you my father went to school with Armand Dickson? Yeah, they're great buddies," she said, thinking fast on her feet, and Dillon's eyes went wide.

"Your dad's friends with the athletic director at UT?"

"They're old Phi Delt fraternity brothers." Laura felt

buoyed by his obvious interest. "They go hunting every deer season, and sometimes J. R. Rhodes goes with them."

Dillon looked like he was about to stroke out. "Your dad knows Coach Rhodes?"

"Oh, yeah, *really* well. My dad's a die-hard Longhorn from way back, and he's one of the university's most generous Texas-Exes." Laura wasn't sure how far to push it, but decided to go for broke. "I'm sure he could talk you up to J.R. big-time, particularly if you did a huge favor for his baby daughter." She paused, tapping a finger to her chin. "Well, actually, if I wanted to, I could convince him to take you on their next trip to the cabin. It wouldn't hurt for you to have some face time with the coach, huh? There's fierce competition to play quarterback for the 'Horns, I'll bet."

"Beyond fierce," Dillon replied. His Adam's apple bobbed as he swallowed hard, digesting what Laura had just said. "Damn," he murmured, and glanced nervously across the room, apparently needing a moment to figure out how to handle the situation.

Laura followed his gaze to the wall of glass that made the room seem to extend into the thick green of Buffalo Bayou beyond. The boughs of a thick oak seemed about to reach through the window, gently brushing the transparent panes with each breath of wind.

"So?" she said, and she tapped his shoulder so he'd look at her. When she still saw confusion on his face, she did what she'd always done whenever her daddy wouldn't cave: she turned on the waterworks. Dewy tears caught in her lashes and slowly rolled down her cheeks, and Laura's lower lip trembled. *"Puh-leeze,"* she got out, prepared to really blubber if necessary.

He hesitated a second, like he was holding his breath, before he whispered, "Okay, okay."

"What?" Laura blinked.

"I said I'll do it. I'll help you out. If you'll work on that hunting trip with the coach and A.D." He leaned toward her, and she could smell the sweat on his skin. "I'll give you a call next time I'm working out here. I can maybe swing a few minutes of supervised instruction once a week, just until you know what you're doing. But that's it, and it's just between us."

Laura sniffed away her crocodile tears. "You mean it?"

"You heard me," he said. "Now I've got to go." He extricated himself from her and the bench, snatching up his cell, the water bottle, and his towel. "C'mon," he called to his workout buddy. "Let's hit the cave."

The older dude popped off the pull-down machine and followed Dillon out of the gym toward the windowless weight room in the back used by the truly serious athletes.

Laura rose from the floor, feeling strangely dazed as she wandered back toward where Mac worked out halfheartedly on an elliptical machine.

"What the heck was that about?" Mac hissed at Laura as soon as she was within earshot. "What could you possibly have to say to Dillon Masters?" Mac had completely stopped moving and waited for an answer as Laura climbed onto the adjacent machine. "Because if you think cozying up to Dillon will help you get Avery back, you're dead wrong. Jo Lynn will despise you even more if she thinks you've been within a hundred yards of her boyfriend. Have you forgotten that she hates your guts?"

No, Laura had not forgotten. In fact, Jo Lynn's attempt to

get her blackballed from the GSC's debutante list was foremost in her mind. It was a little like walking through a minefield every day, not knowing if her next step would set off an explosion, which was why she needed Dillon indebted to her. If anyone could make Jo Lynn bend to his will, it was him.

"I'm taking countermeasures," Laura told her.

"No, you're not, you're committing social suicide," Mac informed her. "Jo Lynn's already declared war. Whatever you're doing with Dillon is only gonna make things worse!"

Laura blew stray hairs from her eyes, not wanting to listen. When Mac was on a roll, she spewed as much steam as boiling water.

"You need to stay away from Dillon, and from Avery, too. For God's sake, Laura, the Ratfink's dating one of Jo Lynn's best friends. He does whatever she tells him to. He's not ever going back to you. You're like Sisyphus, doomed to push a rock up a hill."

God, why did Mac have to go all Greek mythology on her?

Laura wished that Mac could understand what it meant to truly be in love with someone, the way Laura was with Avery. It wasn't something you got over, not when you knew deep in your heart that nothing was impossible.

"The only rock I'm going to keep pushing is Jo Lynn, and I won't stop until I heave that sucker off the hill, or at least get it off of my back," Laura said as she fiddled with the setup buttons on the machine, trying to get the thing started.

"You're either a hopeless romantic or you're a masochist, or maybe a little of both." Mac frowned at her.

Despite the tightening in her chest at Mac's harsh words, Laura managed a shrug.

"Good thing it's my life to live and not yours, huh?" she declared, gripping the bars and moving her legs as the machine began to hum.

Falling in love is so hard on the knees.
—Aerosmith

Hormones make people do crazy things.
And when I say "people," I mean girls.
—Michelle "Mac" Mackenzie

Three

Fresh out of the shower after her morning "workout" with Laura—and she used the term loosely—Mac sat cross-legged on her bed, wet hair wrapped in a towel turban. She'd brought out the shoe box from under her bed and set it down in front of her, carefully removing the lid. Inside were all the letters her mom had written to her before she'd passed away from cancer two years ago. After the morning's frustrations, she needed the positive boost Jeanie Mackenzie's words always seemed to give her.

Mac slipped one particular note from the batch, unfolding the linen stationery and smoothing it out until it was flat. She felt a catch in her throat, seeing her mom's handwriting again, but at least her eyes didn't tear up like they used to (which accounted for the damp smears on most every page).

She ran her eyes down each line of loopy cursive and found just what she was looking for.

I'm going to miss being there to hold your hand when you need it and to remind you how important it is that you always be you. I feel better knowing you've got such true-blue friends in Laura and Ginger. You girls have known each other forever, haven't you? I hope nothing ever comes between you—nothing important anyway, and never for long. And do remember, when you get impatient with your friends, that it's important to live and let live. You're such an individual, Mackie, but so are Laura and Ginger. You have to respect that about them and give them room to grow as well. You won't always agree with everything they do (any more than you always agreed with everything I said!), but you must always support them and love them, much in the same way I will forever love you.

Live and let live.

Mac hugged her knees and sighed, thinking of how often her mom had said those words whenever Mac had complained about people who drove her crazy (and sometimes it seemed like those you were closest to drove you the craziest).

Since Jeanie Mackenzie wasn't around to say it today, Mac mentally repeated it several times—*live and let live, live and let live*—feeling less keyed up and better able to breathe evenly again. She refolded the letter and retrieved her journal, scribbling in it quickly with a pen she kept handy on the nightstand.

It's so hard trying to be "myself" sometimes when everyone around me has a different perception of who I am. Like, there's Brainy Mac, who's enrolled in all AP classes and who aced the SAT. Then there's Goody-Goody Mac, who doesn't really drink, doesn't do

*drugs, and doesn't act like a ho (what's wrong with
waiting to have sex until you're actually old enough
to understand real love, for God's sake?). And let's not
forget Stick-in-the-Mud Mac, who dragged her feet
about debuting. Seriously, I'm still not all-fired sure
about being a Rosebud. Why is it so important to
everyone but me? Talk about pressure!!! Some days I
think I'm going to explode. At least I can be the real
me when I'm with Alex.*

Mac set aside her notebook and pen with a sigh. Laura's
insane behavior this morning had only made her surer that
the road to deb-dom would be more like a roller coaster than
a trick-pony ride. Mac wished that Laura and Ginger hadn't
badgered her into accepting the Glass Slipper Club's invitation. Not that they didn't have really good ammunition for
arm-twisting, considering Jeanie Mackenzie's deathbed desire
that Mac wear the Oscar de la Renta gown that she herself
had debuted in. No pressure there.

Go with the flow, live and let live, Mac told herself, and
tugged the towel off her head. Draping it over her shoulders,
she ran her fingers through the damp curls, working out the
tangles. She thought of a recent kung fu movie that she and
Alex had watched on one of their weekend movie
marathons. The underlying message—besides "Kick the bad
guy's ass"—went something along the lines of "Don't be like
a rock slamming into other rocks. Be like the water slowly
wearing down the rocks."

Not a bad idea. Though it led her to wondering if Alex
still had the T-shirt he'd worn weekly in tenth grade that said
BRUCE LEE IS GOD.

49

Alex, Alex, Alex.

Mac grinned, brightening at the thought of him and their plans to spend Labor Day afternoon together. Her best guy-friend and the resident Geek-Next-Door (as Laura called him) had laid out their schedule in an earlier e-mail:

Alex and Mac's Excellent Labor Day Adventure:
- Ride bikes to Sandalwood, packing picnic lunch (peanut butter and jelly sandwiches— yeah!)
- Water Uncle Ed's plants so they don't croak before he gets back (always work before play—ha-ha!)
- Goof off like a couple of idiots for the rest of the day!

Mac couldn't wait.

Sandalwood was one of their favorite close-by destinations, just a hop, skip, and a jump down Knipp and across Memorial Drive. Alex's uncle Ed owned a house on Longleaf, on one of the three small lakes in the private subdivision, and he was away for a while, doing some kind of statistical analysis for a corporation in India. Alex figured Uncle Ed wouldn't care if they rode over and sat on his deck, dangling their legs in the water while they ate their PB&Js. So there would be no one around to bother them: no parents, no relatives, and no BFF plotting revenge.

Goofing off is just the ticket, Mac decided as she put away her mom's letter and stowed the precious shoe box under her bed. Feeling in the right frame of mind again, she padded into her bathroom to dry her hair until her mud-brown curls were only slightly damp. Then she wandered through her walk-in closet, tapping her lip with her finger as she figured out what to wear. She ended up pulling on her best pair of Gap cargo shorts and her favorite lavender T-shirt with velvet piping on the collar.

"*Mah-chelle!*"

Mac paused and gritted her teeth as her stepmother's annoying drawl traveled up the stairs.

"Coming!" She shuffled out into the hallway and leaned over the railing, spotting the way-too-blond top of Honey's head and her dad's salt-and-pepper crown. "What's up?" she called down, causing both faces to tilt in her direction.

Mac still wasn't used to seeing Honey standing arm in arm with her father. What an odd couple they made: tiny Honey with her flipped-out hair and her big boobs squeezed into a too-bright outfit, and tall Dan Mackenzie with his conservative haircut and golfer's uniform of pastel Polo shirt and tan slacks. Jeanie and Daniel had looked like they'd belonged together, and they had. That Mac's dad had picked Honey of all people to be with after her mom had died didn't make sense. Maybe it never would.

"Do you want some lunch?" her stepmom offered, smiling her toothy Miss Houston Runner-Up smile. "I could make you a grilled cheese before your daddy and I head out for our golf date with the Harrisons."

Like Honey played golf? Or made grilled cheese sandwiches for that matter.

"No, thanks," Mac declined as politely as possible since her dad was staring hard at her. He had a slightly pained look on his face that tied a knot in Mac's belly.

Was he seeing Jeanie in her face? Was he thinking, too,

how the holidays used to be when her mom was alive? How they used to spend time together, doing whatever fun things Jeanie Mackenzie dreamed up: going to the zoo, hitting the art museum for an exhibit, visiting NASA for the hundredth time, or buying ice cream at Marble Slab?

"We could bring you back something from the club," her dad said dutifully, out of pity, Mac was sure. "You used to love their Monte Cristos, didn't you?"

"Daddy, I haven't eaten those in ages," Mac told him, figuring he would've known that by now if he'd spent half as much time with her in the past two years as he did with Honey. "Besides, I'm having lunch with Alex, so you don't have to feel sorry for me."

"I wasn't feeling—" He cut himself off, shaking his head. "Hey, have a great time, kiddo." He gave her a mock salute, like he'd done when she was a kid.

"Don't worry." Mac forced a smile, assuring him, "I will."

"All rightee, then." Honey tapped her glittery diamond watch. "We'd better skedaddle or we'll be late, and you know how snotty Zani Harrison can be."

"You're right, of course, sweetheart."

"Aren't I always, baby doll?"

Ugh.

Mac winced as Honey slipped into PDA mode, slapping a wet one on Daniel Mackenzie and then slipping her arm through his, hanging on possessively.

"We're off then, sweet pea!" Honey trilled. "You be good while we're gone, ya hear?" she added as she dragged Mac's dad out the door.

Like Mac was ever anything *but* good.

She held her breath until the click of her father's shoes

and Honey's high heels on the foyer tiles had evaporated and the front door had closed with a bang. As the silence washed over her, she retreated to her bedroom, her heart twisting in a most uncomfortable way.

Saying hi and bye was about as much communication as she had with her dad these days. Since her mom died, instead of embracing her, he'd done his best to hold her at arm's length, not that tricky to do once Honey had entered the picture. As dead set as Mac had been against the relationship, her mother's own words had advised against it. In fact, one of Jeanie's letters explicitly instructed: *Your dad will get lonely when I'm gone. He'll need to find someone else. When he does, don't hold it against him. Promise me you'll let him move on.*

And maybe someday Mac would figure out how to do that, just as soon as her father had figured out how to relate to her again without Honey standing between them.

Argh! What am I doing?

Wasn't today supposed to be all about goofing off?

She didn't have time to be morose anyway. Not if she wanted to be ready for Alex when he knocked on the door.

Mac had barely pulled on her sneakers when the front bell rang. She rushed out of her room and down the carpeted stairwell, flinging herself at the door and pulling it open, an expectant grin on her face.

Something in her chest fluttered oddly when she saw Alex standing on the welcome mat, his brown hair curling at his collar and blue eyes bright behind the small wire-rimmed glasses. His cheeks were clean-shaven, which made the dimple in his chin especially noticeable.

"You ready?" Alex asked.

"Me? I was born ready," she said, sounding like an idiot.

He grinned a lopsided grin and patted the nylon straps of his knapsack, telling her, "I've got the grub, so grab your bike and let's roll."

"I'll meet you around by the garage, okay?" she said, and abruptly shut the door in his face.

She raced from the foyer through the breakfast room, kitchen, and utility room until she'd reached the door into the three-car garage and let herself out. She hit the garage opener after she'd locked the door behind her. Alex was waiting for her on the driveway as she untangled her bike from her dad's yard equipment.

"Ah, the ancient Schwinn," Alex said, nodding at the restored red bicycle with foot brakes that used to belong to Mac's mom, Jeanie. "Wasn't that appraised on *Antiques Roadshow* for something like five bucks?"

"Bite me, Bishop."

"Someday, you're gonna have to upgrade to keep pace with me."

"Newer isn't always better," Mac retorted, putting the kickstand down before she went back inside the garage to hit the down button.

Then she dashed out beneath the closing door, the sun beaming down on her, a trickle of sweat rolling down her back. She toed back the kickstand, grabbed the handles of the Schwinn, and hopped on.

"C'mon, slowpoke!" she called over her shoulder as Alex scrambled onto his mountain bike. "I'll race you there!"

Mac peddled away from her house and to the end of her street, checking briefly before steering her bike onto Knipp. She heard the crunch of tires on asphalt before she glanced to her left and saw Alex pulling up beside her.

"Eat my dust, woman!" he called out, laughing, before racing in front of her.

Mac shouted back, "No fair, your legs are longer!"

But she was laughing, too.

Man, it feels good to be with him. She could be herself with no worries, no pressure. It was exactly what she needed.

Alex slowed down as they approached Memorial Drive, and she caught up to him as they waited for cars to pass so they could cross the busy street. Then they were cruising again, and she pulled up alongside him as they peddled toward Longleaf. Mac kept up with him until he decided to sprint toward his uncle's house, and he raised one arm victoriously as he braked in the driveway just yards ahead of her.

"Call me Lance Armstrong," Alex said as Mac rolled in behind him and stopped, straddling the bike and breathing hard.

"Okay, Lance, so which celebutard is on your wish list this week? Kate Hudson? Or some other bobble-headed actress?" she joked, getting off the Schwinn and walking beside him as they rolled their bikes around to the rear of Edward Bishop's house.

"Bobble-heads are for dashboards," he shot back. "I'm not into girls who look like lollipops. I actually like brains." He glanced over his shoulder, directly at her, as he added, "Oh, yeah, and a sense of humor. That's vital too."

"Good answer," Mac said, and her heart thumped hard against her chest, no doubt from all the furious pedaling. She turned away from him, glimpsing the lake beneath the canopy of leafy green. It seemed the most beautiful place on earth at the moment, even if it was so sticky that her shirt felt glued to her back and mosquitoes buzzed around her ears.

How many times, she wondered, had they come here since they were kids, leaving their bikes at his uncle Ed's, then exploring the neighborhood? They'd play hide-and-seek, or pirates seeking treasure, or they'd pretend to be lost on an island, like the Swiss Family Robinson, traipsing through brush and foliage around the trio of tiny lakes.

"Remember when your uncle rigged up a tree swing, and you did your best Tarzan, running with the rope and flinging yourself into the lake"—Mac started to giggle before she'd even finished—"and then you hit the water with the loudest smack. I swear, I thought you were dead."

"Ah, yes," Alex said, nodding, "the belly flop heard round the world." He set a hand on his stomach and winced. "It still hurts on humid days."

Mac swatted at him. "You're such a dweeb."

"*You're such a dweeb,*" Alex parroted in his best Texas teen-girl-speak and did an exaggerated eye roll. "Like, that's *so* twentieth century. Hello," he went on, putting his hand to his head, pinkie and pointer fingers extended, pretending he was on the phone. "Oh, hey, Mac, it's for you. It's 1992 calling, and it wants its cliché back."

"Shut up," she groaned, rolling her eyes for real and muttering, "*dweeb.*"

"Love you, too." Alex leaned over his bike and stretched an arm out to muss her already wind-tangled hair.

Mac swatted him away.

"Let's go inside so I can do my thing and then we can eat," he suggested, and Mac didn't argue.

They left their bikes at the bottom of the rear deck and climbed the stairs so Alex could unlock the back door to let them in. He dropped his knapsack on the sandstone counter in the kitchen. Light filled the large room around them, spilling through the two-story windows and bouncing off the stainless steel appliances.

"You can get the food out if you want," Alex suggested. "I'll water the plants and then we can eat."

"Cool," she said, and took charge of his backpack while he filled a pitcher with water at the double sink.

As he wandered over to the sunny living area to douse the plants, Mac heard his cell phone ring—it still played the theme from *Star Wars*—and she caught a bit of one side of the conversation from the kitchen.

"Yeah, we're here," he was saying. "Uh-huh, yes, I'm sure it's okay with her. Hey, that's great."

Who's he talking to? she wondered. His mom, maybe, or his uncle?

Alex's voice became muffled and then inaudible, and Mac glanced up to see he'd drifted out of range. She busied herself, rummaging in the cabinets for plates and then pulling a large bag of SunChips, two apples, and a banana from his knapsack. She removed three Ziploc baggies stuffed with peanut butter and jelly sandwiches—crunchy PB, her fave, as Alex well knew—wondering who the third sandwich was for, not to mention the extra piece of fruit, when Alex sauntered back into the kitchen, swinging the empty pitcher and grinning.

"Your eyes must be bigger than your stomach," she said before he had a chance to speak. "Three pieces of fruit, a huge bag of chips, and three sandwiches, all for the two of us?"

His smile faltered. "Oh, yeah, well, I figured I should come prepared just in case."

"Just in case what?" Mac's antennae went up. What the heck was going on? "Are you a squirrel or something? Getting ready to hibernate?"

Alex shifted on his feet, and Mac caught a flash of the silver swoosh on the side of his black leather Nikes (his "pimp shoes," he called them).

She stopped putting food on the plates and stared across the countertop.

"For God's sake, spit it out, Alex!"

"Don't get mad, okay?" His pale eyes blinked behind the round specs. "But I didn't think you'd mind."

"Mind what?" *For a genius, he can be so dense sometimes!* Mac felt the dull thud of her pulse at her temples.

"I sort of invited someone else to join us today, this really cool girl I met at the auto show last weekend," Alex said, talking so fast that Mac's head started to spin. "Her dad owns an honest-to-God Shelby Cobra, Mac, and not one of the redesigns but one of the originals from the 1960s. It's, like, one of six still around today. I think the others are in museums. She's got one of the new Cobra Mustangs. Those things cost, like, seventy thousand dollars, can you believe?"

Okay, so far, Mac knew more about Mystery Girl's car than about the girl herself.

"Who's this 'she' you keep babbling about?" Mac asked point-blank, hardly able to disguise the irritation in her voice. But then she'd thought they were going to be alone today. She'd been looking so forward to it. "What auto show hoochie have you invited over without telling me, Alex?"

And why was he being so secretive?

"She's not a hoochie," he said just as the doorbell chimed.

They stared at each other dumbly until Alex revved into

58

gear. He shoved the empty pitcher onto the countertop and scurried around the corner of the kitchen and through the great room. There was a vague whine as the carved front door was pulled wide, and Alex's greeting of "Hey, that was fast" followed by a higher-pitched voice, one Mac thought sounded familiar. She knew why soon enough, when Alex reappeared around the corner with a tall girl with shiny black hair and exotic almond-shaped eyes.

"Oh, hey, Mac," the girl said when she saw Mac standing there.

"So you two know each other?" Alex appeared surprised and way too pleased, which somehow irritated Mac all the more.

"Yeah, we know each other. Hi, Cindy, so nice that you could join us," Mac said, sounding flat and insincere despite her best efforts.

Cindy Chow was one of the newer members of the Pine Forest Prep senior class, having transferred from St. John's late last semester. Even if Mac had wanted to hate her guts, she didn't. Cindy wasn't part of the Bimbo Cartel, was rumored to ride a motorcycle, and was, unfortunately, super-sweet.

Damn her.

"So, you live around here?" Mac politely inquired while secretly wishing the car-loving, Harley-riding, *Top Model*–pretty transfer student would vanish into thin air.

"Yep, just up the street," Cindy said, all dimples and toothy grin, casually flipping ink black hair over her shoulder. "Who'd of thought I'd run into you here, Mac? I didn't realize you and Alex were friends. Memorial can be such a small world, huh?"

"Pea-sized," Mac agreed.

"Hey"—Alex gestured toward the food Mac had laid out on the granite island in the kitchen—"anyone else hungry? I'm starving all of a sudden."

"You promised me peanut butter and jelly, right?" Cindy asked, fixing her doe eyes on Alex. "Please tell me it's chunky?"

"Oh, it's chunky all right," Alex said, and pushed at the bridge of his glasses, the way he did when he was nervous. "Smooth is for wussies."

Oh, God, is he flirting with Cindy?

Mac felt like she was watching a train wreck. She couldn't tear her eyes away, but it made her vaguely nauseous.

"Smooth is *so* lame," Cindy agreed with a giggle. "Kind of like driving a Japanese muscle car when you could be driving a Mustang."

"Especially a hot-off-the-line Shelby Cobra Mustang," Alex piped up, and his cheeks flushed. "What kind of power does that baby have under the hood? Five hundred and forty horsepower?"

"Five fifty," Cindy said, causing Alex to whistle.

I'm gonna be sick, Mac thought, trying hard to keep her mouth from hanging open.

"Hey, Mac, you want Coke or Aquafina?" Alex asked out of the blue, and strode purposefully around the granite island.

"You're talking to me?" Mac asked, surprised he'd even remembered she was there. She'd felt invisible during the "chunky versus smooth" discussion.

Alex's pale eyes narrowed behind his preppy lenses. "Yeah, I'm talking to you. I said, 'Hey, Mac,' didn't I?"

"Coke, please," Mac said, deciding to help him with the

drinks. She started toward him only to watch Cindy blow right past her, saying, "No, no, Mac, you should sit down. Let me do something. I mean, y'all are so sweet to let me hang out with you today. It's been kind of lonely being the new girl at PFP."

Reluctantly, Mac settled onto a stool across the counter, watching the way Alex's face lit up as Cindy fussed over their modest lunch, folding napkins and distributing chips onto plates while Alex extracted bottles of soda and water from the tiny cooler in his knapsack.

Something lodged in Mac's throat—it tasted an awful lot like resentment—and she tried to swallow it down, but it wouldn't budge. She had a really bad feeling that her perfect day of goofing off with Alex had flown right out Uncle Ed's window, and there wasn't a damned thing she could do about it.

You live but once,
You might as well be amusing.
—Coco Chanel

Preparing for tea at Rose Dupree's
means putting on my best manners and
accessorizing with a sense of humor.
—Ginger Fore

Four

If there was one thing Ginger figured could spoil a Monday off from Pine Forest Prep entirely, it was being summoned to her grandmother's house in River Oaks for afternoon tea.

Tea at Rose Dupree's boded ill for so many reasons. Usually when Rose invited Ginger and her mother to appear at her pillared mansion on Piping Rock (or rather, *summoned* them), it meant Rose had something up her lace-edged sleeve, some Old South–inspired, matriarchal agenda she wanted to push. And as much as Ginger's mom, Deena Dupree Fore, liked to play the independent divorcée with her constant round of cocktail parties and her residential real estate career, she couldn't seem to say no to her domineering mother, in the way that most well-bred daughters of Texas women never could. Ginger usually ended up suffering the consequences.

Deena had even made Ginger change out of her shorts and flip-flops into "something more presentable," which Ginger interpreted as "put on a dress and real shoes." Grudgingly, she'd donned her rose-colored Earth Creations tank dress and sandals. As if dressing up on Labor Day wasn't punishment enough, before they'd passed through Rose's front door, Deena had used spit in a futile attempt to flatten Ginger's spiky auburn hair *and* she'd pulled out her Dior compact to powder Ginger's freckled nose. But Ginger had flatly refused to swipe on any of Deena's bloodred lipstick.

"For heaven's sake, it wouldn't kill you or the environment if you put on makeup," her mother had chided before Rose's housekeeper, Serena, had let them in. "Somebody must make eco-friendly mascara. You've got such lovely green eyes, Ging. I don't understand why you try to hide the fact that you're a beautiful girl. Is it anti-Earth to be pretty?"

Once they'd all been seated and the tea had been poured, Ginger considered grabbing a poker from the set by the fireplace to stab herself in one of her "lovely" green eyes, anything to get her out of this. But instead she acted like a well-reared blue blood, sitting primly in a stiff-backed Victorian chair in the stuffy formal parlor, sure that the hot buttered scones would go cold before her grandmother got around to explaining why they were there. Until that time came, Ginger stirred her cup of Earl Grey and listened to her mother and Rose Dupree blather on about the latest shenanigans of the Junior League set.

"Did you see that obnoxious Amanda Pepper driving around town in that god-awful tank?" Rose remarked, and Deena cleared her throat before correcting her.

"It's a Hummer, Mother, not a tank."

"Well, it certainly looks like a tank. Is she afraid of a mortar attack while she's drivin' her kids to soccer practice?" Rose's laid-back drawl took on a sharp edge. "Whatever's wrong with a good, solid Cadillac? Your father drove his El Dorado till he drew his last breath."

"There's nothing wrong with a Cadillac, Mother," Deena replied, holding her voice remarkably level. "It's just some folks find them old-fashioned."

"So driving a tank through the streets makes more sense?"

Oh, Lord, here we go again, Ginger mused, and rolled her eyes as she balanced the Sevres cup and saucer on her knee and escaped the inane conversation by taking in the room around her. She was surrounded by ornately carved Eastlake furnishings with overstuffed cushions and cranberry-colored walls smothered in period paintings, mostly landscapes of gloomy-looking glades in Scotland or bleak portraits of relatives who seemed to glower at her from within the gilded frames. The only portrait of interest was an enormous one situated over the marble mantel of a fireplace that was rarely used—Houston wasn't exactly known for its chilly winters—showing Rose Dupree at eighteen, wearing her formal debutante gown.

"Ah, dear girl, I see you're admiring . . . well, me," her grandmother said, smiling, and set down her teacup with the gentlest of clinks.

Ginger nearly dropped the cup and saucer from her knee, surprised that Rose had paid attention to her wandering eye. She usually got reprimanded for daydreaming.

"It's quite an amazing painting, Grammy," she said, and Rose beamed at the compliment.

"I was hoping you'd take an interest in it one of these days, and never better than now." Rose took the monogrammed napkin from her lap, got up gracefully from the settee, and walked slowly toward the fireplace.

Crossing thin arms, the older woman gazed up at the portrait of her much younger self, and Ginger squinted, trying to imagine the grandmother she knew—with the fine lines

67

about her subtly powdered face, the perfectly coiffed white hair and ever-present pearls—having once been the lithe and lovely teenage girl painted in the flowing white dress.

"I was something, wasn't I?" Rose Dupree said, as if reading her mind. "Hard for you to believe I was ever your age once, hmm?"

How to answer that one without inadvertently insulting her? Ginger played it safe, replying, "You were beautiful then, and you're beautiful now."

Rose smiled appreciatively, but there was a knowing look in her eyes. "You are quite the little diplomat. I'm not sure where you got your even temper, not from either of us"—she flicked a hand toward Deena—"and most certainly not from that no-good father of yours."

Deena frowned. "Mother."

"It's true." Rose scowled back at her daughter. "Probably one of the reasons that arrogant bastard you married finally left you. You're both stubborn as mules."

"Please, Grammy, tell me more about the painting," Ginger begged, stepping in before any real fireworks went off.

Besides, she was actually curious. Art had long been a love of hers, ever since she was a kid and Deena had enrolled her in summer classes at the Glassell School, part of Houston's Museum of Fine Art. Though Ginger had redirected her passion toward the environment last year, she figured the beauty of the earth and the beauty of true art went hand in hand, like the Ansel Adams photographs she had hanging in her bedroom. Sometimes she wondered if artistic talent wasn't a big part of what had attracted her to her last ill-fated crush, Javier Garcia—besides how good-looking he was and his activism, of course—and she had to admit that it was. There was something sexy about the smell of oils and the way Javier always seemed to have a smear of paint in his hair. . . .

She cleared her throat, pushing *that* thought away, asking her grandmother, "What was it like posing for a true artist? Did you have to stand there for hours, holding the back of a chair and looking over your shoulder like *this*?" She tipped her head coyly and discreetly arched her back, mimicking Rose's stance in the portrait, and her grandma chuckled.

"It wasn't easy, let me tell you, but it was well worth it." Rose stared up at the mammoth painting and sighed. "That was certainly a time in my life I'd never want to forget. You'll see what I mean, Ginger, very soon. Becoming a Rosebud is an incredible privilege, and I'm so proud you'll be following in my footsteps."

A quiver of excitement traveled up Ginger's spine at her grandmother's words, and she flashed on the sight of the messenger in top hat and gloves who'd delivered her formal Rosebud invitation. What a relief that had been! Especially when her bad judgment in boys had nearly derailed her.

"She'll be following in my footsteps too, don't forget," Deena said, sounding miffed, as if she felt forgotten in the conversation between grandmother and granddaughter.

"Although you weren't exactly the model deb, were you, Dee?" Rose cocked her head, tapping a finger to her chin. "I so vividly recall your refusal to wear my gown or anything else that had belonged to me. Isn't that right, darlin'? And you wouldn't let me have your portrait done either, would you?"

"Good Lord, Mother." Deena set her china cup down so hard upon its saucer that the clank startled Ginger and made

Rose wince. "It was the eighties, for heaven's sake. No one I knew would've been caught dead in her mother's deb gown, much less sat for hours for some fussy old artist."

"Yes, God forbid, you would've actually honored me by donning vintage Givenchy," Rose countered, the creases around her eyes deepening as she added, "particularly when big bows and puffed sleeves were all the rage. You looked like a wedding cake that exploded."

Deena opened her mouth as if to fire back, and Ginger prepared to duck for cover. She hoped things would never get that tense between Deena and her, although chaining herself to a tree with that backstabbing, heartbreaking Javier Garcia and getting hauled down to the police station hadn't exactly made their mother-daughter bond any cozier.

But instead of blowing up, Deena settled her hands demurely in her lap and quietly uttered, "I'm so sorry you didn't like my dress, Mother."

"Didn't like it?" Rose's slim, drawn-on brows arched high above her eyes. "My dear, I *loathed* it. I was ecstatic when you and that cheating, conniving bastard eloped so I wouldn't have to pay for another god-awful monstrous white gown of your choosing."

Stop the madness! Ginger wanted to scream. It was just like Deena and Rose to turn talk of portraits and debuting into a verbal slug-fest that included jabs at Ginger's father. Their squabbling drove her crazy.

"Your portrait, Grandmother," Ginger interjected before either of the two older women could get another word in edgewise. Besides, she'd heard more than enough of what a "cheating, conniving bastard" Edward Fore was since the divorce. "Will you tell me about the man who did your portrait?" she prodded. "Who was he? Someone you knew?"

70

It was as though Ginger had pressed the On button, and Rose let out a squeal of delight (although Ginger knew her grandmother really wouldn't "squeal"—it was unladylike). The elderly woman's cheeks flushed pink beneath the fine layer of powder and she clasped her hands at her breasts, nearly snagging her triple strand of snow-white pearls.

"His name was—and is—Augustus Wakefield," Rose declared, and let out a bawdy, naughty schoolgirl laugh. "And oh, my, but he was the cat's pajamas. The man was utterly divine. He could paint like a master, and he was far too handsome for his own good."

"You had a crush on him," Ginger said, amazed she'd even suggested such a thing, but her grandmother merely grinned.

"A crush? Oh, yes, a big one." Rose reached over the mantel and touched the signature at the base of her portrait, near a barely visible satin shoe, just peeking from beneath her gown's hem. "Sitting for him when I was eighteen almost ruined me for your grandfather. When you're young, love's a dangerous thing."

Ginger wanted to say, "I know what you mean exactly." She'd gotten her heart smashed by Javier. He'd painted an amazing mural of Provence in the Fores' dining room, before his underhanded tactics to use Ginger for a tree-saving crusade had gotten him fired and her grounded for a month. She hadn't talked to him in weeks, and he'd finally stopped calling and texting her. It was better that way, Ginger decided. It was time to move on. She was all for forgiving and forgetting, except when it involved being deliberately misled and used.

"Boys are notorious liars," Rose remarked with that gentle smile on her face, and Ginger thought, *You're telling me.*

71

"Mother, please," Deena said, but Ginger wasn't sure if it was a note of warning or if Deena was appalled that her mother was being so uncharacteristically revealing.

"Well, it's the God's honest truth," Rose insisted, and glided away from the fireplace to stand behind Ginger, placing her hands on the velvet back of the chair. "Gus was a charmer, and I think he had half my debutante class madly in love with him by the time he'd finished with us."

"Finished with you?" Ginger echoed, an auburn brow raised.

Rose shook a finger at her. "Finished with our *portraits*, dear heart—at least, in my case, though I can't vouch for the others," she said, and gave Ginger a wink.

"Augustus Wakefield is a well-respected federal judge, and an incredibly generous philanthropist," Deena interjected, giving Ginger a look that clearly meant "Don't listen to your grandmother."

"Oh, but he wasn't always a judge, now, was he, Dee?" Rose replied. "Or even very respectable, come to think of it. Just because he's well thought of now doesn't make him a saint."

Deena looked primed to respond but Rose beat her to it.

"Nothing happened between Gus and me," Ginger's grandmother clarified with a toss of her silver hair. "I may have been a teenager but I was no fool, though I can't say I wasn't tempted. Gussy certainly knew his way around women, and he still does, if marrying his fourth—or is it fifth?—*much* younger wife is any indication. Let's just hope his desire to be a Lothario wasn't passed down to future generations."

What's the deal with older guys and younger chicks? Ginger wondered, realizing her last few crushes had been on older dudes. Hadn't her own father left them for his twenty-something secretary? And look at Mac's dad and Honey, too. Mac was closer to her stepmom's age than her dad was. Then there was Harrington Bell, who seemed about a hundred years older than Laura's mom.

Mac would probably chalk it up to Darwin's theory of survival of the fittest or something. Ginger just figured it was pure and simple lust.

"So Gus was a player, I get it," Ginger said, ignoring her mother's disapproving sigh. "Still, the painting's so truthful it's brilliant. Whatever this Gus dude was or wasn't to you, he definitely captured your essence. I mean, look at your eyes. . . . They're so alive!" She set aside her cup and saucer and rose from her chair, walking over to stand beneath the seven-foot portrait. "And your skin seems to glow." She clasped her hands behind her back, studying the effects of the colors and texture of the strokes on the canvas. "It's incandescent, Grammy. Really, it is. I know I'd love it if someone ever painted such an honest portrait of me."

Her grandmother looked surprised. "You would?"

"I would." Ginger nodded, thinking nothing of the exchange until Rose Dupree smiled so broadly it looked like her face would crack. A lightbulb went on in Ginger's head, and she quickly glanced in her mother's direction. But Deena wouldn't meet her eyes. She merely concentrated on her teacup as she raised it to her lips and took a sip.

So this has to do with the portrait, Ginger realized, and wondered if perhaps Rose was thinking of donating hers for the upcoming charity auction to raise funds for Trees for Houston, one of Ginger's favorite green causes. But would her grandmother truly part with something so sentimental? It didn't make sense.

"I'm delighted you feel that way, darling girl, because I have a surprise for you." Her grandmother strolled toward her, arms extended, blue-veined hands reaching for Ginger's freckled ones. "I could only hope you'd be pleased, and now I'm sure you will be."

With that, Rose let go of Ginger and scooped up a small crystal bell from a carved sideboard. She rang it with a practiced hand and, within moments, a slender mocha-skinned woman in a neat gray pantsuit entered the room, pausing just inside.

"Are you ready for him now, Miss Rose?" she asked.

"Yes, Serena," Ginger's grandmother responded. "Do bring the boy in."

The boy? *What the hell is going on?*

Was she going to be asked to babysit or was she being set up? And what, if anything, did this boy have to do with Rose's deb portrait?

Ginger didn't like the sound of it. If only she was as good at throwing a tantrum or turning on the tears as Laura Bell. Laura could dramatize her way out of any situation. It was a talent Ginger didn't possess, since she tended to overdo and Deena could see right through her.

Before Ginger could do anything, Serena returned with a tall young man. "Let me know if you need anything else, Miss Rose," the woman said, and nodded at the elder woman before bowing out of the room, drawing closed the parlor doors.

"Ah, Mrs. Dupree, you're looking as exquisite as ever," the fellow said, smiling familiarly at Ginger's grandmother.

He brushed at midnight black hair that nearly reached his collar, and Ginger noticed threads of gold as the light from the chandelier struck the thick waves. Professional highlights, and expensive ones too. *How totally metrosexual,* she thought. She was normally drawn to less materialistic guys who didn't look so picture-perfect (like Javier, for example, though look where that had gotten her).

"Kent, darling, so good to see you," Rose gushed, and made a graceful beeline across the parlor toward the lanky young man in the pin-striped trousers that clearly screamed "Armani." His black T-shirt was neatly tucked into the low-slung waistband of his pants, and he wore a black leather belt with a flat silver buckle.

He looks like Ralph Lauren's version of Goth, Ginger thought with amusement, having passed through a true post-punk dark-wave period herself. She suddenly heard Laura's voice in her ear, whispering disdainfully, "Someone should have told Kent *darling* that black *isn't* the new black."

She had to bite her cheek to suppress a giggle.

"Come in, dear boy, please," her grandmother said, the pitch of her voice rising like a giddy schoolgirl's. Rose drew her guest forward, pausing fleetingly in front of Deena. "You know my daughter, Deena Dupree Fore, of course." She hesitated only long enough for Kent to acknowledge Ginger's mother with a brief "So nice to see you again, Mrs. Fore."

Rose didn't even wait for Deena to reply in kind before dragging the fellow over to Ginger and parking him directly in front of her.

"This," Rose said, waving an arm at the young man as if he were a game-show prize, "is Kent Wakefield, the grandson of my dear old friend, Gus Wakefield."

"Augustus Wakefield?" Ginger repeated, more confused now than ever.

Her grandmother smiled, bobbing her head. "Yes, yes, the artist who painted my debutante portrait. Kent, this is my granddaughter, Ginger. She's the one you'll be painting. How positively delicious is that? Sort of like coming full circle, is it not?" Rose clapped, clearly enjoying Ginger's deer-in-headlights expression too much.

Ginger could only stare as Kent Wakefield stuck out his hand.

"Nice to meet you, Ginger," he said, and she snapped to, shaking his hand. He didn't let go.

"Uh, yeah, hi," she replied, biting on her bottom lip as she took in his patrician features. She tilted her head and squinted. Something about him seemed so familiar, but she couldn't put a finger on it. "Are you at Caldwell?" she asked, easing her fingers from his lingering grip.

"I am now, yes," he replied, his smooth-shaven face taking on a guarded expression. "I just transferred back from prep school up east. I was in Connecticut at Rockhurst, my father's alma mater, until my grandfather requested I come home. He's finagled several local galleries into showing my work, and he arranged for an internship at the Museum of Fine Arts. It was too tempting an offer to resist."

"Gus is the one who suggested I have you paint Ginger's portrait," Rose said, beaming like it was the greatest idea since instant messaging.

Kent cocked his head. "I'm sure his brilliant idea was merely a ploy to keep in touch with you, Mrs. Dupree. Apparently, once upon a time, he was pretty infatuated with you."

Ginger couldn't believe it when her always poised grandmother blushed. "You flatter me, dear boy."

Oh, this dude was smooth, all right. Apparently, he did take after his silver-tongued grandfather after all.

"I'm the one who should be flattered . . . by your interest in my art, I mean," Kent said, ducking his head modestly. "I've no doubt Gus twisted a lot of arms here in town, because my paintings are selling really well and ending up in amazing private collections. I'd like to believe he's so involved in my art because he imagines I'm that good, but I have a feeling it has more to do with his wanting to keep an eye on me."

Rose chuckled. "He's a smart man, your granddad."

"He's certainly got an eye for beautiful things, though I think that runs in the family," Kent said, and smiled at Ginger.

Give me a break!

Ginger cleared her throat and picked up where she'd left off before her grandmother had interrupted them. "So you went to Caldwell for middle school before you left the Wild West for Ivy League turf. Maybe we crossed paths, because there's something about you—I don't know. I feel like we met a long time ago."

Kent's smile evaporated, and he shifted weight from one Gucci loafer to the other. "Um, well, I was only at Caldwell until the sixth grade before my father shipped me off to Rockhurst. Could be we ran into each other at some event or other, since our families run in similar circles."

"I guess," Ginger said. It sounded plausible enough, even if she didn't believe that was it.

"Surely, I would've remembered if we'd met." His gaze

locked on hers, and this time it was Ginger who felt flustered. "You're very different from most girls," he remarked, and seemed to take her in from head to toe. "You're not so . . . obvious."

"You mean, I've actually got clothes on, and I didn't buy half my body parts," she replied, earning her a chastising "Ginger!" from Deena.

But Kent just laughed. "I can already tell that capturing you on canvas is going to be quite challenging."

"In a good way, of course," Ginger teased.

"A *very* good way."

Maybe it was her imagination, but Ginger thought he seemed a little *too* eager; sort of like a boy who'd had too many Krispy Kremes and now hungered for an organic blueberry muffin. Or perhaps like a boy who felt guilty and wanted to make up for it.

"Wonderful," Rose drawled, interrupting them. "It's settled, then. How about we schedule the first sitting for tomorrow evening at, say, eight-thirty, if that works for you, Kent. Do you have a studio?"

"I've been working out of the sunroom at my parents' house, Mrs. Dupree, and I believe Mother's throwing a dinner party tomorrow night, not that I'm invited." Kent shrugged. "My father has business partners flying in from Japan."

"Ah, I see. Well, perhaps we can arrange something else," Rose suggested.

Like, maybe another night and another time?

"Um, excuse me, Grammy," Ginger butted in, not really appreciating the way they talked as if she wasn't even there. "But I have my first Rosebud meeting tomorrow at seven at the Glass Slipper Club. I can't be there and do the sitting, too."

"Pish posh," Rose Dupree said, and dismissively waved a blue-veined hand. "That initial meeting's merely a formality. It won't take all night. It never lasts longer than an hour or so, does it, Deena?"

"Never," Deena dutifully agreed.

"But I already have plans," Ginger tried to beg off. She wanted to go to the first Rosebud meeting with Mac and Laura, and definitely didn't want to carpool with Deena any more than she wanted to return to her grandmother's afterward. "No, I'm sorry, but tomorrow night won't work for me."

"Hush, please, darling. Let Grammy think." Rose cocked her head and fiddled with the pearls around her neck, a sure sign that she was cooking up something that suited her, regardless of what anyone else had in mind.

Ginger felt completely at her mercy. Not even a pre-arranged call from Mac faking car trouble could bail her out this time, she thought with a sigh.

"I know." Rose brightened. "How about y'all come here? Ginger can model my debutante gown so you can take pictures or whatever it is you do to prepare, Kent, dear. You can even use the library for as long as you're working on the portrait. It's where Gus painted me, if you hadn't already guessed."

"What a lovely idea," Deena piped up with a smile—the first real smile that Ginger had seen on her mother's face all afternoon. She turned to Ginger. "Sweetie, we can go together, if you'd like. I have to be at the meeting anyway."

Would anyone listen if she said no?

Kent obviously noticed her frustration. But instead of making it easy on her by suggesting another date, he stepped toward her, explaining, "I promise it won't take long. We'll just do some preliminary staging, and I'll take some photographs. It'll be over in a flash."

"A flash, huh?" Ginger sighed, realizing this wasn't something she could get out of gracefully—or at all. She nodded reluctantly. "Okay. So long as I'm allowed to come by myself. Thanks anyway, Mother."

She glanced at Deena, who shrugged, which was as good a nonresponse as any. Ginger had expected a bit of an argument, but her mom seemed too happy about the turn of events to put up a fight. That got Ginger to wondering if this whole scenario hadn't been cooked up between Deena and Rose to keep her occupied for a while so she wouldn't waste her time on "unworthy boys" like Javier Garcia. Ginger wasn't normally a conspiracy theorist, but she found the idea entirely plausible.

"So there we are," Rose said, and her pale eyes lit up within the soft folds of her face. "I'll see everyone back here tomorrow night at around half past eight. Ginger?" Her grandmother's penciled brows arched.

"Yes, Grammy, I'll be here," she agreed, wishing it didn't mean skipping out on her two best friends.

Trust has nothing to do with love.
It's vigilance that's important.
—Tallulah Bankhead

Love may be blind, but I'd rather
keep both eyes wide open.
—Jo Lynn Bidwell

Five

"No freakin' way!" Jo Lynn squealed into her iPhone as she drove her Audi one-handed down tree-shaded Bunker Hill toward the cul-de-sac where Dillon lived, already late for his family's Labor Day barbecue. "You saw *Laura Bell* working out at the club? Sure you didn't sprinkle crack on your Frosted Flakes?"

"It was Laura, I swear to God," Camie Lindell assured her.

"Damn, I would've paid to see that! Does the Hostess Cupcake even know how to break a sweat?"

"Only if it involves shoveling food into her mouth," Camie said, laughing.

"Snap!" Jo wondered if Laura's workout was in any way inspired by the edible gifts she'd been getting from her phony admirer. She smirked at the thought. If Laura seemed panicked about her weight, then maybe Jo's plan to bulk her up and get her booted from the Rosebuds was right on track. Being a Glass Slipper Club deb was a privilege that a debu-tank like Laura didn't deserve. "Was she alone?"

"Do Randoms ever travel alone?" Cam retorted. "She was with that mousy Mac Mackenzie. Although they were both gone by the time Trisha and I finished with yoga. They probably had heart attacks after five minutes on the treadmill."

"I doubt Laura even lasted that long." Jo snorted.

"Dillon was there too. We ran into him before our class."

"Oh, really?" Dillon had mentioned working out before the party, but still Jo's pulse picked up at the idea of Dill and Laura being in the same room when she wasn't around. It was that conniving slut she didn't trust. "Was he with anyone?" Jo Lynn ventured to ask.

"Just some other jock."

Jo's heartbeat slowed, and she told herself, *See, nothing to worry about!*

"I'm on my way to Dill's house now," Jo Lynn told her friend, and took her hand off the wheel long enough to hit her right blinker, before she turned onto Dillon's street. "I'm a little behind, so I've gotta run. I'll catch up with you later so we can talk smack. Did you hear that one Rosebud already bit the dust? Though Bootsie wouldn't tell me who."

"Omigod," Camie breathed. "It must be Mindy Sue Mabry. My mom was yakking on her cell this morning about the Mabrys going bankrupt and Donatella Versace refusing to do Mindy's dress on credit."

"Mindy Sue? Are you sure?" Jo couldn't help feeling disappointed it wasn't the Hostess Cupcake or one of her troll-like friends.

"Like, ninety-nine percent sure, but I guess we'll find out all the gory details tomorrow night at the first deb meeting, right?" Camie said, adding giddily, "God, I can't wait!"

"The first deb meeting, yes," Jo said, playing down her own excitement when just uttering those words gave her an unbelievable rush. The Rosebud orientation was the official start to their debutante season, and it couldn't begin soon enough for her.

"So you're going to Dill's barbecue?" Cam asked, changing the subject. "Tell me if you see Avery, and take notes on anyone he talks to, pretty please? He didn't ask me to go with him, the jerk. He told me he wanted to chill with his homies."

"I'll keep an eye on him," Jo promised, wondering what the hell was going on with Avery. Ever since Jo had caught him kissing Laura-the-Party-Crasher at Jo's end-of-summer bash, he'd been acting more and more like a loose cannon, doing things his own way instead of following her advice. Jo just hoped it wouldn't get to be a real problem, or she'd have to yank him back in line again.

"At least Brody didn't invite Trisha either," Cam rambled on. "They probably just want to get drunk and act like idiots, which is why the coaches aren't ever invited." When Jo didn't respond, Camie sighed. "So, anyhoo, we'll be getting mani-pedis at the club spa while you frolic poolside with the football studs."

"Look, I gotta go. TTFN," Jo Lynn drawled into her phone and hung up before Camie could say more. She dropped the cell into her lap.

She glanced at the clock on her dash. It was fifteen past one, which she'd hardly consider late for a formal dinner, much less a casual barbecue. Besides, it wasn't as if Dillon ever expected her to be on time, and Jo liked being unpredictable.

For anybody else, being late might mean parking miles away, particularly since the line of cars in front of the Masterses' house went from one end of the street to another. But Jo wasn't just *anybody*.

85

She smiled to herself, knowing that Dillon had arranged for her to park in the driveway. So, no worries about having to wedge her pristine Audi between any of the dusty vehicles perched on the grassy shoulder between the dip of the drainage ditch and the road, thank God.

As Jo slowly rolled forward, she glimpsed Avery Dorman's burnt-orange Corvette stuck between two over-sized Chevy pickups with tires so huge they came up to her hips. One truck wore a bumper sticker that read: WARNING TAILGATERS! DRIVER CHEWS TOBACCO.

Ugh, rednecks, Jo thought, and stuck out her tongue. *Dillon might play football with a few cowboys, but he definitely isn't one.*

Jo slid her Audi between the rows of cars on either side of the street, cruising toward the sprawling Mediterranean-style mansion at the cul-de-sac's far end. Within a blink, she spotted a handmade sign tacked to a stepladder at the foot of the driveway, the only open space, as it looked like a parking lot with the BMWs, Mercedes, and Escalades packed in like sardines. *Reserved for Jo Lynn* the sign read in Dillon's handwriting. *How precious is that?* she thought as she put the car in park, jumping out long enough to get the stepladder moved, and then hopping back in the driver's seat to pull the car in. Dillon always made sure she was taken care of. So few guys even bothered to hold doors open for their girlfriends these days, and here Dill had gone and made her a front-row parking space.

Before Jo Lynn turned off the engine, she sat in the cool of the air-conditioning and dabbed another layer of MAC gloss on her lips until her mouth looked slick and luscious. She checked her hair, the pale tresses worn long and straight, which made her blue eyes pop.

Can't improve on perfection, she told herself, and grinned as she slipped her Prada shades on. Then she cracked the windows in the Audi before she locked up, even though it wouldn't help much. It might officially be September, but a high of near ninety was predicted, which meant her thighs would stick to the leather seats when she got back in, no matter what. Looking on the bright side, at least living in H-town meant she never had to break out the snow tires, right?

She tugged on the hem of her brown BCBG miniskirt and turquoise-striped tee before striding toward the front door of the Masters mansion in her matching turquoise Max Azria sandals.

With each long-legged step, the sun warmed her arms and the top of her head. A prickle of anticipation raced through her as she followed the curve of the driveway toward the custom new-construction home that looked very much like a Texas builder's idea of an Italian villa. Dillon and his family had moved in just about when he and Jo had started dating. She recalled Ray Masters mentioning that his "baby" exceeded ten thousand square feet, and figured Dillon's dad had definitely wanted to outdo the Joneses in a big way. According to Dill, the contractor had torn down two adjacent McMansions to make way for Big Ray's showplace.

Not bad for an ex-football jock who peddles cars for a living, Jo Lynn mused as she reached the sandstone path set precisely between rows of Royal Palms that towered overhead at least twenty feet. Ahead lay a two-story entrance with a carved teak door below the second-story balcony with its hand-forged iron railing.

Beyond the pale peach stucco facade, she heard Willie

Nelson wailing, "You were always on my mind," from the backyard speakers. Dillon's dad did love his Willie . . . and his barbecue. Jo sniffed the air, thinking she could smell that, too.

"Hey, there you are!"

Dillon burst through the front door before Jo Lynn had even reached the welcome mat. He must've been on the lookout for her, she figured, and her heart nearly jumped from her chest.

"I was wondering when you'd show."

"Like I've ever been on time to anything," Jo teased with a smile, taking in the sight of him as she walked forward. He had on Quiksilver board shorts, slung low on his hips, and his chest was bare and bronzed, sculpted muscles everywhere she looked. His blond hair was slicked back from his head and appeared dark, damp with pool water.

God, he's too good to be true.

She had to stop herself from drooling. "Did you miss me?"

Instead of answering, Dillon pulled her in for a bear hug, and Jo Lynn breathed in the warm smell of him, like tanning oil and beer. It was like nectar to a bee, and she couldn't resist catching her fingers in his hair and pulling him in for a deep, wet kiss that sent heat oozing through her belly and left Dillon's lips covered in MAC gloss.

"You're a mess," she said, and ran a thumb over his mouth, wiping away the pink smear as he grinned and tugged her by the hand.

"My dad's been asking where you were. Hell, most of the team has been wondering, too. I think they just want to eyeball you in your bikini," he said, leading her through the ginormous foyer with its patterned marble floors, pink marble columns, and double staircase with a stylized wrought-iron banister that split and swirled above them.

Jo nearly tripped as he drew her into the step-down great room with sliding doors that lead to the patio outside.

"Dad's manning the grill, as always, but everyone else is either drinking something cold or they're in the pool. You did bring your swimsuit?" he asked as he pushed a glass door wide and led her outside.

"I'm good to go," Jo promised him, having worn her turquoise Vitamin A halter top and low-rise bottoms underneath her shirt and mini.

Once they'd left behind the quiet interior of the Mediterranean mansion, the noise level rose appreciably. Willie Nelson's voice twanged loudly, though the buzz of conversation and shouts and splashes from the pool nearly drowned poor Willie out. The immense patio area swelled with bodies: mostly muscular dudes in bathing trunks, roughhousing in the pool or lounging on the sidelines swigging beers—always Shiner Bock in cans, of course, since Big Ray didn't cotton to glass in the pool area. Even the balcony area swarmed with people. Jo made out Dillon's mother in a group of women sipping margaritas from pink Lucite glasses, and she gave a little wave.

"Hey, Jo Lynn! Looking *gooood*!" a chorus of boys called out from the shallow end of the pool, and Jo blew them kisses. They grabbed at their hearts and fell backward in the water.

"This way," Dillon fairly shouted in her ear, and tugged her toward one of the many umbrellaed tables arranged on the patio around the pool. He pulled out a chair for her, giving her no choice but to settle in and put her purse down.

"Can I get you a drink? You know my dad never invites the coaches, so there's plenty of beer, and Mom's got pitchers of mojitos and margaritas," her boyfriend said, poised to take off if she said yes. But she shook her head.

"Just sit with me a minute, okay?"

"Yeah, sure." He grabbed the next chair, pulling it nearer, and sprawled out beside her. "Nice day for this, huh? And the forecasters predicted rain. Those doughnuts never get it right. Better to just look out the window."

"It's a perfect day," Jo said, reaching over to squeeze his hand. "Looks like the whole team's present and accounted for."

"Just about," Dillon confirmed. "Plus, friends of Mom and Dad's. Seems like it gets bigger every year."

"Good thing you've got the space."

Dillon laughed, leaned back in his chair, and stretched out. The sun slanted below the umbrella overhead, catching the blond hair on his chest and legs and turning them gold. "Why do you think Big Ray bought this place? The man likes to party."

Jo figured it was more like Big Ray needed to impress people now that he didn't have the cachet of being a pro football player to brag about, which is probably why he bragged so much on Dillon and put such emphasis on Dill becoming someone *special*.

"Your pal Avery's here," Dillon remarked, and Jo looked around them. "Apparently, he came alone."

"Yeah, Camie's pretty frosted about that."

"I'll bet she is."

Without too much trouble, Jo Lynn spotted Avery across the way, sitting on the pool's edge, his muscular legs dangling in the water, talking to some pretty brunette Jo didn't recognize. *Has he tired of Camie already?* she wondered, eyes narrowing as she watched them flirt, splashing water on each other and laughing. Jo hated the thought of him getting itchy and drifting back to Laura Bell. The cow wasn't near good enough for him, but Avery didn't seem to always see what was best for him, which was where Jo came in. Maybe it was time they had another little heart-to-heart chat, so she could remind him how unpleasant things could get when he didn't listen to her. He surely wouldn't want the past coming back to haunt him, would he?

As if sensing her eyes on him, Avery lifted his head, looking right in her direction, and Jo stared right back. He raised a can of Shiner in mock salute.

She frowned and turned toward Dillon just as a shadow fell over the table.

"Aha, so she did show up after all," a hoarse voice twanged, and Jo glanced up to find a very large middle-aged man hovering above her. Gray fuzz covered his head and chest, and a Texas-sized beer belly hung over his swim trunks. "How's the prettiest gal in Texas?"

"Big Ray!" Jo jumped out of her seat, giving Dillon's daddy a couple of dramatic air kisses. "You think I'd ever miss one of your barbecues?"

"As long as you're datin' this son of mine, you'd better not!" he said, and pulled her into a bear hug, rocking her back and forth, nearly smothering her with his oversized arms. He smelled like hot sauce and grill smoke. "You're just the kind of young woman my boy needs to keep him on track," Ray declared as he let Jo Lynn go and patted his son on the back. Dillon looked about as comfortable as a possum crossing the Katy Freeway in rush hour traffic.

"A hotshot blue-chip quarterback should have a knockout

91

babe on his arm," Ray Masters stated, scratching his jaw. "Being a total package only makes his value skyrocket, 'cause everyone's always looking for the next Broadway Joe. These days, it's as much about your image as your arm." He slapped Dillon again. "Am I right, or am I right?"

"It's gotta be right if you say it is," Dillon dutifully replied.

"Smart-ass." Ray lovingly cuffed him. Then he rubbed his hands together. "Burgers are almost ready. It's all Grade A sirloin, darlin', nothing but the best," he told Jo, giving her a wink. "Just like you, sweet pea."

With that, he walked away, greeting others in his path, and Jo heard Dillon let out a held breath.

"Jesus, I think I know how you felt when you were doing all those pageants," he said, running a hand over his damp hair and shaking his head. "It's, like, not just about you, is it? What you want and how hard you work to get it doesn't even come close to the image you project. I feel like I'm under a freaking microscope."

Jo's heart tugged at his confession, and she reached out to lay her palm against his cheek. For a second, he leaned into her touch. But instead of something sympathetic coming out of her mouth, she rambled on like an idiot: "I don't even know who Broadway Joe is. Is he an actor or something?"

Dillon instantly lifted his head, drawing away again. "Are you kidding me? You've never heard of Joe Namath?" he asked, sounding miffed. "He's a Hall of Famer, played QB for the New York Jets most of his career." When Jo still drew a blank, Dillon pressed on. "He's the first quarterback to throw more than four thousand yards in a season, for Christ's sake. Joe's an effing legend."

Jo shrugged. She couldn't have cared less about some old jock who was probably dead by now. What she wanted was to take that fleeting moment of real intimacy between them and make it permanent, like concrete. "I don't care about Joe What's-His-Name, Dill, because I have you here right now, and you'll be a legend, too, one of these days. Like your daddy said, every star needs the perfect woman on his arm. Am I right, or am I right?" she said, only half teasing.

"Big Ray has you well trained," Dillon remarked, and his mouth curved ever so slightly.

"I think I would like that drink now," she said, and slipped her shades atop her head so she could look him in the eye. "If you don't mind fetching one for me."

"Big Ray would kick my ass if I didn't." He slapped his hands on the chair arms. "Be back in five," he said, and started to rise, but Jo pulled him back down for a second.

"I love you," she whispered, and leaned forward to kiss him soundly on the lips. He did a good job of responding, even reaching over to give her ass a squeeze as his tongue slipped into her mouth, expertly twisting and twirling around hers. She grabbed his shoulder, holding on tight as she tipped her head, making the kiss even deeper, earning them a shout of "Get a room, Masters!" from the guys at the next table, before Dillon drew away, looking pleased with himself.

"Now I'll get drinks. Two margaritas, coming up," he said, trailing a finger across her cheek before he headed off.

Jo Lynn propped her sunglasses back on her nose and watched him walk away, his broad shoulders maneuvering between crowded umbrella-topped tables. He paused to chat and slap a few backs along the way, as was his nature. At that rate, Jo figured it'd take him fifteen minutes to deliver her margarita. So she might as well put the time to good use, right?

She retrieved her iPhone from her bag and speed-dialed, looking straight across the pool at Avery as he picked up.

"So you're such a princess you can't walk around the pool to come talk to me?" he said, waving at her from where he dangled his legs in the water, the brunette, who stuck to his side like fungus, looking pissed off.

"I'm waiting for Dillon to get back with our drinks." In other words, Jo wasn't going anywhere. Avery caught on quickly.

"Which means you want me to come to you?"

"Bingo," she said, and hung up on him, tucking her cell back into her purse.

While she waited for him to ditch the brown-haired babe and wend his way toward her, Jo Lynn shimmied out of her T-shirt, pulling it over her head without disturbing her sunglasses; then she unzipped the mini and slid it down her legs. With only her turquoise bikini strategically covering her body, she settled back in her chair, crossing her legs and tipping her face to the sun. Behind the dark lenses of her shades, she saw Avery approach.

"You summoned?" he said as he plopped into the chair beside her.

"I thought we should chat," Jo said coolly, noting the subtle dip of his chin, and then she caught her breasts reflected in his sunglasses, the curves barely covered by the small triangles of fabric.

"Chat about . . . Damn, what the eff?" His gaze dropped to his lap, and he made a face as he fished under his thigh.

"Is this yours?" he asked, pulling a cell from beneath his leg and setting it on the table.

"Thanks," Jo said, and palmed the phone. It must've dropped out of Dillon's pocket when he got up to leave.

"So, whassup?" Avery prodded, elbows on his knees, leaning forward. His perfectly toned abs rippled above the low-slung waistband of his brown Ed Hardy shorts. He looked even better now than a few years ago when Jo had been dating him. Her gaze strayed down toward his muscled thighs until she saw the skull and heart design on his shorts that read LOVE KILLS SLOWLY and her smile died.

"Why didn't you bring Camie?" she said, getting right to the point. "You're not breaking up with her again, are you, Av? Do you need me to remind you of why she's right for you, as opposed to"—she hesitated and lowered her voice— "less desirable girls."

"Less desirable, huh? According to the Gospel of Jo Lynn." Avery's smile tightened, and he tugged at his earlobe. "Maybe it's time I figured out what I want all by myself. Maybe who I want isn't who you want for me. You can't hold the past over my head forever."

Oh, can't I? Jo Lynn's whole body tensed. "If you go back to Laura, I swear to God, I'll—"

She stopped herself, and it was a good thing she did. Avery's square jaw tensed, his eyes darkening to black.

"You'll what?"

Jo frowned at him. "Nothing."

"Right." He shook his head and stood up. "I'm not doing this today, okay? I'm not arguing with you about my love life. I'm here to chill, which is *exactly* why I didn't bring Cam. You might want to think about relaxing too. It's gotta get tense running everyone's lives all the time. God help Dillon if he ever slips." A devilish smile took shape on his lips. "Or has he already?"

"What's that supposed to mean?" Jo reached for his arm, wanting him to sit back down and explain himself, but Avery wasn't having it.

"Watch out for the sun, sweetheart," he drawled. "It's hot enough to burn today." With that, he gave her a backhanded wave and strolled away.

Well, damn his stubborn hide, she thought, unconsciously curling her fingers around Dillon's cell phone, wanting to pound the table with it. *Probably not a good idea.* She reconsidered, and set the cell in her lap.

"God help Dillon if he ever slips . . . or has he already?"

What was that, a warning or just spite?

Jo stared down at Dillon's phone in her hands and gnawed on the inside of her cheek. Dill would never betray her. Big Ray would strangle him, for one thing, and Dillon hated having his father on his ass.

Still—she flipped the cell open with a fingernail—what harm would it do if she checked who he'd been calling? It wasn't like reading his text messages or e-mail.

She glanced around her, but no one was paying her the slightest bit of attention, and Dillon was nowhere to be seen. He'd probably had to duck inside for the drinks and gotten cornered by somebody. At the very least, she had a couple of minutes until he got back.

Her heart thudding in her chest, she quickly scanned his recent calls, checking out the numbers from this morning, which all looked benign until she got farther down the list: Coach Ben, Brody, Mike, Mom, Big Ray, Laura Bell. . . .

Laura Bell?

WTF???

Had Dill really phoned Laura Bell at—she squinted at the time stamp—a few minutes past nine that very morning?

Jo's stomach lurched. She had to ask him about it. Surely, he'd have a logical explanation, because there was no way he was two-timing her with that fat bitch. *He couldn't be, could he?* It would explain why he'd been so distracted these past months and where he'd gotten that whack idea about slowing down, as in no sex for longer than Jo Lynn could remember.

Chillax, she told herself. *It's got to be a fluke, something weird.* Someone else could have borrowed his phone, right? Maybe even Avery, just to mess with her. Well, it was possible, wasn't it? Av and Dillon played football together, had shared the practice field and the locker room every day even if they weren't best friends.

Jo had nearly convinced herself of that until she got into Dillon's address book, and suddenly she couldn't swallow. Because there it was, that name again: Laura Bell. And hideously enough, it was listed right in front of *her* name. Bell before Bidwell, perfectly alphabetical.

OMFG.

Jo started to stand up, her legs wobbling. Where was Dillon? Why was it taking him so long to get their margaritas? She wanted the truth right this minute!

Whoa, girl, whoa.

She took a deep breath, willing herself to calm down, which is when it clicked in her brain that confrontation was the wrong approach entirely.

What am I, crazy?

Jo sank back down into her chair, and her course shifted 180 degrees. Clear as day, she realized she couldn't ask Dillon why he had that skank's name in his phone without him knowing she'd snooped, without him thinking that she didn't trust him. And for someone like Dillon Masters, who constantly had people grabbing at him and wanting things from him, trust meant everything.

No matter how much it hurt, Jo had no choice but to stay cool and pretend she'd never nosed around in Dillon's cell. Until she could figure out the truth on her own, she'd just keep finding more ways to dig an even deeper grave for Laura Bell.

A loving heart has a cataract
and cannot see.
—Louise Colet

What's so wrong
with believing in true love?
—Laura Bell

Six

Since Labor Day had begun less than optimally, with Mac dragging her out of bed and to the country club gym, Laura spent the afternoon doing something requiring zero exertion or sweat: she lounged on the sofa in the downstairs den, pale hair pulled back in a madras-plaid headband, dressed for comfort in a pair of hot-pink Capri pants, white T-shirt, and bare feet. The room was large but cozy, filled with over-stuffed furnishings, walnut bookshelves, faded Turkish rugs, and potted palms. The sun streamed through the slanted shutters on the windows, dimming the screen of the sixty-inch TV, but Laura didn't care. She'd set it on mute while MTV counted down the top ten most bling-filled episodes of *My Super Sweet 16*.

She focused on the fall issue of *Brides* magazine in her lap, poring over the pictures. She kept dog-earing pages that featured elaborate to-die-for gowns so Tincy could forward her ideas to Vera Wang for her custom-made Rosebud gown. Hers had to be *perfect* in every way, more so because she wasn't a size nothing like most of the other girls. She was determined to outclass and outgorgeous Jo Lynn

Bidwell, no matter what it took, and it was going to take plenty.

Ding-dong!

Laura lifted her head at the sound of the doorbell, though she made no move to get up. She wasn't expecting anyone, what with Mac on a bike ride with Alex Bishop, and Ginger doomed to spend the afternoon at her grandmother's house.

"Baby, will you get that?" Tincy yelled from another room as the bell chimed again.

"I'm busy!" Laura called back, and returned her eyes to the pages of *Brides,* not moving except to scratch an itch on her nose.

"Never mind, I'll do it myself!" her mother hollered back, and Laura soon heard the click-clack of high heels on the polished floors.

With the housekeeper and even Babette, Tincy Bell's social secretary, off for Labor Day, it was Tincy herself who brought a pink-cheeked Mac into the den where Laura was sprawled out.

"You've got a guest, sweetie." Her mom paused in the doorway, her skinny arms crossed, looking pink and green in her preppy Lilly Pulitzer sundress. Her face still seemed shiny and flushed from a morning spa treatment. Mac might've appeared a little flushed too, though she was anything but shiny in her rumpled shorts and purple T-shirt, a gloomy look on her bespectacled face.

"Thanks, Mother," Laura said, sitting up on the sofa and setting the fat magazine aside so Mac could flop down beside her.

"Let me know if y'all need anything," Tincy said.

"We will."

Once her mom had pulled the pocket doors closed behind her, Laura pounced on her pal. "What're you doing here, *chica*? You're supposed to be spending all afternoon with the Geek Next Door. Did he blow you off so he could stay home and watch the *Battlestar Galactica* marathon on the Sci-Fi Channel?"

"Ha-ha, very funny." Mac grabbed a pillow and hugged it, sighing heavily. "I'm just a little bummed. Why can't things ever turn out the way I plan?"

"Welcome to my world," Laura said with a laugh, though Mac didn't even crack a smile. In fact, she hadn't seen Mac looking so grim since her dad had married Honey Potts, something she still hadn't gotten over. "Good God, Mackenzie, what's wrong? Did you and Alex have a fight? You look like the world's about to end."

"It's not quite as bad as Armageddon," Mac insisted, and tossed the pillow aside, pulling her knees up to her chest. "Everything was going great until we had a stupid *picnic crasher.*"

"A picnic crasher?" Laura raised her eyebrows. She'd heard of wedding crashers and party crashers—hell, she'd *been* a party crasher—but never that.

"I had no idea Alex had invited anyone else until I realized he'd packed too much food and then I heard him on the phone," Mac rattled off breathlessly, looking relieved to finally be able to spit it out. "We were about to have lunch and then all of a sudden *she* showed up. I had to sit there like a drone and watch her and Alex flirt like we were back in junior high. I know it shouldn't bug me this much, but it does." Mac tapped her chin on her knee, arms wrapped tightly around her bent legs.

"She who?" Laura asked, since Mac had left a big freaking

blank in the story. "And, wait, did you say *invited*? So Alex knew she was coming, but didn't tell you? No wonder you're pissed."

Mac nodded. "I guess he thought I wouldn't care, but I do, even though we're just friends, right?"

"For God's sake, Mac, *who*?" Laura tried again.

Mac opened her mouth to reply.

Ding-dong!

Once the doorbell chimed, Mac zipped her lips.

"Ignore that. Go on, spill," Laura prodded, but her friend's head had turned toward the pocket doors, as voices grew louder beyond it, accompanied by the staccato tap of footsteps in the hallway.

"Someone's coming," Mac said just as the pocket doors slid back open and Ginger strolled into the room. Her red hair stuck out in messy peaks around her freckled face, which broke into a huge pixie grin the moment she spied Laura sitting there with Mac.

"Nice! It's like a Three Amigas surprise reunion!" Laura hopped up from the sofa and gave Ginger a hug. "But I thought you were grounded. How'd you get away?"

"Deena gave me a reprieve since I played nice at Rose's." Ging ruffled Mac's hair before she plunked down on the floor, tucking the skirt of her dress around her as she sat cross-legged. "You won't believe what happened at Grammy's tea party."

"I'm still waiting to hear what happened with Mac," Laura said, settling back down beside Mac and giving her a nudge. "She was just about to dish on some girl who showed up and ruined their Labor Day picnic by flirting with Alex Bishop, which apparently made our little Mackie a wee bit jealous!"

"Am not," Mac said defensively, her face beet red, prompting Laura to chant, "Liar, liar, pants on fire," until Mac whacked her with a throw pillow and begged, *"Shut up."*

"What girl are you talking about?" Ginger asked, leaning forward. "Someone we know?"

"I was getting to that," Mac said, clearly irritated. "It was Cindy Chow, the transfer from St. John's. She and Alex met at a stupid car show, and I am *so* not jealous." Mac gave the bridge of her smart-girl glasses a shove. "You're making a big deal out of nothing. I just wanted some time with Alex alone, and I didn't get it. That's all there is to it. End of story." She raised her chin as if daring anyone to refute her.

Laura glanced at Ginger, knowing that she didn't believe Mac any more than Laura did. Still, you could only push Mac Mackenzie's buttons so many times before she shut down. And Mac's posture—knees to her chest, arms hugging them, lips pursed—meant they wouldn't pry anything more out of her, not right now.

So she turned to face Ginger, nudging her with a bare foot. "Guess it's your turn to share, since Mac's being a party pooper." Laura ignored Mac, who stuck out her tongue. "How's Rose Dupree?"

"As sly as ever," Ginger said, blowing out a slow breath. "Y'all wouldn't believe how she set me up." Her petite hands fluttered, gesturing as she told them, "I'm having my portrait done in my grandmother's debutante gown, and the artist painting me is the grandson of the guy who painted Rose when she was a Rosebud."

"Does that sound like an old *Gilmore Girls* rerun or what?" Mac cracked. "But if you tell me how hot he is, I'm gonna gag."

"Okay, I won't tell you"—Ginger grinned mischievously, looking fit to burst—"but he is."

Mac pretended to stick a finger down her throat.

"Only I've got these strange vibes about him, like I met him a long time ago, and it wasn't good," Ginger said, causing Laura to squint with confusion.

"So, it's a past-life thing?" she teased, but Ginger shook her head.

"More like a middle school thing. He's a senior at Caldwell now," Ginger explained. "He's been up east in boarding school. Someplace called Rockhurst, I think. He moved away after sixth grade."

"What's his name?" Mac prodded, beating Laura to the punch.

"Kent Wakefield," Ginger supplied.

"Wakefield," Laura repeated, and shrugged, not recognizing the name. She looked at Mac, who shrugged as well.

"Um, Mackenzie." Ginger sat up on her heels. "Any chance you could ask Alex if I could borrow an old Caldwell Academy yearbook from when we were all in sixth grade? I want to look Kent up, see if anything jogs my brain."

"Sure," Mac said before asking, "You really have to sit for him? Won't that be boring?"

"Well, *I* think it's très exciting," Laura said, wishing Mac would stop being such a drag. "Do y'all remember the scene in *Titanic* where Kate Winslet poses for Leo, and she's wearing, like, *nothing* except that necklace and you can tell right then and there how much they're in love." Laura feigned a swoon, falling back on the cushions. "Oh, man, that was beautiful!"

"I think I just threw up in my mouth a little," Mac said dryly.

But Ginger looked amused, at least momentarily. "The

106

only bad thing about it is I'll have my first sitting tomorrow night at Rose's right after the deb orientation meeting." She winced. "So I can't sneak off to Marble Slab with y'all afterward."

"Wait a minute, wait a minute." Mac gesticulated wildly. "I thought we were doing all this deb crap together. You can't bail on us," she groaned.

"Yes, she can, if it's important," Laura chastised, and Mac scowled in response. Then she turned to Ginger and gushed, "How totally cool to have your deb portrait done. The rest of us will just have dumb old photographs to show for it, but you'll have real art."

"I hoped you'd understand," Ginger said, sounding relieved. "And I promise I'll meet y'all there, and we can all sit together." Her wide mouth curved into a full-fledged grin. "It's gonna be so amazing, being with you two at Rosebud orientation, getting our handbooks—"

"And watching Jo Lynn Bidwell and her Bimbo Cartel squirm, knowing how much they *loathe* the fact that we're there at all," Laura said, butting in, and Ginger giggled.

"Let's just hope Jo-L doesn't get wind of your messing around with her boyfriend at the club gym this morning," Mac said pointedly.

"I wasn't messing around with him," Laura snapped back, wanting to put the smack-down on her for even bringing that up, when Laura hadn't spilled that part of her plan to Ginger yet.

Ginger wrinkled her pert nose, looking clueless. "What's this about you and Dillon? What'd I miss?" was all she got out before the melodic *ding-dong* of the door chimes interrupted them.

Before Laura could open her mouth, Tincy called out,

"*Sweetheart!* Would you come out here, please? You've got another delivery!"

"*Another* delivery?" Mac squinted. "Have you been watching QVC? You didn't order, like, fifty lip-gloss holders with mirrors or something?"

"No, smart-ass, I didn't order lip-gloss holders," Laura said, getting up from the sofa and marching barefoot toward the pocket doors, sliding them open. "I think it's from my secret admirer," she tossed over her shoulder before she raced toward the foyer, the noise of Mac's and Ginger's footsteps right behind her.

"Where is it?" Laura ran up to Tincy, who was carrying a box toward the kitchen.

"It's all yours," her mom said once she'd set it down on the glass and wrought-iron breakfast table.

Hardly aware that Mac and Ginger had gathered around her, Laura glanced at the Fairytale Bakery return address, her adrenaline rushing. She didn't waste a minute, ripping the package open and spilling out its contents from a nest of Styrofoam peanuts. She plucked out a purple box from its center and opened it wide to reveal dozens of brownies, a bag of cashews, and a big jar of caramel sauce for dipping. Like the gifts before—the Godiva chocolates and the gourmet cupcakes—there was a simple message included: *From your admirer.*

Laura dug through the box, hoping to find more, wanting to see a name on the invoice to tell her exactly who her mysterious admirer was. But there was nothing.

"Who's it from?" Mac asked, impatiently snatching the card from her hand and murmuring, "Don't you find this kind of creepy?"

"No, it's romantic," Ginger piped up, and reached over to the box to inspect Laura's gifts. "You still think Avery's the one who's been sending stuff?"

"It has to be him," she said, knowing she'd racked her brains to come up with someone else who'd want to secretly court her and coming up empty.

"Avery Dorman?" Tincy said shrilly, reminding Laura she was there. Her bracelets jangled as she fingered her tousled hair. "If *that boy* is sending these things, what the devil's wrong with him? Doesn't he know it's deb season and you're watching your weight?"

Laura sighed, wanting to snap, "No, Mother, *you're* the one watching my weight." But Tincy did have a point.

Tincy crossed her arms snugly over her chest, half obscuring the green and bright pink pattern on the bodice of her sundress. "I'd hate to see what happens if the GSC selection committee decides you're too *stocky* to come out. And that's just what's gonna happen if you keep wolfin' down all this chocolate sabotage. You won't even fit in the Vera Wang gown we've commissioned!"

Mac and Ginger stood silently, eyes downcast, saying nothing.

Laura couldn't blame them. Even she wasn't sure how to react to her mother's outburst. Like ninety-nine percent of the super-skinny socialite moms in the Villages, Tincy lived by the motto "You can never be too rich or too thin," even if being too thin meant looking like a Tootsie Pop. *I am who I am*, Laura reminded herself, taking in a deep breath. *And I will never be Tincy.*

She gathered up the box of brownies and said, "Don't worry about me, Mother. I know what I'm doing. C'mon, amigas"—she jerked her chin at her two BFFs—"let's go upstairs."

"*Laura.*" Her mother made a tsk-tsk noise. "Please don't be like that. I'm only trying to help. I wouldn't say these things except that I love you so much. Sami always told me I was too overprotective, and maybe she was right."

Ya think?

"Whatev," Laura murmured, and strode purposefully upstairs, holding her door open for Mac and Ginger before shutting them all in her bedroom. "Who wants a brownie?" she asked as she dropped onto her bed with the tub of treats.

"I'll have one!" Mac volunteered, adding with a grumble, "Since I didn't exactly eat much for lunch."

"Are they organic?" Ginger asked, bending over the box and trying to read the list of ingredients.

"Organic-schmanic. They smell amazing!" Laura declared. "I worked out this morning with Mac, so one won't kill me in spite of what Tincy thinks." That said, she grabbed a chocolate-mint brownie, ripping off the wrapper and biting in. She rolled her eyes dreamily as she chewed. *Ah, heaven!*

She was tempted to try another until she remembered that her favorite True Religion jeans felt kind of snug yesterday—the housekeeper had probably washed them on hot and put them in the dryer—but instead, feeling emboldened, she reached for her BlackBerry and started to text. Thanx 4 the brownies, she thumbed at warp speed. But U don't have 2 keep sending stuff. U know how I feel abt U.

"What are you doing?" Mac grabbed her arm, trying to look at the tiny screen. "Please, don't be texting Avery."

"What if I am?" Laura said, and snatched her arm back.

Who was Mac to give her advice on her love life? She couldn't even acknowledge that she had a thing for Alex Bishop.

"Laura." Ginger looked at her quizzically with those big green eyes, and Laura wondered if even Ginger understood, what with the way she was always crushing on someone who ended up treating her like crap. Not that Avery had done everything right—because he hadn't—but Laura had no doubt he was her one true love. Had Ginger ever truly felt that way about anyone yet?

"Okay, so it's totally uncool," Laura admitted, because she knew it's what they wanted to hear. "But I know it's him. I just wish he'd admit it."

"You're hopeless," Mac muttered, and Ginger just bit her lip, which Laura figured was as good as her agreeing.

"I need to use the bathroom," Laura lied, walking off with her BlackBerry in hand and enclosing herself in her granite-tiled bath. She turned the fan on just to drown out any sounds, and she sat down on the toilet lid. When it came to Avery, she wasn't good at holding back, or playing the well-mannered debutante. She couldn't help herself: she *ached* to talk to him.

She'd barely waited half a minute before her cell began purring. Her breathing quickened as she read the return text from Avery. It read: Brownies???

Laura wrinkled her brow, about to reply that he knew *exactly* what brownies, when she realized this was the "secret" part of his being her secret admirer. C'mon. He wasn't exactly going to confess.

Nevermind she wrote back. Where R U?

Leaving Big D's BBQ Heading 2 the cave Need 2 work out.

111

So Avery was heading to the weight room at the club. Laura's house was only five minutes from the Villages Country Club. Not that she wanted to go back to the fitness center—twice in one day seemed *way* over the top—but she really wanted to see him. Besides, what harm would it do if she bumped into him accidentally on purpose?

Maybe I'll C U, she typed. On my way 2 club spa.

OK. Kewl.

Her heart beat double time. So she'd told a little white lie. Like people didn't do it all the time.

"Laura, are you all right in there?" Ginger gently rapped on the door. *"Laura?"*

"I'm fine," she called out. "I'll be out in a sec." Her mind raced, already thinking that if she left now, she could beat Avery to the club and could intercept him. She'd pretend she had a massage scheduled. That was certainly believable enough. But she had to hurry, unless she wanted to hunt him down in the weight room (and she definitely didn't).

Laura took off her headband, ran a brush through her straight blond hair, and stuck the band back on again. With one hand, she dabbed on extra lip gloss and with the other, she brushed brownie crumbs off her white Alexander Wang T-shirt.

She nearly ran smack into Ginger and Mac both as she flew out of the bathroom and into her walk-in closet, where she slipped on a pair of gladiator sandals and snagged her white Betsey Johnson bowling bag (well, no white bags or shoes after Labor Day anyway, so she might as well give it a final fling, right?).

"I've gotta go," she told her friends as she emerged from the closet, stuffing her BlackBerry into her purse and pulling out her keys. "Hey, take as many brownies as you'd like!" she told them, hurrying out of the room before they could stop her.

Once downstairs, she raced past Tincy in the kitchen, murmuring, "I'll be back in a bit," before she escaped to the garage.

Two minutes later, she was in her Mercedes Roadster, heading to the Villages CC, retracing the route she and Mac had taken just that morning. When she pulled onto the grounds, she noticed the parking lot was definitely more crowded than before. But she saw no sign of Avery's burnt-orange 'Vette with the GR8HANZ plates.

Whew, she thought as she scrambled out of the car. She hurried toward the clubhouse, knowing Avery would have to walk through it to get to the fitness center and the weight room. The pro shop was open for business, as was the Grill, judging from the hum of conversation drifting from the restaurant.

Laura made a beeline for the spa doors, trying to decide what to do, how best to wait for Avery to appear and make it seem coincidental.

Should she go in and peer through the glass until she spotted him, then leap out into the hallway? Should she linger outside, fumbling in her purse as if she couldn't find . . . something?

"Hey, Laura," she heard over her shoulder, and her knees threatened to buckle. "Lucky me, I guess I caught you just before your appointment."

She turned so fast she nearly tripped over her own feet. "Avery? For heaven's sake," she said, acting surprised to see him, though the blush in her cheeks was a hundred percent real. "I wasn't sure if I'd run into you or not. This place is so big," she rambled on. "But I'm glad I did. I wanted to tell you something, in person if I could."

"Oh, yeah?" He crossed his arms so that his biceps bulged. "What's that?"

"Um, it's just that I—well, how do I put this?" She clutched her oversized bag, wishing her pulse wasn't galloping like a Derby pony on its final lap. *Why does he always have to look so damned good?* Yummier than any gourmet brownie. He had an American Eagle tee pulled over his Ed Hardy shorts, his gym bag slung over his shoulder. His pale brown hair curled around his ears and neck, where it was damp.

"Laura?" he prodded when she didn't explain herself right off the bat. But she was so distracted, being so close to him.

"You smell like chlorine," she said, then leaned closer, breathing him in. "And Hawaiian Tropic."

He smiled, his dimples carved into his cheeks. "And you smell clean and soft, like flowers. You always do."

Wow, Laura thought, and blinked at him dumbly.

Avery had this way about him that sucked her in, no matter how she tried to resist it, only she never tried very hard. He made her feel completely at ease and nervous all at once. She hugged her purse more tightly when she wanted so badly to drop it and throw her arms around him. They hadn't kissed since that awful night at Jo Lynn Bidwell's guesthouse when the Queen Bimbo had reamed Laura out before shoving her into the pool, and Laura was dying for another smooch.

"You wanted to tell me something," Avery reminded her, and uncrossed his arms, reaching out to tuck a thumb beneath her chin.

"Oh, yeah, that," Laura said, hoping she sounded casual even when his mere touch made her want to throw herself on top of him right then and there. "I figured we could be honest with each other, right?"

He nodded. "Sure."

"So you don't have to pretend anymore. I really appreciate all the things you've been sending me, not just for the brownies and the cupcakes and the candy, but also for the flowers you sent on D-day when invitations to the Rosebud dinner were delivered." She paused to take a breath. "It's very sweet and all, but I've got to watch my figure or else I'll screw up the measurements for my deb gown, and Tincy will strangle me with her French manicure," she rambled on, blurting out before she could stop herself, "I'm tryin' hard to get in shape so I can do the Dip without seriously embarrassing myself. I even begged Dillon Masters to train me. . . ."

"Whoa, hold on there, babe." He deposited his gym bag on the floor and caught her by the arms. "All right, you got me. I'll confess that I did send the flowers as an apology for hurting you again, and because I was happy you got your deb invitation. You deserved it."

"Thank you for that. Very much," she whispered, unable to resist leaning forward and rolling up on her toes to kiss him firmly on the lips.

As soon as their lips touched, Laura felt herself melt into him, pressing against his chest so his heartbeat and hers seemed one and the same. His hands slipped to her waist, fingers spanning her lower back, holding on to her tightly, and the rest of the world completely faded away, as if there were only the two of them, as though nothing had ever come between them.

Avery made no move to draw apart, not until a white-haired clubber with tennis racquet in hand cleared his throat and said, "Excuse me, please." They quickly separated, allowing him to pass.

"Laura, look at me," Avery demanded.

She sagged against the wall beside him, still light-headed from their kiss. They were so close their shoulders touched. Somehow, she managed to turn her head so she could gaze right into his puppy-dog eyes.

"Like I said before, I gave you the flowers, but I didn't send brownies or anything else." His forehead wrinkled. "And what's that about Masters training you? You sure that's a good thing?"

"Yes . . . no . . . oh, God, are you serious?" Laura stopped smiling. "You're not my secret admirer? Who then?"

"I wish it were me," Avery said softly, and shifted in his Converse high-tops.

"Oh?"

"Because I do admire you, Laura, a lot," he whispered, tipping his head toward hers so they were nose to nose. "Maybe more than I should." His brown eyes clouded. "It's just really . . . complicated."

Why? she wondered, when it didn't have to be.

"Avery," she sighed his name and placed her hand on his heart, wanting to ask him, *Why are we doing this? We should be together. Why can't you break free of Jo Lynn and her toadies and just BE with me? What does she have on you?*

But she didn't get the chance to say anything at all.

Across from where they stood, the doors to the spa burst wide open. A ponytailed brunette and a flat-ironed strawberry blonde in micro-mini-shorts shuffled out in post-pedicure flip-flops, tissues tucked between their toes, and stumbled right into Laura and Avery.

"Hey, get your sleazy hands off my boyfriend!" Camie Lindell shouted first, before Trisha Hunt exclaimed with a wave of glossy manicured fingers, *"Omigod!"*

Camie's hard sea green gaze bounced from Laura to Avery. "What the hell is going on here? And don't even tell me you took her to Dillon's barbecue instead of me?"

"Yeah, don't even tell her that," Trisha repeated the threat.

"Is there an echo in here?" Laura was not about to let herself become roadkill again like the last time she encountered the Bimbo Cartel. "Oh, wait, it must be your brainless skulls doing that Grand Canyon thing." Then she turned to Avery and said, "I've got to go."

"But don't you have a spa appointment?" he asked as Laura edged around him.

"Hey!" Camie grabbed her shoulder and growled, "Don't you walk away from me, bitch."

But Laura yanked her arm free and kept going, her heart slamming hard against her ribs. She didn't even stop to take a breath until she was outside the clubhouse, stabbing the key into her Mercedes. For a minute, she thought they might follow her and continue the scream-fest outside, but when she glanced back, no one was there.

Still, her hands shook as she got into her car and held the wheel, lowering her forehead against it and gently banging.

Idiot, idiot, idiot, she told herself, until a huge honking light went on inside her skull.

Laura lifted her head from the wheel as she realized two very important things. The first was Camie's assumption that

Avery might have taken *her* to the Masterses' annual barbecue. That meant he'd gone alone, or at least without the Brunette Bimbo, which had Laura grinning for a minute. Until she thought about Thing Number Two: Avery wasn't her secret admirer. Which meant someone else out there was toying with her heart . . . or . . . maybe just her head. *But who?*

Laura gnawed on her bottom lip as she started the car, an ugly thought creeping into her consciousness, wondering suddenly if she was being played for a fool by the dirtiest player of all.

If you want the rainbow,
you've gotta put up with the rain.
—Dolly Parton

Some days aren't worth
even getting out of bed for.
—Mac Mackenzie

Seven

Beep, beep . . . beep, beep . . . beep, beep.

Dragged from unconsciousness by the incessant tweeting, Mac rolled over and slapped off her alarm clock, then flopped onto her back with a sigh. *How could it possibly be Tuesday morning already?*

The long weekend was history, even though she felt like she had so much unfinished business. Her picnic with Alex had turned into "three's a crowd," Laura had blown off her BFFs for yet another Avery chase-down, and Ginger had dropped the bomb about ditching the Three Amigas' planned Marble Slab outing after the first Rosebud meeting tonight.

Their first Rosebud meeting.

Ugh.

Just the thought of having to sit through their deb orientation at the Glass Slipper Club's headquarters nearly drove Mac back under the covers.

She forced herself to get up and shuffle toward the bathroom, where she mechanically flipped on the light and stripped off her nightshirt. Eyes still half closed, she stepped into the shower, only to find there wasn't anything left in her bottle of Pantene. She nixed a dripping-wet trip to the linen closet to forage for spare shampoo, instead washing her hair with the unused Terressentials Organic Left Coast Lemon Body Wash that Ginger had given her for her birthday last October. It was either that or suds up her curls with glycerine soap. So Mac opted for reeking of lemon from head to toe.

She stood under the spray for as long as she could to rinse off the citrus scent and then stepped out of the glass-walled stall, wrapping herself in an ultra-plush Egyptian cotton towel (Honey insisted on them). Eyes wide open now, she padded over to the sink and wiped at the steam on the mirror to create a circle where she could see herself, only to wince when she spotted a bright red pimple smack in the middle of her chin. It was like the Zit That Wouldn't Go Away.

Now I'll stink like furniture polish and *look like the "before" part of a Proactiv infomercial,* she thought, frowning.

Glumly, she searched for her Bliss spot fix, but she couldn't find it. She must've run out and forgotten to reorder.

Crap and double crap.

Mac did the best she could with a nearly dried-up cover-up stick, but the pimple merely glowed like Rudolph's red nose. Too bad it wasn't Christmas.

Come on, sweetie. Look on the bright side. At least it's not permanent, she imagined her mom consoling her, and she found herself wishing Jeanie Mackenzie was downstairs, watching the clock for Mac and kissing Daddy goodbye. Honey Potts could never fill Jeanie's shoes, no matter how hard she tried, Mac decided, which only made her mood worsen.

It didn't improve even a smidge when she pulled on her last clean white button-down shirt and dropped a blob of toothpaste down the front. Though she rubbed the spot with a damp washcloth, it proved impossible to get out.

"Bugger," she groaned as she realized she'd either have to live with the outline of a Crest blob on her boob all day, or dig out an old shirt since Honey had forgotten to do a dry-cleaning run on Saturday. Her tan Pine Forest Prep blazer would've covered up the stain nicely, but it was still too hot to wear it without sweating profusely. So Mac raided the storage closet for last year's uniforms and grabbed the first white shirt she came across. When she pulled it on, she realized that it was too short in the sleeves and too tight around the bust.

Perfect.

Mac rolled up the sleeves but there wasn't much she could do about the straining buttons. Good thing she hadn't had her breasts done, like half their senior class, or she would've literally been popping out all over.

She managed to finish dressing without further crises, but as she started to work on her tangled, lemon-scented hair, the blow-dryer gasped its last breath and died in her hand.

Oh, man, what else can go wrong?

"*Mah-chelle!*" Honey trilled from downstairs in that high-pitched Scarlett O'Hara drawl. "Alex is here! He's waitin' for you in the car!"

Weird. Mac didn't remember having arranged a ride this morning.

"Hurry up, sweet pea, or you'll be tardy for class!"

She cringed as Honey shouted again, thinking it couldn't be that late. The shampoo conundrum and the shirt change must've cost her precious time. So she grabbed her book bag from her desk and glanced at the clock, which showed it was already a quarter to eight.

Her black-rimmed glasses securely on her nose, she ran her fingers through the messy tangles of her hair, which had turned the collar of her old shirt damp. She looked like a drowned rat with a Texas-sized zit, but she couldn't worry about that. Mac had never been late for school, and she didn't aim to start now.

She flew down the stairs and sped past Honey in her pink bathrobe and orange juice can–sized hot rollers, ignoring the brown paper sack that her stepmom held out to her.

"Don't you want a healthy lunch, sugar? It's fresh veggies and a little Tupperware tub of ranch dressing for dipping."

Yuck. "No, thanks," Mac hastily replied.

"Good Lord, what's that on your chin?" Honey yelped as Mac opened the door and stepped out, slamming it closed behind her.

Alex Bishop's gray Saab idled in front of the stoop, and Mac took a deep breath before flinging herself inside, mumbling an apology for being slow as she tossed her bag at her feet and buckled her seat belt so they could get rolling.

"Hey," he said, once he'd maneuvered out of her street and onto Knipp, heading toward Taylorcrest, where traffic would doubtless be bottlenecked. "Are you feeling okay? You hardly ate a bite of your lunch yesterday, and you had this constipated look on your face."

"Oh, gee, thanks," Mac said dryly. "You sure know how to make a girl feel good, Bishop."

Alex glanced at her, and a wicked smile slid across his mouth. "So I guess I shouldn't comment on that miniature of Mount Saint Helens you're cultivating on your chin? Didn't that thing blow a few weeks ago?"

"Shut up, or I'll kill you with my mechanical pencil," Mac threatened, thinking it was shaping up to be the worst day in history. *Is the pimple that bad?* She flipped down the visor mirror, looked at herself, flinched, and slapped it closed again. *Yeah, it's that bad.*

As if the Zit from Hell wasn't enough, Alex sniffed the air like a hound dog. "Is that lemon?" he remarked, before taking his eyes off the road to glance at her again. "Don't take this the wrong way, but did you shower in Country Time?"

Was there any way to take that *but* wrong?

Mac scowled and crossed her arms over the straining buttons on her shirt, figuring that would surely be his next target. She stared out the window, chewing on her lower lip. Normally, his candid observations didn't bother her at all, but for some reason, this morning they seemed to sting. What was up with that? When had she suddenly become so sensitive around him? Things had been fine with him before the summer. It was like everything changed after he returned from computer camp, taller and more self-assured, yet still the Alex who'd always been there for her, especially after her mom had died.

Maybe it was just her bad mood, facing her senior year without her mother, having to go through her debut season for so many people other than herself.

"She was just about to dish on some girl who showed up and ruined their Labor Day picnic by flirting with Alex Bishop, which apparently made our little Mackie a wee bit jealous!"

125

Laura's remark from yesterday came back to haunt her, and Mac cringed, thinking, *Oh, God—she couldn't be right. Could she?*

"So did you have a good Labor Day weekend?" Alex asked. "I know I had fun with you yesterday." He shifted his hands on the wheel, not looking at her as he added, "Oh, and, um, thanks for being so great about Cindy coming to our picnic. I should've said something to you sooner, but I wasn't sure if she'd show, you know."

"Hey, no problem," Mac said, maybe a little too quickly.

"It's hard for her, being the new girl at PFP and all." He shot her a sideways look and a lopsided smile. "I think she's only just started to feel like she fits in."

"Bully for her." Mac turned toward him and tried to smile back, causing the seat belt to tug tightly across her chest. She ran her fingers beneath the nylon strap and loosened it so she could breathe.

Alex reached over to pat her shoulder. "You're a real pal, you know that?" he said, and Mac felt a tightness in her chest, like the seat belt was squeezing her too tightly again. Only it wasn't.

What was her frickin' problem?

Her mouth went dry, and her brain felt empty of things to say.

Luckily, Alex started babbling about some new gadget he'd acquired from Newegg. "It's a slide scanner, Mac, so I can convert all these pictures on E-six film. . . ."

"Sounds awesome," she remarked when he paused for breath, though she wasn't really listening. Her gaze drifted toward the window as they rolled down Taylorcrest toward Strey Lane. She had a pretty good idea of what was going on with her and Alex. Only she was too chicken to face it.

"Here we are . . . school, sweet school," Alex joked as he pulled into the turnaround to drop her off in front of the columned facade of Pine Forest Prep.

Mac had her seat belt off, her book bag in her lap, and one hand on the door latch before the car had even come to a stop.

"You're sure eager to get to class," Alex remarked, catching her by the hand before she could flee. "Was it something I said?"

She turned to look at him squarely, seeing the face she knew so well, finding it different somehow. So grown up, like he was the boy next door she'd played with since they were babies, but he wasn't a kid anymore. And neither was she. Whatever she was going through, she was going to have to deal with it. She just wasn't sure exactly how to do that at the moment.

"Mac?"

"I'm fine," she assured him, only half a lie. "Thanks for the ride. I'll see you later, okay?" She flashed a lame smile and started out the door before she remembered to ask him a favor. "Oh, hey, could I borrow your old Caldwell annual from middle school? Ginger has some guy she wants to look up. I could pick it up before the deb meeting tonight."

"Yeah, that'll work," he said and nodded.

"Great."

She shut the door and hiked her bag up on her shoulder, rushing past a couple slow-moving students up the stone path toward the brick facade smothered in climbing ivy. She raced up the front steps and flung open the door, ducking into the building, the heels of her loafers clicking fast on the tiles. Mac was late enough that the hallways had thinned out already, and just a few stragglers remained at their lockers.

The clock in the hall showed a minute to spare as she hurried up the corridor toward first-period chemistry. The bell clanged just as she dodged through the doorway, out of breath.

"How nice of you to show up, Miss Mackenzie," Ms. Kozlowski said by way of greeting, and Mac realized she was the last to appear.

"Sorry," she apologized for the second time that morning, heading for her usual stool at the front-most lab table before she realized it was occupied.

"Why don't you share the table with Miss Chow," the teacher suggested. "I'm sure you'll make fine partners in our experiment with hydrogen peroxide."

"Miss Chow?" Mac repeated, and Ms. K raised painted-on black eyebrows.

"Yes, Miss Chow. Are you suddenly hard of hearing, Miss Mackenzie?"

"No, ma'am."

"Good. Then take your seat."

Mac detected a good deal of snickering coming from the table where two of the Bimbo Cartel, Trisha Hunt and Camie Lindell, sat, and she found herself hoping the hydrogen peroxide experiment would blow up in their faces and bleach off their eyebrows.

"Can you hear me now? Can you hear me now?" she heard them whispering as she passed, and Mac felt her cheeks heat. She resisted the urge to bang them upside the head with her book bag as she headed toward the back where Cindy waited.

The girl smiled, tucking shiny black hair behind multi-pierced ears—though only one earring per ear was allowed, per dress code rules in the PFP student handbook.

"Hey," Cindy said under her breath, as Mac set down her book bag and slid atop the stool. "You barely made it under the bell."

"Tell me about it," Mac whispered back as she rummaged for her chemistry text and her notebook.

"About yesterday," Cindy started to say, but the headmistress's voice interrupted as it poured forth from the intercom speakers, forcing Cindy to zip her lips.

"Good morning, Pine Foresters, and welcome back after your holiday weekend. I trust you're all well rested and ready to learn," Dr. Percy intoned. Mac propped her chin atop her hand, pretending to listen, although her mind was somewhere else entirely during the morning messages. She barely realized that Ms. K had begun instructing them on their experiment until Cindy nudged her under the table with the toe of her shoe.

". . . what you'll be doing is sometimes called the 'Aladdin's Lamp' reaction using hydrogen peroxide and solid potassium iodide," the teacher explained in her usual monotone. "Please find your instructions on the sheet of paper on your table. Do wear the rubber gloves and goggles provided for you. You have fifty minutes. You may proceed."

Once Ms. K had finished talking, she did her usual slow stroll around the room, looking over everyone's shoulders. She was at the farthest corner now, so Mac wanted to get started before the teacher wandered their way.

She checked over the instructions, making sure they had the correct ingredients, including a large bottle with a stopper, a tea bag, thirty percent hydrogen peroxide solution, and the potassium iodide.

When she finished her checklist and looked up, Cindy was slipping her cell into her lap. Her eyes glancing down discreetly, she started to text.

"What are you doing?" Mac hissed, feeling like an alien with her goggles on over her glasses and a pair of red rubber gloves on her hands. "We're not supposed to have our phones turned on during class. They'll confiscate your phone for that, or suspend you if they're really pissed off."

"I just need to answer—"

"Well, answer fast, would you?" Mac urged, glancing Ms. K's way.

Cindy stopped texting long enough to smile sweetly and say, "Dr. Percy's not going to mess with me, I promise you. So stop worrying."

For a moment, Mac stood there mutely, thinking there was more to Cindy Chow than met the eye. She obviously had little fear of authority figures, and she hung out at car shows. She definitely wasn't a typical PFP girl, and Mac had yet to get a handle on her.

Still, she wasn't about to let Cindy get her in trouble for not doing her lab work.

They now had forty-five minutes to finish the experiment and write down their results.

That was enough cause for Mac to get antsy.

"Look"—Mac rounded the table, pushing the second pair of goggles and gloves toward Cindy—"we're using potentially dangerous chemicals here. You might at least want to put on your equipment and pretend you're helping out."

Cindy looked up from the cell in her lap, amusement sparkling in her brown eyes. "Okay, okay, I'm done anyway."

Mac glanced down at Cindy's slider screen just before the other girl popped it closed, catching something that made her heart skip: a name. Alex's name, to be precise.

"What's going on here?"

Oh, crap.

Mac lifted her head to find Ms. Kozlowski standing not three feet away from their table. She looked fierce with her short black buzz cut, her arms crossed over her chest, a thin-lipped frown on her nut-brown face.

"Were you using your cell phone, Miss Chow?" the teacher asked bluntly as Cindy tried to hide the slider in the pleats of her skirt. "Because if that's what you were doing, I'll have to ask you to step out—"

"No, Ms. K, I wasn't doing anything, I swear," Cindy said innocently, her almond-shaped eyes wide and guileless.

Heck, if Mac hadn't known the truth, she would've believed her.

"Is that right, Miss Mackenzie?" The teacher turned her attention to Mac.

"Me?" Mac's hands began to sweat inside her rubber gloves.

"Yes, you, Michelle," Ms. K said, brow wrinkled with impatience. "Was Miss Chow on her phone?"

"Can I plead the Fifth?"

"No, Miss Mackenzie, you may not."

Mac felt as if the whole room had stopped working and was staring at her. Cindy certainly was anyway. So what was she supposed to say?

Yes, she was on her cell, and she didn't care if she got caught!

Okay, that was what Mac wanted to say. But instead of blurting out the truth, she found herself muttering, "I don't know. I guess if Cindy says she wasn't on her cell, then she wasn't."

Mac couldn't believe she'd actually covered up for the girl, and her heart thudded nervously against her ribs. She *so* wasn't good at lying.

The teacher squinted at her for an eternity before she said, "All right, girls, get to work now, please."

Then Ms. K walked away to hover over another lab table, and Cindy leaned over to whisper, "Thanks for not ratting me out. I owe you one."

Mac pushed the goggles and gloves toward her. "Just put your stuff on, okay? I'll start pouring the hydrogen peroxide into the bottle."

It took all of Mac's concentration to get the lab work done—replacing tea in a tea bag with potassium iodide, dropping the modified bag into the hydrogen peroxide, and creating a cloud of oxygen gas and water vapor—with minimal help from Cindy. Mac was still scribbling her notes when the bell rang.

"Gotta run!" Cindy chirped, popping out of her seat like a rocket. She dropped her own notes off on Ms. K's desk and disappeared before Mac frantically finished up and turned her work in.

Mac grabbed her book bag and took off, hitting her locker since she hadn't made it there before her first class.

Laura and Ginger were already huddled at their lockers, heads bent together, looking grave and whispering.

"What's going on?" Mac asked as she approached, quickly unlocking her combination and opening her locker door. She tossed in a few books and removed several others while Laura and Ginger converged on her. "Whatever it is, y'all don't seem any too happy about it."

Ginger solemnly informed her, "Word is that Mindy Sue Mabry won't be debuting in May after all."

"Looks like her family's declared bankruptcy," Laura jumped in, "and the Glass Slipper Club's worried the Mabrys don't even have the cash to buy a table at the Rosebud Ball, much less pay for Mindy's dress or photographs or anything else that goes along with being a deb."

"Wow." Mac closed her locker deliberately, thinking what a blow that had to be for someone like Mindy Sue, who'd spent her entire existence at PFP acting like a Jo Lynn Bidwell wannabe; now her chance to be on level footing with the school's reigning queen had gone up in smoke. That had to hurt.

It almost made Mac feel guilty for accepting her Rosebud invitation when she really didn't want it, not as badly as Mindy Sue surely had. She cleared her throat. "She's out for real?"

"Yeah, for real." Ginger nervously fingered her razor-cut layers of red, nodding. "But that's not even the worst of it," she added. "I've heard that Mindy Sue might get kicked out of PFP unless she can finagle some kind of scholarship. I haven't seen her in class today, so maybe she's already gone."

"Oh, man, that sucks," Mac murmured, unable to fathom what it would feel like to get tossed out of school. That idea pained her far more than being dumped by the Glass Slipper Club.

"I caught Tincy yapping on the phone before I left this morning, and it sounds like the GSC has already decided on Mindy Sue's replacement," Laura said, one hand loosely cupped to the side of her mouth, as if afraid of being overheard.

"Who've they picked?" Mac asked, hugging her book bag to her chest. There weren't that many more senior girls at PFP to choose from, considering their class totaled all of thirty. Well, twenty-nine, if the gossip about Mindy Sue getting booted was true.

"That's just it. I don't know, and neither does anyone else I've talked to," Laura said with a sigh, and glanced over at Ginger, who shook her head and uttered, "I haven't a clue."

"Guess we'll find out at the meeting tonight, huh?" Mac remarked, when she really wanted to say, "Who cares?"

Her head was somewhere else entirely, and it had zilch to do with anything deb.

He's just about the nastiest little man
I've ever known. He struts sitting down.
—Lillian K. Dykstra

Everyone isn't always worth liking,
but that doesn't mean you can't be nice.
—Ginger Fore

Eight

The Tuesday-night orientation for new Rosebuds took place at the Glass Slipper Club's official headquarters on Briar Oaks Lane in Post Oak, just east of the 610 Loop and northeast of the Galleria. The four-story building sat on the same block as the Junior League and up the street from the St. Regis Hotel, where Ginger's mom and Rose Dupree used to take her for Sunday afternoon tea when she was a child, though it wasn't called the St. Regis until Ginger had nearly graduated from middle school. That was right about the time she'd begun to feel too old for their weekly bonding over finger sandwiches, teapots, and harp music.

Only now, having glimpsed the facade of the hotel before she turned in to the parking lot at the Glass Slipper Club's entrance, Ginger's chest swelled, like a million bubbles floating to the surface. It was amazing to think how much she'd grown since her tea parties with Deena and her grandmother. She'd been so shy back then, maybe too much a daddy's girl. The past few years she'd come into her own after her parents' divorce, with Edward Fore moving out of the Castle and in with his then-girlfriend. Ginger had to figure out who she was, apart from all the junk in her life, and she liked the person she was becoming, even if she made some stupid mistakes now and then.

She'd gotten stronger in so many ways, and she felt like she had something to give to the world. That was part of the reason she was so psyched about being a Rosebud. She wanted to flip the stereotype that all debutantes were ditzy rich girls with nothing better to do than spend their daddy's money. The Glass Slipper Club's deb program was about philanthropy, too, and Ginger had plenty of causes she wanted to bring to the Club's attention. But first she had to find an empty parking space. . . .

Just as she eased her Prius into a spot between Jo Lynn Bidwell's shiny Audi and Laura's red Mercedes, her cell rang. It took a second or two to dig it out of her bag, and when she did, a familiar voice barked at her.

"Where are you?" It was Laura, totally impatient. "The meeting starts in, like, ten minutes and Bootsie Bidwell's already looking nervous 'cause plenty of Rosebud seats are empty."

"I'm parking as we speak," Ginger assured her, "right next to your Roadster. How cosmic is that?" She didn't mention the fact that Jo Lynn's Audi was on her other side. Laura would probably urge her to key *bitch* into the door. "I'll be up in a sec," she promised.

"Oh, hey, Mac said to tell you she brought that Caldwell yearbook you were wanting."

"Great!" Ginger said, grinning, before she hung up.

Now she'd have the chance to look up Kent Wakefield's school picture from middle school and see if it jogged any old memories.

She cut off the engine, snatched out her keys, and grabbed her bag. Then she hurried through the parking garage and through the glass doors leading into the GSC's lobby.

"Well, hey, pretty girl!"

A petite woman with a lipsticked grin and teased Texas-sized hair called out, and Ginger wiggled her fingers at Laura's mom, Tincy.

"Hi, Mrs. Bell," Ginger said, sizing up the GSC's official greeter, who was as tiny as Laura was tall, and as brunette as Laura was blond. Tonight, Tincy's copper-streaked chocolate-brown hair was arranged in a typical Houston helmet around her taut-looking features. "Am I late?"

"Not a bit. You're not even the last to arrive. I'm still waiting on a few others. Oh, yes, and the girl who's taking Mindy Sue Mabry's place," Tincy Bell drawled. Then she sighed and made a little tsk-tsk noise. "Sad about that, isn't it?" she remarked, though Ginger didn't think she sounded sad at all. "It's just amazing how fast things can change. One bad turn and it's over, just like *that*," she added, snapping her fingers.

"Yeah, right." Ginger's throat went dry. She thought of how she'd barely escaped getting nudged from the Rosebud list when she'd been hauled down to the Villages Police department. If her daddy hadn't smoothed things over with everyone like he had, she might be in Mindy Sue Mabry's position right now, meaning O-U-T.

"Well, let's get you fixed up," Tincy said, and gave her form-fitting silk blouse a tug so its hem fell neatly over her long black skirt. "C'mon and follow me." Her high-heeled boots clicked on the peach-colored marble tiles as she strode toward a table with its WELCOME, ROSEBUDS! banner and enough white ribbons to wrap half the gifts in the Neiman Marcus Christmas catalog.

Tincy scooped something up from a white box on the table, hunted for another item, then turned around. "Here you go, sweet pea, rosebuds for a new Rosebud," she said, her voice molasses-sweet, as she proffered a nosegay of tiny white rosebuds, their stems wrapped in white ribbon.

Ginger held the small bouquet, which made her feel oddly bridelike. "Thank you," she said, feeling like her cheeks might crack from smiling so big.

"Now let me pin this name tag on you. It's silly, I know, since everybody knows who you are. But there you go!" She finished fastening the tag and gave Ginger's shoulder a pat. "Now you can hightail it to the big meeting room on the second floor. Your mama's already up there, and I'm sure Laura and Mac are dying to see you."

"Thanks, Mrs. B, for everything," Ginger said, clutching the nosegay and glancing down at the crookedly pinned name tag on her chest: VIRGINIA DUPREE FORE, it read. Then in smaller print below: GLASS SLIPPER CLUB ROSEBUD (LEGACY).

A tiny shiver shot through her at seeing her deb status printed out in black and white. *It's really happening,* she thought, wondering if this was how Rose and her mother had felt before her, like they could walk on clouds. She was doubly glad that she, Laura, and Mac would be going through it all together. Though getting Mac to accept the inevitable hadn't been easy, and Ginger always thought *she'd* be the one to drag her feet. Things so often didn't turn out the way she expected.

I'm here. . . . I'm here. . . . I'm here echoed in her head as her boot heels tapped quickly up the marble stairs. She glimpsed Laura and Mac, waiting for her outside the "big meeting room," which was really more like a small auditorium.

"Thank God!" Mac leapt away from the wall she'd been leaning against, lined with elegant black-and-white photographs of Rosebuds from years past. She looked rather girlish in her Anna Sui floral-print dress and braided sandals. Ginger wondered if Honey had anything to do with the outfit. "What took you so long?" Mac grilled her as she approached.

"Sorry, but traffic was terrible," she lied, unwilling to admit she'd changed her clothes, like, five times before she'd left the house. She'd finally settled on an organic bamboo tunic in teal over organic cotton leggings from GREEN by Adeline. The black faux-leather Diba boots weren't exactly eco-friendly, but she'd had them forever and loved them to death.

"Get off her case, Mac, at least we're all here now," Laura said, her smile wide and cheeks rosy-pink. "Can you believe we're actually doing this? Isn't it divine?" She kept lifting her flowers to her nose and inhaling, obviously enjoying the moment as much as Ginger.

Mac rolled her eyes at Laura then turned back to Ginger, shoving a shiny black and red book at her. "Here's the Caldwell annual. Alex said just to give it back when you're done."

"Thanks." Ginger juggled the yearbook, the flowers, and her hemp shoulder bag, hoping she didn't drop something on her way in. She could hear the buzz of voices from inside, and it made her feel strangely light-headed.

"Should we make our grand entrance?" Laura prodded, shifting nervously on her retro black-and-white spectator pumps, which looked perfect with her simple black linen dress. "Everybody ready?"

"No," Mac grumbled, and Laura gave her a stare that said "Yes."

"Just let me take a deep breath first," Ginger told them both, standing in place and inhaling before slowly letting out the air. Her nerves calmed enough so that she nodded. "Okay, I'm good. Let's do it."

"After you, Virginia Dupree Fore," Laura teased, gesturing with her tiny white bouquet as Ginger took a step forward to lead them in.

Only her path was cut off abruptly by a cluster of girls who appeared out of nowhere.

"Ex*cuse* me!" Camie Lindell sneered, nudging Ginger aside and making way for her and Trisha Hunt to pass. Like a queen expecting her handmaids to sprinkle flowers in her path, Jo Lynn Bidwell brought up the rear.

"Hey, who do y'all think you are?" Laura snapped as Ginger nearly toppled back into her and Mac.

Jo Lynn stopped in front of Laura and turned her head in a swish of pale blond hair. "No, you pathetic loser, who do you think *you* are? You'd better stay away from what's mine, you hear me? Unless you want more trouble than you can handle."

Ginger shuffled her armload so she could catch Laura's wrist. "C'mon," she quietly urged, but Laura shook off her grip.

"What do you mean *'yours'*?" Laura moved in so that the two tall blondes stood nose to nose, although Jo Lynn's figure seemed twiglike compared to Laura's curvy body. "Are you talking about Avery, by chance?" she drawled, and she set a hand on her hip, adding provocatively, "Or maybe it's Dillon you're worried about losing?"

Jo Lynn's high-boned cheeks flushed, and she raised a hand, fingers pinched together. "You're this close to being *over,* you hear me?" Her ice-blue gaze looked Laura up and down. "Good to see you've got a black dress that fits your fat ass, since you'll need one soon . . . for your funeral."

That said, Jo Lynn pushed past them into the meeting room, leaving Mac staring openmouthed, and Ginger trying hard to calm Laura down so she wouldn't do anything rash.

"She's not worth it," Ginger reminded her. "Let it go."

"I could snap her neck like a chicken," Laura remarked under her breath, but the anger started to fade from her eyes.

"Is anyone game to spray Pam on the soles of her shoes so she falls on her butt in her fancy white gown?" Mac cracked, adding, "That would almost make debuting worth the headache."

Ginger couldn't help grinning.

Though Laura still seemed uptight from her encounter with Jo Lynn, there was the barest hint of a smile on her lips when she said, "C'mon, y'all, let's go in," clutching her skull bag and flowers, her head held high.

Ginger fell in step behind her, crossing the threshold into the Rosebud's meeting room. The scent of roses mingled with expensive perfumes clouded the air, as vases filled with tall-stemmed white roses abounded, seeming to cover almost every surface. She spotted a fancy, catered spread of champagne and cheese atop a linen-clothed table in the back of the room, and Glass Slipper Club members milled about, glasses in hand, mingling like they were at an elegant cocktail party.

"Ladies, if you'd please take your seats." Bootsie Bidwell stood at the front of the room, gently clapping her hands to get things in motion.

Ginger scanned the chairs as the women began sitting down, singling out Deena and nodding as she waved. Separated from the rows where the GSC members took their places sat ten white Chiavari chairs in the front of the room. Each chair had a gauzy white silk chiffon ribbon tied around its back.

Ginger eyed the Bimbo Cartel, who had yet to sit down, hoping to keep as far away from them as possible. She'd hate for World War III to erupt in the middle of their deb orientation.

"We don't have to sit alphabetically, do we, Mrs. Bidwell?" she approached Jo Lynn's mother and asked politely.

"It's not necessary, no," Bootsie replied, her thin brows furrowed.

"Thank God," Ginger said, and rejoined Mac and Laura, who'd already found three seats on the far side of the row from the ones that Jo, Camie, and Trisha had settled down in.

Before she took her place between Mac and Laura, she went over to the three girls positioned in between the Bimbos and the Three Amigas. She uttered warm hellos to Hailey Duffy, Prissy Schaeffer, and Courtney Millstadt, then she paused at the empty chair where Mindy Sue Mabry should have been sitting.

"Makes you wonder who'll end up there, huh?" Laura remarked as Ginger plunked down beside her, balancing the yearbook and flowers on her lap.

"They're sure keeping it secret," Ginger said.

"According to Tincy, no one knows but the GSC selection committee, not even the other members," Laura explained as she clutched her nosegay while carefully stowing her large bag with its skull design under her seat.

Ginger winced at the sight of the Shelly Litvak duffel from the Abejas boutique on Kirby that Laura had drooled over last time they'd gone shopping, though Ginger had begged her not to get it. It was elk skin with python. *Yuck.* PETA would kick Laura's ass if they caught her carrying it.

"I wish they'd get this show on the road," Mac whispered, glancing around them. "But I guess they're waiting on the substitute deb, whoever she is."

"So long as it's not another bimbo, I'm cool," Laura whispered, leaning across Ginger.

Bootsie Bidwell put an end to conversation in the room as she marched toward the center of the floor, between the GSC members and the debutantes.

"Welcome, everyone, or rather, *almost* everyone," she said, looking cool and calm in an eggshell pink Chanel suit, her inky dark hair cut precisely at shoulder level, providing a dark contrast to the pale fabric. She held a slim book against her flat stomach and tapped it anxiously with French-manicured fingers. "Apparently we're still missing a Rosebud, though I'm told she'll be here shortly."

A low murmur ran through the rows of women as heads bent together, and Ginger thought Bootsie Bidwell looked pleased to have so many on the edge of their seats, waiting for the mystery deb to show up.

Ginger realized she was digging her nails into Alex Bishop's yearbook and forced herself to relax. It wouldn't look good for a new Rosebud to pass out on the floor during their first meeting, just because she'd forgotten to breathe.

"As chair of the debutante selection committee, I have a few introductory words for our moms and debs. First of all, I'd like to welcome our latest class of Rosebuds," Bootsie said, and turned her focus on the girls. Ginger blushed when Mrs. Bidwell's gaze touched on her. "Some say that debutante balls are archaic and irrelevant in today's society, and to them I say, you're so very, very wrong. Tradition is never irrelevant, and what we're doing here at the GSC is encouraging young ladies to behave like ladies and continuing our tradition of philanthropy. I ask you, what's more relevant than that?"

Tradition and philanthropy, yes, Ginger thought, nodding, her skin tingling with goose bumps as she listened.

Bootsie held up the slim tome she'd been holding and patted it firmly. Its cover looked like parchment paper, and elegant calligraphy across the front read:

The Glass Slipper Club Debutante Program
Overview of Rules

"Darling Rosebuds, *this* will be your bible for the next eight months," she told them. "It's your debutante handbook. In it are guidelines and guidance. You'll find reminder dates for meetings, always the first Monday of the month unless there's a holiday, as is the case with tonight's meeting. You'll have the Glass Slipper Club's rules of decorum at your fingertips, and you'll find a bit of history about this special rite of passage. There are requirements for volunteer service for any number of club-approved charities, and there are rules regarding selection of your gown for the Rosebud Ball next May. It must be white, of course, and mustn't be too revealing, among other things. And don't forget, your gown must be registered by the November meeting, please, whether you provide a copy of your design or a photograph of the dress itself. Like snowflakes, no two can be alike."

Ginger took a deep breath and glanced sideways at Mac, whose stoic expression implied that she'd rather be anywhere else, and then she looked at Laura, whose eyes sparkled with excitement. No matter how different they might feel, they were all in this together, she mused, and reached over for each girl's hand, catching their pinkies with hers and holding on for a minute.

"I hope you're all ready to be very, very busy," Bootsie went on, pacing in front of the row of debs, her high-heeled Chanel pumps making soft sighs on the Berber carpeting. "Prepare yourselves for a bombardment of invitations to mother-daughter teas, chaperoned parties with your peer escorts, and various charity functions in the months ahead. You'll have refresher courses in etiquette and deportment," she added, grinning as some of the girls audibly sighed. "Oh, yes, and you'll be coached exhaustively in how to properly curtsy, and I do mean the dreaded *Texas Dip*," she intoned, garnering a twitter of laughter from the ladies of the club and groans from the girls.

"But we have a crackerjack instructor to whip y'all into shape, so no one need fear falling," Bootsie finished, and gestured broadly toward the seated club members. "Honey Potts Mackenzie, will you stand up? Honey's one of our newer members and had a lengthy career in the world of beauty pageants, as well as a background in ballet and dance, so there's no one better to teach you Rosebuds how to make your entrance and how to bow."

Ginger watched Mac's stepmom stand up, flip back her feathered blond hair, and wave perkily at everyone.

"Hey, y'all! First practice is Wednesday night at my house, ladies. That's tomorrow, seven o'clock sharp, and wear flat shoes and something comfy," she instructed in her Betty Boop drawl. "I'll have to work y'all up to doing the Dip in high heels, but we've got plenty of time for that."

Mac started coughing, bending head over knees like she was choking. Ginger patted her on the back until she stopped. Bootsie didn't seem to notice. She'd already turned toward the doorway. There was a rustle of fabric and creak of chair legs as most of the room followed suit. Laura elbowed Ginger, and she looked away from a red-faced Mac to see Tincy Bell ushering someone into the room: a serious-looking woman in a chic Armani suit-dress.

"Well, look who's here," Tincy called out. "It's the mother of our newest Rosebud and her— Wait a sec." She paused, glancing behind her and waving an arm. "Hon, we're right in here," she said, which was when the slim girl in deep teal strolled through the door, her shiny black hair swinging as she moved.

"Welcome, Ambassador Chow and daughter, Cindy," Bootsie said, taking the lead again. "The Glass Slipper Club is honored to have you both here tonight. Cindy, why don't you settle in between Michelle and Prissy? And, Ambassador, why don't you take a seat in the front row beside Tincy?"

Cindy Chow is the new Rosebud?

Mac let out a strangled "Uhhh."

Ginger and Laura exchanged bug-eyed glances.

"Can you tell whoever's got a voodoo doll with my name on it to stop sticking pins in me?" Mac said through gritted teeth.

"Shhh, she's coming," Ginger warned as Cindy walked their way, smiling and holding her white nosegay like a perky bridesmaid.

"My, oh, my," Laura whispered from Ginger's other side. "This just keeps getting more and more interesting."

Cindy did a little wave and uttered a soft, "Hey, girls," as she slid into the empty chair next to Mac, who slouched down in her seat, hardly looking very ladylike.

Poor Mac, Ginger thought, hoping this wouldn't be too hard on her. She patted her friend's knee, which garnered a groan in response.

"All right then, Rosebuds, more about your duties as GSC debutantes," Bootsie Bidwell said, resuming her monologue, waving the debutante handbook as she spoke.

"You'll each be representing the Glass Slipper Club during your Rosebud season, so how you behave at each function, in public, or anywhere another clubber's eyes may fall upon you will determine whether you make it through to the spring. If you should let us down in any way, there will be serious consequences."

Was it Ginger's imagination, or did Bootsie Bidwell stare right at her as she'd uttered the warning?

A blush crept high into Ginger's cheeks. She wanted to lift her nosegay to her face and hide behind it.

Would she ever live down the embarrassment of crushing on a guy who'd used her? Even if Javier had good intentions, like saving a historic oak, it had felt like being stabbed in the back *and* in the heart, and it might've cost her any chance to deb. Thank God it hadn't come to that. Neither her mom nor Rose Dupree would've ever forgiven her. No boy was ever going to get the best of her again, not if she could help it, anyway.

* * *

Ginger arrived at her grandmother's house right on time—because to do otherwise would be to incur the Wrath of Rose—though Deena had beat her there by a hair to lay out "The Dress," as Ginger was beginning to think of it.

She hauled the Caldwell annual inside with her since she hadn't gotten a chance to look at it yet—though she could see Mac had bookmarked a page with a sticky note. Unfortunately, her mother intercepted her the moment she walked through the door.

"C'mon, Ging, let's get you changed into the Givenchy ASAP."

"Can't I even say hello to Grammy first?" she protested, but Deena just shooed her toward one of Rose's guest rooms in the west wing of the house.

"Kent's been here for a while already, and it's going to take a good fifteen minutes to get you buttoned up in the dress," her mother droned on as she guided Ginger past the library.

From behind the closed pocket doors, Ginger could hear her grandma's molasses-slow drawl going back and forth in animated conversation with the deeper voice of Kent Wakefield. If only she could pop in . . .

"Ginger, *move it*," Deena ordered, and poked her in the

shoulder, prodding her toward the large sitting room connected to the spare bedroom.

The Dress was laid out across a vast embroidered bedspread, the under-petticoats beside it. There was even a pair of sheer silk stockings, a strapless La Perla bra, white kidskin elbow-length gloves, and pristine white Christian Louboutin peep-toed pumps that Ginger had never seen before.

"They're your size," Deena said as she caught Ginger eyeing them. "Your grandmother wants this done right, and that's how we'll do it. So get undressed, sweetie, and I'll help you into the gown."

Ginger was left completely speechless, knowing that her mother had gone to the trouble of finding her lingerie, gloves, and the perfect shoes. She wondered how Deena had found the time, between her busy social life and selling expensive real estate to her expensive friends.

As her mother fluttered around the bed, gathering up the petticoats, Ginger sat down on a carved Victorian chair, unzipped her boots, and pulled them off, leaving them on the floor at her feet. She peeled off her tunic and leggings next and draped them over the chair's back. As quickly as she could, she rolled on the silk stockings. She normally refused to wear panty hose, but figured getting dressed up for a portrait sitting merited an exception. Before pulling on the Louboutins, she ran a finger across the almost iridescent sheer chiffon and the matching satin trim. She felt like Cinderella as she slid her feet into each one. They fit perfectly, as if they'd been made for her.

Deena tapped a toe on the floor, waiting with the petticoats in hand, and Ginger went over to her, basically stepping into them and then standing still while her mother fastened her in. The dress came next with Deena holding it wide over her head, leaving Ginger with nothing to do but raise her arms as her mother directed hands through sleeves and then guided the gown down Ginger's hips and to the floor. It was undeniably breathtaking, and Ginger couldn't suppress a tiny giggle of amazement, imagining walking into the Grande Ballroom at the Houstonian in Rose Dupree's incredible gown.

Ginger swirled around in the gown, stopping when she spied her reflection in a floor-length oval mirror. She stood stock-still and looked at herself in the dress, her mind instantly popping back to the sleepover she'd had before school started when she, Laura, and Mac had played Truth or Deb. Ginger had picked "Deb"—meaning a deb-related dare—and Laura had dared her to don Rose Dupree's price-less gown. It hadn't fit then. Laura couldn't even get all the buttons done. But Rose had agreed to have it altered, and Ginger couldn't believe the way it fit. She cocked her head, studying her image in the mirror, deciding the Givenchy appeared as if it was made for her.

"The alterations were beautifully done," Deena remarked as if she was reading her thoughts. Then she stood behind Ginger and began working on the tiny pearl buttons going up the back. "The seam work is flawless."

"Yeah, flawless," Ginger said with a grin. She still recalled all too clearly that it was her mother who'd been dead-set against Ginger wearing the Dress at her coming out. If Rose Dupree hadn't insisted—and had her trusted seamstress do the alterations—the vintage Givenchy ball gown would have remained entombed in its archival box forever.

How quickly her mother had done a 180-degree turn

when Rose had put her dainty size-five foot down. Ginger could only imagine how it felt to have such power over people, though maybe it just took living longer than anyone else around you. Or else it was something in the water that made Texas matriarchs so potent they could silence a room with one look.

"Stand still, please," Deena directed. Her nimble fingers had Ginger buttoned up in no time.

All too soon, Ginger found herself being plunked on a stool in front of a maple vanity so Deena could attempt to tame—with spit, ugh!—the short layers of her warm auburn hair. But when her mother brought out a makeup bag, Ginger pushed up from the stool, snatched up the cosmetics case, and said, "I'll take it from here, okay? Just give me a minute or two alone."

"Don't forget the lipstick," Deena told her.

"Yes, Mother."

"And the gloves, of course."

"I won't," Ginger promised, and Deena finally left the room—albeit reluctantly—closing the door behind her.

As soon as she was gone, Ginger pushed the makeup bag aside and retrieved the Caldwell yearbook, hastily flipping to the page Mac had earmarked with a bright pink Post-it. *Is this him? It's the only Wakefield I could find in Alex's sixth-grade class or any other class from that year,* Mac had written.

Ginger scanned the black-and-white faces, running her finger beneath the names until she came upon the only Wakefield, as Mac had written. Her brow wrinkled.

"William K. Wakefield," she read aloud, studying the photograph from all angles. Surely that had to be him: same moody eyes and straight nose, same petulant lips.

Her gaze wandered to the opposite page, where a small feature touted Caldwell's Budding Picasso. It displayed a slightly larger photograph of a lanky boy posing beside an abstract painting that nearly dwarfed him. The caption proclaimed, *William Wakefield with his prize-winning oil on canvas. Wakefield's work stole the show at the annual citywide competition for middle school artists.*

Wait a second.

William Wakefield . . . prize-winning . . . competition for middle school arts.

She skimmed the article, pausing on one quote in particular: *"It's cool being considered such a good artist at my age. I feel like I'm following in my grandfather's footsteps."*

That was Kent, all right. She had no doubt about it. And now she knew for sure why the name Wakefield had jogged something in her brain, beyond the fact that his grandfather had been infatuated with Rose Dupree. No wonder she'd had butterflies in her stomach when Rose had introduced them. It wasn't because of his Gus Wakefield–esque charm, but because of the way he'd cut her down back when she was a sensitive and impressionable twelve-year-old. It flooded back to her, the things he'd said, every single word. . . .

It was a long time ago, Ginger told herself, snapping the yearbook closed. She was older now, with a thicker skin. But that hardly made her feel better.

She tossed the yearbook on the bed, telling herself to chill as she grabbed the makeup bag and dug through it, pulling out a sheer pink lipstick and applying it with a trembling hand. She hastily dabbed some blush on her cheeks and a coat of mascara on her lashes, and that was that. If "prize-winning" artist Kent aka William Wakefield was going to paint her, he might as well paint her looking like herself.

She stood up, teetering a bit on the Louboutin heels as she crossed the bedroom and opened the door, holding up her skirt as she carefully walked up the hallway toward the library where her mother, Rose, and Mr. Wakefield awaited her. The rustle of silk petticoats filled her ears, and an anxious frown pursed her lips.

What if I jog his memory? she asked herself, stepping into the room. Would he still deny they'd met before? Like his insult had meant nothing at all?

"My Lord, you look gorgeous!" Rose Dupree's wrinkled hand went to her heart the moment Ginger came into view. "Why, you're a vision!" she gushed, raising a glass of cognac in salute. "You look like a real princess."

"The lipstick's a definite improvement," Deena remarked in her usual reserved fashion, but the way her face lit up told Ginger that she, too, approved.

Ginger blushed and said, "Thank you," but her eyes were on Kent Wakefield.

Like Rose, he held a snifter of cognac, which he nearly dropped when he turned away from the mantel to gawk at her. He'd apparently been admiring Rose Dupree's endless silver-framed photographs of her and Granddad Dupree posing with famous blue bloods and politicians from all over the world.

"Wow," he uttered, and his gray eyes took her in. He looked pretty "wow" himself, Ginger thought, in a black jacket, gray T-shirt, and washed-out blue jeans, and the admiring look on his face made Ginger's heart melt a little. "Your grandmother's right," he said, shifting his glass of amber liquor from one hand to the other. "You look every bit like royalty."

Ginger glanced at the hand-cut crystal decanter filled with

155

Rose's treasured Hennessy cognac, which was practically empty. She wondered how long ago Kent had arrived and how much brandy he'd been drinking. It got her guard up again, just as she'd begun to lower it.

"Is it against the law to get an underage artist liquored up before he paints?" she said, and headed toward him. "I'd hate to come out looking like a sixth grader's attempt at a Picasso."

If he caught the reference, he didn't show it.

Instead, he laughed. "Do I look like a sixth grader? I'm eighteen," he corrected her. The way his black hair was slicked back from his face gave his patrician features a vaguely rebellious bent. He had a wicked glint in his eyes and an amused smile on his lips. "And I'm not liquored up, just enjoying myself."

"If the boy's old enough to vote, he's old enough to drink, I say," Rose proclaimed.

"Hear, hear," Kent said, and raised his snifter to her.

"Well, I'm not sure the police would feel the same, and I'd rather have him sober than silly, if that's all right with you," Ginger declared, rounding a tufted settee to close the gap between them.

"Seriously, Ginger, I'm fine, just relaxed and ready to get to work," Kent assured her, though she was close enough now to notice that his eyes seemed just a little bloodshot.

"Look, Kent . . . oh, wait, or is it William?" she said as evenly as she could, nervously smoothing the skirt of the gown. "I finally know how we met before," she announced as he raised his dark eyebrows. "You were the artistic savant in sixth grade who squashed everyone at the local art competitions. In fact"—she cocked her head, staring right at him—"you're pretty much solely responsible for my putting away my paints forever."

"Me?" He brought the snifter to his chest. "How could I be responsible?"

"You still don't remember?" She couldn't *believe* he was callous enough to forget how he'd crushed the dreams of a girl still struggling to find herself. After his demoralizing comment, Ginger had even stopped with her art classes and put away her unpainted canvases, dyeing her hair pink and going punk for a while, and then going blond as a rock chick and then black all over as a Goth before she'd found environmentalism and embraced it.

"What did I say?" Kent asked, looking like he wanted to laugh rather than seeming ashamed.

"Ginger, please, you're being silly," Deena tried to dissuade her, but it was too late.

She raised her chin and said in a slightly quivering voice, "You remarked that my attempt at Impressionism looked like a cat had booted all over the canvas."

"I said that? Oh, God. It's kind of funny, don't you think?" Kent said, and grinned, but it was an uncomfortable grin, and he looked across the room to Rose and Deena for help, though neither offered him any defense at all.

"Yes, you said it, and I didn't think it was funny at all. Just plain mean," Ginger blurted out, a tremor of anger rushing through her. How could he hurt someone like that and so easily block it from his mind? "I threw away my honorable mention ribbon and cried myself to sleep for, like, a week."

Kent took a slow sip of cognac, cleared his throat, and said, "If I was an ass back then, I'm sorry."

But there was something in his voice that sounded oily to Ginger's ears, like he was doing what he had to do to appease her so he wouldn't look like a total shit in front of Rose Dupree and Deena. Ginger knew how some guys liked to take advantage of gullible girls. She'd already been there and done that with Javier Garcia. She wasn't about to go there again with Kent Wakefield.

Her grandmother had hired him to paint her portrait, nothing more. So that was all there would be between them, she told herself, not about to let him get to her.

Ginger straightened her shoulders, lifted her chin, and said, "You're right. It was forever ago." She crossed her arms, hugging the bodice of the dress. "I've done a lot of different things since then, found more worthwhile ways to spend my time. Maybe you actually did me a favor."

"Kids say stupid things." He shook his head, gesturing toward her with his glass of cognac. "So I'm sorry if I did anything to hurt you . . . in the *sixth* grade," he added, and Ginger felt like he'd come just short of calling her silly, like Deena.

If she'd been smart like Mac, she would've let it drop then and there. But she had more in common with Laura when it came to dealing with guys. Neither seemed inclined to use their common sense until it was too late.

Ginger wanted to show him that she was in charge this time, that nothing he could do would intimidate her.

"If you wouldn't mind, Mr. Wakefield, why don't you give me that glass so I don't end up looking like something the cat booted all over the canvas," she said, and reached for Kent's glass, grabbing at the stem.

"What are you, the alcohol police?" He pulled the snifter back toward him. "I'm not finished."

"Ginger . . . Kent, let's not squabble over this," Rose Dupree insisted, and Deena chimed in, "Yes, let's move on."

But Ginger didn't listen.

"I don't care if you're finished or not"—she made a final attempt to snatch Kent's glass from him, jerking it in her direction—"so give it to me. . . . *Oh!*"

She felt liquid splash across her skin even before she glanced down and saw the deep amber stain on her white glove . . . and down the front of the Dress. Her mother and grandmother let out audible gasps. At that moment, Ginger figured it would have been better if she'd actually been stabbed. She'd ruined Rose Dupree's vintage dress, which was *far, far* worse.

"I'm so sorry, it's my fault completely," Ginger heard Kent saying over and over again, though it wouldn't undo the done, would it? It wouldn't change the disastrous thing that had just happened because of his stubbornness.

She felt frozen in place, like she was going through an out-of-body experience, looking down on the room and herself from somewhere above, trying to stay cool while everyone else swirled around her.

"Try club soda!" she heard Rose squawk at Deena, and soon Ginger felt hands patting damp napkins all over her chest, all the while her mother muttered under her breath, "I knew something bad would come of your wearing this dress. I knew it."

I'm sorry, Ginger tried to get out, but her voice seemed paralyzed as well.

Rose threw open the library doors and started howling, "Serena! Serena, come here right this minute! It's an emergency! God help us all."

It was like someone had died, not just spilled a drink.

Ginger squished her eyes closed, fighting tears and wishing she was anywhere but there, sure that Rose would kill her if the Dress was ruined for good. And if she didn't, Deena surely would.

A man can have a love affair that means
no more to him than a good meal.
—Barbara Cartland

Guys who cheat on hot girls obviously
can't tell dog food from Texas prime.
—Jo Lynn Bidwell

Nine

Jo Lynn took an impatient sip of her Skinny Cinnamon Dolce Latte, set it down with a thwack, and scowled at Camie and Trisha across the table.

"Thank God *that's* over," she said, and her two comrades nodded. They surely knew exactly what she meant: the first Rosebud meeting, where she'd had to endure Laura Lard-Ass Bell getting up in her face yet again. "How am I going to make it through the next eight months without her provoking me into doing something crazy?" she moaned. "Just looking at her makes me want to spew."

Trisha reached over to pat her hand while Camie murmured a sympathetic, "It's too bad she wasn't the one who got booted instead of Mindy Sue."

"But deb season's just begun, hasn't it?" Jo replied, looking on the bright side. "There's still plenty of time for her."

Her two friends had followed her to the Starbucks on San Felipe, not far from the Glass Slipper Club's building. She'd been tempted to drive to Antone's instead so she could stuff down a mayo-drenched tuna po'boy. She'd loved those things ever since her daddy had first taken her to Antone's when she was, like, five. But Bootsie had cut her off as soon as she'd started entering pageants, and Jo wasn't sure she could stomach one now. What she did need was a jolt of caffeine and a little advice from her BFFs, which was exactly what she was getting.

"I'd rather have that freaky Angela Dielman as a Rosebud than Laura," Trisha blurted out, obviously showing she was Team Jo-L.

"Angie Dielman?" Camie squawked. "Are you high?"

That actually got Jo to crack a smile. Like Angie Dielman—the bucktoothed, chain-smoking editor of the school newspaper—would've made a worthy Rosebud. *Ha!* But Trisha wasn't far off. Jo almost didn't care who'd replace Laura, so long as the Cupcake got dumped.

Trisha stirred her coffee overzealously. "Okay, maybe that's not the best example. But it's true that Laura has no respect for herself or anyone else. She's just not fit to be a debutante."

Jo rolled her eyes, wanting to say, *No shit, Sherlock.*

Camie wrinkled her nose like she'd smelled something foul. "She's totally disrespectful," she agreed, her slim forehead rumpling. "And I think she's up to something, Jo Lynn. Why else would she show up at the country club yesterday afternoon, conveniently bumping into Avery, when she was there just that morning?" Cam flipped her dark hair over her shoulder, green eyes flashing fire. "She's still after Avery, I know it, despite all your warnings. It's so damned obvious." Her navy-blue-tipped fingers tightened around her cup as she raised it to take a slow slip.

"Hey, rewind there, will ya! What's this about Laura

going back to the club?" Jo asked, because that was the first she'd heard of it. Why hadn't Camie told her earlier? "When was this?"

"Like, right after Avery left Dillon's barbecue. He said he drove straight to the club to work out in the cave. Trish and I bumped into him when we were coming out of the spa," Camie explained while Trisha nodded. "I lost it when I saw the slut with her hands all over him." Her cheeks turned even pinker than the shade of her MAC blush. "I went off on her, and she gave me some lip. Then she waddled out before I could kill her! But Avery swore he didn't take her with him to Dillon's party." Camie shifted in her chair, biting on her bottom lip as she peered at Jo Lynn. "She wasn't there with him, was she?"

"No, she wasn't at the barbecue with Avery, and I personally reamed him out for not taking you," Jo assured her. She debated whether to tell them about finding Laura's name in Dillon's cell phone with the Cupcake's number listed as one of his recent calls, but decided it was too humiliating to talk about. So instead, she said what she'd been mulling over for the past twenty-four hours, her heart thumping a million miles a minute: "I'm not really sure that Laura's set her sights on just Avery anymore. I think she might be after Dillon."

Trisha made a choking noise and stopped slurping on her latte. "Did you say *Dillon*?"

Camie nearly knocked over her espresso, sloshing brown liquid over the edge of her cup. "Why would you even say that? The bitch can't be dumb enough to pursue Big D. Everyone knows he's your boo." She shook her head, indignant. "And there's no way Dillon would give her the time of day besides. She's the size of an offensive lineman."

"Yeah, she's a hippo all right," Trisha echoed. "He'd have to be stupid to fall for her."

Okay, even Jo Lynn realized the "size of an offensive lineman" remark was a stretch, but it was good to know Camie and Trisha were firmly on her side.

Jo folded her arms on the table and leaned toward them. She kept her voice low as she confessed, "I'm so freakin' tired of that girl being all up in my business. Since using that messed-up photo of Laura blew up in my face and having loads of chocolate delivered from a made-up secret admirer isn't working fast enough, it's time to move on to Plan C."

"I thought porking her up on the chocolate *was* Plan C," Trisha said, twirling a red-gold strand of hair around her finger and looking befuddled.

Jo Lynn ignored her and pulled their debutante handbook from her brown leather D&G bag. "Check out all the rules we're supposed to follow for the next eight months," she said, running her finger down the list of them and reeling off, "Good grades, high morals, ladylike demeanor, no visible tattoos, no drugs or alcohol."

She snapped the book closed, stuffed it back in her tote, and propped her elbows on the table. Smiling, she settled her chin atop her interlocked hands. "There are *so* many ways a girl could stumble."

Camie's face lit up. "You've got something cooking, haven't you? Another way to trip up Ding-Dong Bell."

"Yeah, Jo-L, spill, spill," Trisha begged, bouncing up and down in her seat like a little kid.

Camie looked fit to burst too.

"That's just it." Jo Lynn sighed and settled back in her chair. "I don't know exactly what my next step is yet," she admitted, "but it's going to have to be something dirty and über under the radar."

So under the radar that the GSC could never trace it back to her, she realized, thinking of Bootsie's warning: *"You need to watch yourself. All it takes is one slip, and the GSC will review your Rosebud status. If that happens, I won't be able to do a thing about it."*

"Come on, Jo, you were in, like, a trillion beauty pageants," Camie reminded her. "You must have plenty of tricks up your sleeve."

"You mean like lacing brownies with laxatives? Rubbing poison ivy inside a competitor's sequined gown? Spiking protein drinks with Everclear?"

Cam and Trish both began giggling.

Jo Lynn flicked a manicured hand. "Unfortunately, none of that will work here." She pushed away her Skinny Latte, which had gone mostly untouched. "That irritating stepmother of Mouse Mackenzie's is totally on to my, um, pageant history. So I can't do anything that'll leave fingerprints."

"The only thing that never seems to leave a trail is gossip," Trisha suggested, popping the top of her latte and stirring it with a fingertip. "Think of the buzz that went around the Web about the Lauren Conrad sex tape. No one could ever prove who started the rumor. It was the perfect lie." Trisha's round face screwed up thoughtfully. "I wonder if Laura has a sex tape floating around somewhere?"

Bingo.

Jo Lynn stared across the table at Trisha and goose bumps prickled the hairs on her arms. She was tempted to shriek, *Oh. My. God. That's it!* But she bit her lip and kept mum.

Somehow, she figured it'd be better if she plotted Plan C all by herself. She'd be less likely to get caught if no one knew precisely what she was up to.

She couldn't use the sex tape thing, not with Trisha just having mentioned it. So what kind of lie would do the trick?

It had to be so juicy and believable that it'd be hard to convince anyone it wasn't true once it leaked. Jo Lynn needed to sleep on it. This wasn't the kind of thing she wanted to rush into. She had to mull it over first.

"I don't know." Jo sighed, feigning disinterest. "Maybe Laura's past will catch up with her without any help from me at all."

"It'll all work out," Cam said.

Like clockwork, Trisha chimed in, "Doesn't it always?"

They didn't stick around much longer, and Jo Lynn waved off Trisha and Camie as the two got into Camie's sapphire-blue Lexus coupe and drove away. She started her Audi but wasn't sure where she wanted to go. So she sat there, parked in the Starbucks lot for a few minutes with Finger Eleven playing on her iPod, hooked up to the hands-free stereo, until she pulled out her iPhone and dialed Dillon.

He picked up immediately. "Hey," he said. "What's up? I thought you had your first deb meeting tonight?"

"I did. Cam, Trisha, and I just finished our post-orientation lattes." She ran a finger down the curve of stitched leather on her steering wheel, wishing it were Dillon's abs. "I'm just missing you is all, and I was hoping I could drop by—"

"Right now?"

That was hardly the answer she'd expected.

"I haven't seen you since the barbecue yesterday," she reminded him, not wanting to sound desperate even if she felt it, "and you know I like hooking up face to face. Texts and phone calls aren't exactly personal."

"It's late, Jo, and I'm beat," he begged off.

Late? It was barely nine o'clock, for God's sake.

Tempted to grovel, she stopped herself. "Sorry I bothered you," she said, her heart clenching at his relieved "That's okay."

She started to say "I love you," something she tried to do every time before they hung up, but Dill murmured, "G'night, babe," and suddenly he was gone.

Jo Lynn sat there for a moment, staring at the cell phone in her hands while Finger Eleven's "Paralyzed" surrounded her, thinking that if Dillon would rather go to bed alone than see her tonight . . . well, screw him. Maybe she'd just go see someone else instead.

Jo put the car in gear, slipping out of the Starbucks lot and heading toward the house in Hunters Creek where Avery Dorman lived with his parents and two younger sibs. She was afraid to call him in advance to warn him she was coming because he'd tell her it was too late *for sure.* Jo knew how his ultra-strict dad put him under lockdown on school nights.

She didn't dial Avery's cell until she'd pulled her car against the curb in front of the two-story French-style home with the mansard roof. She turned off her headlights, cut off the music, rolled down the window, and shut off the engine. The occasional car passed by with a sweep of headlights, but otherwise it was quiet except for the twitter of a bird or the chirp of crickets. The night air smelled of lemon, which Jo knew was from the clumps of lemongrass in the Dormans' landscaped front yard. The flowers and shrubs that curved alongside most of the stone path leading to the front door looked shades of gray in the dark, with only a few glowing windows illuminating the facade. But in the daylight, the gardens were a riot of color.

Avery had told her once that his mom was a master gardener and had a green hand, not just a green thumb. Jo Lynn couldn't even keep a houseplant alive to save her life.

Jo Lynn's pulse picked up at the sight of movement beyond the bay window. Someone obviously was awake. She just hoped it was Avery. *Please be up,* she thought, plugging in his number and waiting through two long rings before hearing his voice.

"What'd I do?" he groaned. "Is Camie bitching about me again?"

"This isn't about Camie," she told him. "I need to talk to you right now. It's personal."

He sighed, clearly not getting that it wasn't a request. It was a summons. "It's late, Jo and I'm brat-sitting. My folks are out. Some bank function. Why don't you just tell me what's on your mind, and I'll see if I can help."

"No," she said quickly, her heart skidding. She couldn't risk him hanging up, and she had to see his expression. When it came to a guy, the look on his face was worth a thousand words. "I'm right outside your house, Av, sitting in my car," she said, and within seconds, she saw the drapes pull back and he stood in the window. "Can I come in, or you want to come out? *Please.* It's important."

"Daisy and Lily are already asleep. I put them to bed half an hour ago." His drawl didn't sound welcoming so much as reluctant. "I'll come out, okay? But just for a few minutes. I don't want to leave them alone for long, and not just because my dad would rip my head off if he caught me sitting in your car when they got home."

"A few minutes is all I need," Jo told him before he hung up and disappeared from the window, the drapes dropping.

Soon after, the front door opened and Avery emerged barefoot, wearing jeans and a Longhorns T-shirt. He jogged across the front lawn and ducked into her Audi, closing the door with a firm thump. He filled the space so solidly that Jo Lynn felt crowded in for a moment, like there wasn't enough air for them both. He was nearly the same size as Dillon, she realized, but they were so completely different. One had made a mistake that had changed their lives, and the other . . . well, she was hoping that Dillon wouldn't ever do anything nearly as heartbreaking as Avery had done to her.

"Hope you don't mind," he said, and moved the seat back so he could stretch out his legs. Then he turned to look at her, the lack of light creating shadows beneath the strong bones of his face. He brushed brown hair from his brow, unconsciously flexing rock-hard muscles in his arm. "Okay, what is it?" he asked without even a "Hey, how're you doing?" first. "And make it short and sweet. I need to get back inside."

His eyes were usually so easy to read, but she couldn't read them now, and she didn't think it was because of the dark.

She wet her lips, wondering how to approach this, wishing she knew how to be delicate about things, but she didn't. "I need you to be straight with me," she said, diving right into the heart of the matter. "Did you and Laura hook up—I mean, *really* hook up—when she got back from fat camp? Because if you did, I'll know that everything I'm imagining is wrong and she's just messing with my head."

Usually so quick to flash his dimpled smile, Avery frowned at her instead. "How can you ask me that?"

171

"You owe me the truth, Avery," she insisted.

"Owe you?" he said, and shook his head. "I don't have time for this, Jo Lynn. You can't keep trying to run my life just because of something that happened a long time ago. I did all I could . . . nothing's ever enough. Oh, hell, forget it." He was reaching for the door handle when she put her hand on his knee, stopping him.

"Wait! I'm sorry. I just . . . I'm worried about Dillon, Av. I think he might be cheating on me." She hesitated, grimacing as she got out, "With Laura."

Avery's fingers let go of the handle, and he stared at her. She withdrew her hand from his leg. "You think Laura hooked up with Dillon behind your back?" He made a noise of disbelief. "You've got to be kidding. You're trying to make me as crazy as you are, is that it?"

"I'm dead serious. I think he's screwing around with Laura Bell," Jo Lynn said, laying it all on the table, because she had no choice. "I found her number in his cell, and I found a recent call to her. Very recent."

Avery laughed. "Well, you just called me, and that doesn't mean we're sleeping together, at least not anymore." He shrugged. "It probably means nothing."

"There's more to it than that," she pressed her case, her shoulders tensing as she opened up to him. "Dill's been kind of distant all summer and then, right before school starts, he suddenly decides to slow down our relationship. He's blown me off a couple times and he comes up with the lamest excuses—"

Avery butted in, saying, "We had two-a-days most of the summer, and he works out like a madman. His dad's on his case to be the next Tom Brady."

"Isn't Tom Brady the one who got that actress knocked up and then hooked up with Gisele?"

Avery gave her this look like she was impossible. Then he rubbed his chin. "I don't know Dillon all that well except as teammates, but I haven't heard any rumors about him and any other girls. I'm not sure when he'd have time." He shook his head. "And there's no way he's seeing Laura."

Jo Lynn would've loved to believe every word, but, she didn't, plain and simple. "Camie and Trish saw Dillon at the club yesterday, working out. They said Laura was there too. That call on his cell was made to her yesterday morning. What if he'd arranged to meet her there?"

"Whoa." Avery braced a hand on the dash. "You're way off base, Jo. I know what this is. Laura said something yesterday about Dillon helping her get in shape so she can kick ass in her gown at the deb ball. That's all it is. She didn't act like it was any deep, dark secret."

Whaaaat?

Jo hoped her eyes weren't bulging, but she couldn't hide her shock. If Dillon had agreed to whip Laura Bell into shape—and that would take *some* whipping—and it meant nothing to him, why hadn't he mentioned it? Why'd she have to hear it from Avery first? And wasn't it a little too convenient how the Lard-Ass suddenly wanted to exercise? If she wasn't sure before that Laura was trying to come between her and Dillon, she was certain of it now.

"Someone's been sending Laura gifts," Avery went on when Jo Lynn didn't respond. "Apparently, she has a secret admirer. She thought it was me, but it isn't. I can't believe it's Dillon."

"It's not." Jo jumped in so fast that Avery seemed taken

aback. "I mean, he wouldn't do something like that . . . sending Godiva and brownies with anonymous notes," she stammered. "It's not his style."

Avery arched his thick eyebrows. "I didn't say anything about Godiva or brownies." He narrowed his eyes on her. "What's going on? Are you up to something?"

Uh-oh.

Jo quickly changed the subject. "Laura's trying to get back at me," she asserted, hoping she hadn't said too much already. "She wants to tear my heart out and embarrass me in front of everyone just like—" She stopped herself and took a deep breath, glancing down at her fingers, tightly curled around the steering wheel.

But Avery calmly filled in the blanks. "Just like you did to her?" He shook his head. "God, Jo, it's like you're out to destroy her because something about her pisses you off. I'm not even sure you know what anymore. Is it because I started dating her right after you shut me out, or because she's who she is, and she doesn't give a damn whether you approve or not?"

He reached toward her shoulder, like he wanted to grab it and shake her; then he drew back his hand, dropping it helplessly onto his thigh. "You *have* to let it go. You and I, what happened between us, that was years ago. And you can't keep punishing Laura. She had nothing to do with what broke us up. You need to get over it."

Let it go? Get over it? Jo Lynn couldn't believe he'd even suggest that, not after what she'd gone through.

Her chin trembled and she glared at Avery, emotions flooding her like a tsunami. She had to fight to keep tears from her voice as she told him, "All I want to know is did you sleep with her or not, Avery? Yes or no? Which is it? It's

174

not like I'm going to tell anyone, because it's not like you don't have a reputation as a player anyway, so who would care? I just need to know for me," she lied, "because then I can be sure Laura's not after Dillon, and I'll stop worrying that she's coming between us."

Avery's Adam's apple bobbed as he swallowed hard. "What if I did?" he said quietly. "That's no one's business but mine and hers. At least, it shouldn't be."

If he'd screamed "Yes, I slept with Laura," it wouldn't have been any clearer in Jo's mind. And it gave her a brilliant idea.

Jo turned away from him, hoping he didn't see the sudden look of triumph on her face. She fully intended to use the truth against Laura and twist it into the most believable lie. Now she had all the ammunition she needed to set in motion her plan to smear Laura Bell's name so throughly that the GSC wouldn't want to touch her. It was too perfect.

"What's going through your head?" Avery asked, sounding worried. "You're way too quiet."

Jo Lynn composed herself before she faced him again. "You're right," she told him. "I need to stop looking behind me and focus on what's in front of me."

He shifted his oversized shoulders so he could better face her. "What's the catch?"

"No catch," she told him, and took her hand off the wheel long enough to give his leg a squeeze. Even through the denim of his jeans, she could feel the tension in his thigh. "What's the matter, Av? Don't you trust me?"

Avery looked at her without saying anything for what seemed an eternity. He finally gave a nod, said, "Promise you'll be good?"

"Oh, I'll be better than good."

He squinted at her through the dark. "Why does that scare me?"

Jo Lynn took her hand off his thigh and put it back on the wheel. "Thanks for coming out to chat. I feel completely reassured. So go on back inside to your brat-sitting," she said. "I'd better get home."

She had things to do, like tear a girl's reputation to shreds.

"Jo." He had such a serious look on his craggy face.

"Get out." She laughed and practically pushed him out the door.

Just wait and see what happens to your darling Laura Bell now, she mused, giving Avery a wave as she started the Audi and put it in gear. Then she hit the gas, peeling away from the curb, leaving Avery splashed red in the flash of her taillights.

A lie will go round the world while
the truth is pulling its boots on.
—Old Proverb

Guys can break your heart,
but girls can cut you in two.
—Laura Bell

Ten

Laura stayed up way too late on Tuesday night. She couldn't get her brain to quiet down, not when vivid scenes replayed themselves over and over again in her head, like Jo Lynn warning her off Dillon (*please!*) before their deb orientation and her equally nasty encounter with two of the Bimbo Cartel after she'd "bumped" into Avery at the country club on Monday afternoon.

Maybe she would've felt calmer if she'd had a chance to vent. Only Mac had been so freaked by Cindy Chow's becoming the newest Rosebud that she'd whined about her stomach aching and bailed on their plans for ice cream après–Rosebud meeting. In desperation, Laura had tried to call Ginger, but kept getting her voice mail. Something bizarre must've happened at Rose Dupree's, because Ging never turned off her cell unless it was an emergency.

With neither of her BFFs available to talk trash, she'd ended up texting Avery, asking, How can U hang out w such MEAN girls?

He'd come right back with: The world's a mean place. Get used 2 it.

Wow, that sounded cynical enough for Mac.

Thx 4 the tip, she'd texted back sarcastically, which is when he'd written something that made *her* stomach ache.

B careful OK? Watch out 4 JL

Well, hell, like she wasn't doing that already.

She'd tossed her BlackBerry onto the chaise longue in disgust, and had tried to calm her nerves by eating the remains of a pint of Häagen Dazs chocolate chip cookie dough and scrolling through the latest Vera Wang bridal collection online, looking at potential designs for her deb gown, before she'd finally fallen asleep well after midnight.

When Wednesday morning dawned, and Tincy popped into her room with a cheery, "Rise and shine, my Texas Rosebud!" Laura had groaned and pulled a pillow over her head, lying there for another good ten minutes until she'd dragged her butt out of bed, showered, and started getting dressed. She knew it was going to be a rough day when she had trouble putting on her uniform.

Laura stuck out her tongue as she tugged at the zipper on the side of her tan and black plaid pleated skirt, finally nudging it all the way, up. *Damn PMS,* she cursed, feeling bloated and edgier than before, if that was possible.

"*Laura Delacroix Bell!* What on earth's taking you so long?" Tincy called from the doorway. "Oh, Lord, don't tell me your new uniforms are already too snug? Did you sneak an ice cream last night after the meeting? And don't lie, because Cookie found the empty container in the kitchen this mornin'."

Found it? More like Tincy had her staff snooping for signs that Laura had started bingeing after her stint at fat camp this past summer.

Laura slowly turned away from the mirror to face her mother. Tincy had her fists firmly planted on her tiny hips, and her glossy lips were arranged in a disapproving frown.

"Um, *hello*?" Laura said, staring at her mom. "Perhaps you've heard of knocking? You ball up your hand and bang it on the door, like so." She curled her fingers into a fist and rapped the air in front of her.

For some reason, Tincy had begun to think it was her prerogative to burst into Laura's bedroom whenever she felt like it. Laura was going to have to start locking her door if this kept up. She wasn't at Camp Hi-De-Ho, where the counselors rarely gave the campers any privacy for fear someone would bolt and hit the nearest 7-Eleven for a Big Gulp and a king-sized Snickers.

"Thank you, Ms. Smarty-pants, but in my house, I do as I please." Her mother marched across the room, came up beside her, and began tugging on Laura's skirt and shirt, like she'd done a bad job of dressing herself and needed adjusting. "I can't believe these are the new ones," Tincy murmured. "I wonder where Babette's been sending them out. I think the cleaners must be shrinking them."

Tincy might only come up to Laura's chin—well, maybe up to Laura's nose if she was wearing heels—but that didn't make her any less terrifying. God, Laura mused, her older sister was beyond smart to have taken a PR job in San Francisco, far away from Tincy and her criticism. How had Sami survived her debutante season without strangling Mummy Dearest? Maybe Laura should give her a call one of these days and get some frank advice.

"*Laura.* I'm speaking to you."

"Yes, ma'am."

"Next time a package of sweets arrives from that anonymous Romeo of yours, it's goin' straight in the trash," her mother said in no uncertain terms. "I thought it was cute at first, that maybe it'd be good for you to have another boy interested in you so you'll forget that Avery Dorman. It isn't him, is it?"

"No, it's not him," Laura told her, the only thing she did know for sure, which made her all the more nervous about who was sending the mysterious packages. She'd already checked off the bow tie–wearing boy she'd served lunch with at the Bread of Life last weekend (who she was sure was gay) and Neville Hopkins, who'd professed a crush on her since first grade but who'd been practically engaged to Winnie Van der Haven since their sophomore year. Laura knew her on-and-off relationship with Avery had scared most other guys off. One of the only options left was one she didn't care to think about: that it wasn't a guy at all, much less someone who admired her.

"Maybe it's someone you met at camp," Tincy suggested, and Laura had to bite her lip to keep from guffawing.

The only men she'd met at Camp Hellhole worth five seconds of her attention had been the counselors, but they were all in college and none would ever send a Hi-De-Hoer *chocolates,* for God's sake. Now, if she got an anonymous gift of soy milk and alfalfa sprouts, she'd have a damned good idea where it came from.

"No more talk about my weight, Mother, please," Laura said, trying to step around her mother, only to have Tincy lift a hand to stop her.

"You can't afford to gain another ounce, sweet pea, or you're gonna give the GSC selection committee something more to talk about. I don't want to sound mean, but you're in by the skin of your teeth. If you weren't a legacy, why, they'd never even consider a girl of your, um, build," Tincy got out, then seemed to realize she'd said too much. She drew in a sharp breath and clamped her mouth shut.

Regardless, Laura felt the sting. She hardly needed constant reminding that being her "build" put her on precarious footing with the GSC. All Laura had to do was glance in the mirror to realize she didn't come in the two sizes preferred by the deb selection committee: small or extra-small. Tincy had raised her with the belief that becoming a Rosebud was one of life's most important things. It was just a lot more pressure than she'd ever imagined.

"I won't screw this up, Mother," she said quietly, smoothing a hand over her skirt where it stretched across her belly. "I promise."

"I only say these things because I love you so much," her mother cooed, laying a cool palm against Laura's cheek. Tincy's carefully made-up face softened, though the Botox injected into her forehead every few months kept the skin there from creasing even slightly. It was as if part of her was made of wax. "Now finish getting ready for school." Her mom patted her behind. "You're running late, as always."

Laura stood stock-still until her mom had left the room and then she turned to face her reflection again. She attempted to tuck in her button-down shirt, but ended up leaving it hanging out instead. She debated adding a belt around her hips, but nixed that idea. It would only emphasize her middle. Then she turned left and right, smoothing a hand over her stomach, squinting as she eyed her body critically. She could definitely stand to tone up, but if she started working out with Dillon that would take care of things, wouldn't it?

If you weren't a legacy, why, they'd never even consider a girl of your, um, build.

What was wrong with her build? Why did every fashion magazine in the industrialized world have to promote the idea that only skin-on-bones was pretty?

Think "Diva," she told herself, picturing the photo of the white-gowned debutante taped to her bathroom mirror with her face Photoshopped onto it. She'd written affirming things like *Rosebud* and *Goddess* beside it, and she focused on those words now and all the things she liked about herself.

She turned this way and that, so her skirt swayed across her thighs. Yeah, her legs definitely rocked. They were long and shapely and still a little tan from spending most of the summer outdoors. Camp Hellhole had been good for something, at least. Hadn't Avery once said that her legs were her best feature? Okay, and her boobs, which were one hundred percent real. And hadn't he always loved her eyes? Judging by the way he'd kissed her when she'd run into him at the country club, he didn't seem to have any complaints about how she looked. He'd always accepted her for who she was, even if his crowd—the *in-crowd*—at Caldwell and PFP hadn't approved.

I do admire you. A lot. Maybe more than I should.

Avery might not be her secret admirer, but he *had* sent her the flowers to celebrate her Rosebud invitation. Even if he'd been spending time with Camie Lindell, Laura knew he was still drawn to her. She'd felt it when she'd kissed him. The attraction between them was undeniable.

I am who I am, she silently repeated her personal mantra, adding to it, *and I will get Avery Dorman back somehow.*

She went over her mental to-do list for this year, and finding a way to snag Avery was at the top. Number two was conning Dillon Masters into helping with her pre–Rosebud Ball workouts, which doubled as a slap to Jo Lynn. *Check, check.* Vera Wang was all set to design her ball gown. *Check.* And Jo Lynn Bitchwell's blackmail attempt hadn't stuck, so she had nothing on Laura anymore. *Check and checkmate!*

Ginger had once told her that red meant energy in feng shui—okay, she'd also said it meant danger, too, but Laura ignored that part of it—and she definitely felt red today. To further pump up her mood, she slipped on a pair of red patent leather BCBGirls flats, threw on a pair of red Anne et Valentin sunglasses, and grabbed a red Coach tote. It didn't hurt that her Mercedes Roadster was red also. She could use all the extra energy she could get!

Her laptop kept pinging from her desk, like someone was desperately trying to IM her. But Tincy was right: she was running late and definitely didn't have time to chat. As if to underscore that fact, her mother's voice blared from the intercom: *"Laura, you'd better get going!"*

"Okay, okay!" She scrambled to collect her things. Her Patek Philippe confirmed that she was way behind schedule, so she had to book. If she was late for first period, Señora Rung would make her speak in Spanish for the entire class.

"Goodbye, Mother!" she yelled as she raced through the kitchen and out the back door. She put the top down on her Roadster and flew out of the garage, her blond hair blowing as she hightailed it toward Piney Point, kicking up dust in her wake. The traffic was lighter than expected, and she made quick progress. She put on her XM radio, turning it up when she heard the Red Jumpsuit Apparatus in the middle of "Seventeen Ain't So Sweet."

Maybe it'll turn out to be a red day after all.

She took a fast corner at Taylorcrest and she sailed ahead toward Pine Forest Prep, only occasional stop signs slowing her down. Her BlackBerry went off in her bag, and she dug for it one-handed, answering with a snippy, "What?"

"Where *are* you?" Ginger drawled in her ear. "Mac and I hung out at our lockers forever, waiting. I'm about to head into class, but I'm dying to tell you what happened at Rose's after I left y'all last night—"

Laura cut her off. "Well, it must've been something crazy, 'cause I tried calling you and left a million messages. Look, I'm about to pull into the parking lot. I'm gonna have to run to beat the bell. Can we sit down and dish at lunch?"

"Sure, lunch it is. Now go on and scoot! Don't want you getting detention again for racking up tardy slips," Ginger urged.

Laura tossed her cell back into her bag as she rolled into the senior lot, finding the last available space. She climbed out of her Roadster, not bothering to put the top back up. The sky above was a crystal-clear blue, not a cloud in sight.

She heard the warning bell ring as she reached the grassy courtyard between the ivy-covered brick buildings. Students clustered on the stone benches outdoors began to gather up books and bags.

Perfect timing, Laura thought, passing a group of girls as she strolled up the sidewalk. She smiled and waved at a couple of juniors she knew.

"Hey, Becca, nice kicks!" she called out. "Cute bag, Danielle!"

They stared at her wide-eyed, not even hollering out a thanks before ducking their heads and scurrying off. Another pair of girls nudged each other then started to giggle and point.

What's up with that? Did she spill mouthwash on her white shirt or something?

She casually glanced down, but didn't spot so much as a speck of lint on her starched button-down.

"How's it going, Laura?" a voice piped up from behind her, and Laura looked up from her shirt into the bucktoothed face of the editor of the school paper, Angie Dielman.

An O of smoke eased through her thin lips, and a tiny leaf clung to her sleeve. Had she been puffing away in the shrubbery? Such a disgusting habit.

"Gotta dash," Laura said, and started up the stone steps toward the door.

The girl crushed an outlawed cigarette under her heel and followed Laura. "You feeling okay these days?"

"I'm feeling great, Angie, thanks for asking," Laura said, thinking, *Hello? The Freaky Factory phoned and wants to recall all its Angela Dielmans.* She walked faster, so that she was breathing hard by the time she pushed through the doors into the building. But at least there was no sign of Angie.

The girl's certifiably weird, no doubt about it.

The halls had pretty well emptied out when she got to her locker. She rushed to put her history book in and grab her text for Spanish. She glanced up at the clock on the wall above her, saw she had, like, a minute to go. Just as she slid into her assigned seat in Señora Rung's class, her BlackBerry started to ring, but the chime of the school bell disguised it, giving her a chance to turn it off. She didn't want it confiscated.

The Brillo-haired teacher raised her eyebrows, but if she'd heard Laura's cell, she didn't say anything. She returned her attention to her attendance book while the morning announcements crackled from the school's intercom.

Camie Lindell poked her from behind as the headmistress, Dr. Percy, rambled on about this weekend's schedule for SATs. Usually they ignored each other, so what was up with that? Laura resisted the urge to turn around.

"Now everyone knows what a slut you are," she hissed at the back of Laura's head. Her disgusting breath ruffled Laura's hair.

Laura didn't rise to the bait. Her attempt at revving up her day with her energizing red bag and shoes didn't seem to be working. Since she'd gotten to school, her edgy vibe had only gotten worse, what with all the odd looks and whispers, whacked-out Angela following her around, and then Camie calling her a slut. Okay, that part wasn't so off the wall, but the rest was plain odd.

"*Hola, niñas,*" Señora Rung said, rising from her chair, once the announcements had finally stopped. "*Abre tus libros de textos y da vuelta a la página viente, por favor.*"

Laura had never been so relieved to start a lesson before, even though she stumbled through her conversational Spanish, and the hour seemed to drag on forever. When the bell finally rang, Laura grabbed her things and fled the room as fast as she was able. The last thing she wanted was to have Camie breathing down her neck, whispering more spiteful things. Though she passed Mac and Ginger at their lockers and in the hallways several times between their next two classes, Laura didn't have a real chance to talk to them until they snagged the best out-of-the-way corner table in the cafeteria for lunch.

"What the hell is going on?" she asked her BFFs, leaning over the untouched Caesar wrap she'd bought at the snack bar. "It's like girls either ignore me, or they look at me funny and then start whispering. I checked my shoes for toilet paper trails, and my skirt wasn't tucked into my panties. So I haven't a clue."

Laura paused and glanced around them. Something even felt odd about the cafeteria today, and it wasn't just the lingering odor of French fries. Maybe it was the noise level, which seemed more hushed than was usual. The room generally buzzed with voices, seeing as how the first lunch-period class mingled with the juniors. Maybe she was being paranoid, but Laura felt like all eyes were upon her. She even caught one of the girls at the next table pointing.

"Did you see that?" she asked, putting up a hand to shield the side of her face. "I haven't sprouted antennae, have I?"

"Face it, Laura, people are weird," Mac tossed out, taking a bite of her peanut butter and jelly sandwich and adding through a full mouth, "and girls are the weirdest people of all."

Figuring Mac would be little help—she was always the last of the Three Amigas to know *any* scoop—Laura turned to Ginger. "I swear I'm not hallucinating about this. That freaky Angie Dielman dogged me earlier, asking how I was feeling, like she was preparing to write my obituary or something. Then Camie the Bimbo practically spits in my hair in

Spanish class, telling me what a whore I am." She squinted. "Although I guess Camie dissing me really isn't that off the wall, is it?"

"Sorry, chica, but I'm as out of the loop as you," Ginger admitted, and dumped dried cranberries into her tub of vanilla organic yogurt. As she stirred the mixture, she wrinkled up her forehead and said, "I've been kind of distracted this morning, though. Things went from bad to worse at my grandmother's last night."

, "Well, go on," Laura urged, because anything to take her mind off her very bizarre morning would be a relief. "I want to hear how things went with that Wakefield dude who's painting you."

"She found out who he is . . . I mean, was . . . from looking at the picture I tagged in Alex's old yearbook," Mac jumped in, and her thick eyebrows peaked above the frames of her glasses. "Turns out he's some creep that insulted her in sixth grade—"

"You mind if I tell it?" Ginger said, and Mac winced, murmuring, "Sorry." Ginger cleared her throat, her green eyes bright as she looked at Laura and explained, "He used to call himself William Wakefield—Kent's his middle name—and he was, like, a child prodigy, winning all these local art competitions and acting like a snot. He said my artwork looked like a cat had blown chunks on the canvas."

"Nice," Laura remarked, trying to focus on Ginger's story. "So you called him on it, right?"

"Of course I did." Ginger looked pleased with herself for an instant before something dark clouded her eyes. "Which led to kind of an, um, argument—"

"You fought with him? In front of Rose and Deena?"

190

Laura couldn't imagine tiny Ginger picking a fight with anyone, much less with her mom and very proper grandmother as spectators.

"I just tried to get him to stop drinking my grandmother's cognac and take me seriously, which is when his drink spilled down the front of Rose's deb ball gown," Ginger confessed, her voice going softer as she recounted the painful event.

"Oh, shit," Laura said, and Mac leaned in, obviously unable to keep quiet a minute longer.

"Ginger said it looked like a dog had pissed on it," Mac volunteered while Ginger's cheeks flushed, turning nearly as red as her hair.

"I'm lucky I'm alive." Ginger's tiny white teeth tugged at her bottom lip. "But I probably won't stay that way if Grandmother's cleaner can't get the stain out. I could hardly sleep last night"—she gestured at the shadows beneath her eyes—"I had such a stomachache."

"You poor thing," Laura commiserated, selfishly feeling better all of a sudden, knowing she wasn't the only one of the Three Amigas having a hard go of it lately. "Speaking of stomachaches, how's yours this morning, Mac?" she asked with a wink.

Just as Mac started to answer, Laura's BlackBerry went off in her bag.

"Hold that thought," she said, and dug in her red tote to retrieve it. She didn't recognize the number, so she answered with a cautious "Hello?"

"Laura, it's Cindy," a breathy voice said, and Laura's eyes went to Mac. "I sent you an e-mail just now. Did you get it?"

"I haven't checked e-mails in a while," she admitted.

, you might want to look at it now. And if you
:een it already, then you'd better brace yourself."

scrunched up her brow. *What the hell?* "Okay" was
... ... ,ot out before Cindy was gone.

She stared at her BlackBerry for a moment after, and
Ginger asked, "Who was that?"

"Mac's new pal Cindy," Laura said, ignoring Mac's cry of,
"What did she want?" Her eyes were on the screen of her
cell, where she noted half a dozen messages highlighted by
the little yellow envelope. She went to the message list and
found one from CChow at the top. Instantly, she opened it
up to find a link to a MySpace page.

She clicked on it and up popped an old photo of Laura in
a bathing suit from a swim party at Melissa Beeler's from two
summers ago. In it, she stood in a silly and unflattering pose
with her back arched so that her belly stuck out; one hand
was on her hip and the other behind her head, smiling an
exaggerated faux beauty-queen smile. Beneath the photo was
a caption that said: *Anyone else notice that LB's gained weight
since fat camp? A little bird tells me that it's not from eating
Twinkies.*

Her fingers trembled as she scrolled down to see some of
the two dozen comments already in play, hardly able to
breathe as she read the first two, one posted by Anon and
another by someone calling herself BuzzGirl.

*I heard she hooked up with a certain Caldwell's BMOC right
after she got back N town. Could it B his?*

And right below that:

*Girlfriend can kiss her debut goodbye once the GSC hears she's
got a bun N the oven! Even if she deniesdeniesdenies, she'll B big
as a brick house soon enuff N then she's thru.*

Oh, shit, oh, shit, oh, shit.

Laura sat there, staring at her BlackBerry screen, unable to move.

"What is it?" Ginger pressed, coming out of her chair and hanging over Laura's shoulder. Pretty soon, Mac was hovering on her other side.

She felt Ginger's breath on her cheek, as her friend realized what was on the MySpace page and whispered, "Oh, my God."

"You know who did this, don't you? You know it's Jo Lynn Bidwell and her Bimbos." Mac plunked back down into her chair and grabbed Laura by the wrist. "You have to tell Dr. Percy. You have to report them, Laura. You can't let them get away with something like this!"

"Just ignore it, Laura. It'll go away if you pretend it doesn't exist. Besides, how can you prove who started it?" Ginger advised, so that Laura felt like she had the devil whispering to her from one shoulder and an angel from the other.

Laura couldn't breathe. All the voices around her seemed to suddenly grow louder, smothering her. She jerked out of Mac's grasp, pushed away from the table and stood. "I've got to get out of here," she said hoarsely, and shoved her cell in her bag and then snatched up the tote.

She hurried from the lunchroom, keeping her eyes dead ahead. Her face felt feverishly hot, as she imagined everyone in the room staring after her, cracking jokes and making snide comments.

"Wait up!" Mac's voice called from behind her, and she heard several pair of footsteps running after her.

But Laura didn't slow her long-legged stride, not until

she'd turned the corner of the hallway to her locker. Then she came to a dead stop.

A baby rattle hung by a ribbon from her combination lock. A small card had been taped to the front of her locker. Laura didn't need to step any closer than she was to see its printed message offering BEST WISHES FOR THE NEW BABY.

"Are you all right?"

"Laura?"

Her friends' voices sounded eerily distant, drowned out by the pounding of her pulse in her ears.

Bile rose up in her throat as she ripped the card down and flung it to the floor. She put a hand over her mouth, mumbling through it, "I think I'm going to be sick."

Laura raced down the hallway, her red shoes noisy on the patchwork of tiles, eyes blurred with tears as she pushed her way out the side doors. Though out of breath, she kept going, down the stone steps, up the sidewalk through the grass courtyard, and into the parking lot. She didn't slow down until she'd reached her Mercedes, its top down, just as she'd left it. She tossed her bag into the backseat and turned her face to the once-blue sky, now an ugly steel gray.

"Oh, hell," she said aloud, allowing the tears to fall just as the clouds opened up.

She felt the dampness on her cheeks as the rain began to come down.

Her reflexes ultimately took over, and she jumped in the car, turning on the engine so she could close the ragtop. Afterward, she simply sat there with damp hair sticking to her face and drizzle pattering on the roof, seriously contemplating chucking the rest of the school day and going home. But something inside her knew it would be wrong to run away now. Much as it twisted her guts to have to go back inside PFP and face the whispers and pointed fingers, she realized she had to do it.

If she didn't, Jo Lynn would win, and Laura found *that* harder to stomach than the rumor that she was sperminated.

So she blew her nose and wiped her eyes, grabbed her bag, and headed back inside.

The hardest years in life are those
between ten and seventy.
—Helen Hayes

When a day sucks less than the one
before it, I consider myself lucky.
—Mac Mackenzie

Eleven

For Mac, the only good thing about the Wednesday night curtsy practice (aka "How to Do the Texas Dip-ity Do," as Honey had stupidly dubbed it) was not having to leave her own house. Everything else completely blew, like having to get her homework done extra-early so she could help set up and, worse still, knowing that her stepmom was their teacher.

Despite Honey's orders that she stick close to home after dinner, Mac managed to slip out for a few minutes, ducking over to the Bishops' house to return the borrowed yearbook. It was as good an excuse as any to see Alex, and Mac figured if anyone could cheer her up about this evening's deb doings, it was him.

While Honey yakked at Mac's dad, following him into their master bedroom so he could wash up after dinner, Mac snuck out and cut across the backyard, edging through the fencelike boxwoods and emerging on the Bishops' lawn. After she picked a few leaves from her hair, she traipsed past a swing set, beneath towering oaks and bald cypresses, hearing a mosquito buzz somewhere near her left ear as she stopped to glance up at Alex's old tree house. It had been eons since she'd been up there with him, and she missed it. She felt the mosquito land on her arm, and she slapped at it with her free hand, wiping its tiny dark carcass on her jeans before she climbed the steps to the Bishops' back deck. Through French doors smudged with Elliott's fingerprints, Mac could see Alex's mom moving around in the kitchen.

Mac rapped on the doorframe, and Mrs. Bishop looked up and waved as she walked over.

"Well, hey, Mac," she said, drying her hands on a dish towel, which she causally flipped over her shoulder. She had on a yellow T-shirt stained with what looked like spaghetti sauce, and her brown hair was tied up in a messy ponytail. "What brings you over?" she asked, a genuinely pleased smile on her bare face. She had fine lines that crinkled at her eyes and the corners of her mouth, which Mac found reassuring. So many mothers in the Memorial Villages looked like they'd smoothed their faces with steam irons. "I assume you're looking for Alex?"

Mac patted the yearbook. "Yeah, I need to return this."

"Be my guest." Mrs. Bishop pulled the door open wide. "Last I saw him he was playing games with Elliott upstairs. Oh, and will you tell them dinner will be ready in ten? Actually, tell El to put down the joystick and come on down." She set an unmanicured hand on Mac's shoulder as she walked in. "You want to stay and eat with us?"

"Thanks, but we already ate," Mac answered, pausing in the breakfast nook, which was cluttered with discarded jackets, shoes, and knapsacks. "Besides, I've got to get back to the house and help Honey set up for curtsy practice tonight."

"Sounds like fun," Mrs. Bishop said, and ruffled Mac's hair. "Don't be a stranger, okay? We miss you around here," she said before starting back toward the stove top to monitor a pot spewing steam below its rattling lid.

Mac ducked through the doorway and toward the front hall, then climbed the stairs, which were littered with socks, coloring books, and even a Nerf gun. *Elliott's stuff,* she thought. Sometimes it looked like the house had exploded and no one had noticed. But she knew Alex's mom liked to do everything herself. It was no wonder she couldn't seem to keep up.

Elliott and Alex shared the beat-up leather love seat in front of the TV in Alex's room, laughing as they held their Wii wheels in the air, steering the race cars that careened around the giant TV screen hanging from the wall.

"Ah, for the good old days of Doom," she said as she came to stand behind them. "I hate to break up this speed-fest, but your mom said to get downstairs, El." She patted Elliott's head, a riot of blond hair sticking up in every direction. "Dinner's almost ready."

"Okay, okay, just let me blast this last one—yay!" He looked positively gleeful as he smashed his race car into the side of Alex's before dropping his wheel onto the couch and scurrying out the door.

"I tell you, the Idiot's gonna be an expert at Wii before he turns ten," Alex teased as he shut down the game and turned to face her. "So what's up?"

Mac plunked down where Elliott had been sitting. The cushion was still warm. "Just making a return," she said, and set Alex's old yearbook on the space in between them. "Ginger said thanks again."

"Did she find what she needed?"

Mac nodded. "Unfortunately, yes."

"That's good, I guess." He swiped errant strands of dark blond hair off his brow, then removed his preppy glasses to wipe the lenses on his T-shirt before sticking them down on his slim nose again. "I heard you got a surprise at your deb meeting last night. Cindy told me that she's a Rosebud now, just like you. She's really psyched."

"Yeah, it was a surprise, all right," Mac agreed, wishing the idea of being thrown together with Cindy, not only in school, but for the next eight months of the debutante season, didn't bother her so much. But it did. She glanced down at the palm of her hand and started picking at a callus. "Seems like this whole year's going to be a bumpy ride."

"Bumpy sounds about right, especially for your friend Laura right now, huh?" Alex volunteered, and Mac's head came up.

"Why'd you say that?"

He shrugged. "I don't know. It's just that Cindy mentioned someone spread a rumor on MySpace that Laura's, um, knocked up." He hesitated and squinted at Mac. "I mean, it *is* a rumor, right?"

"Of course it's a rumor! God!" Mac jumped down his throat, more upset by the fact that Cindy had mentioned it than by her uncertainty about whether the gossip was true.

He quickly moved to appease her. "I'm sorry, okay? I wish there was an easy way to hack MySpace and lay waste to that page, but if there's anything else I can do—"

Mac had another guilt attack, listening to Alex stumble all over himself, scrambling to apologize when he hadn't done anything wrong. It wasn't him at all. She took a deep breath, telling herself to chill. It didn't do any good to take her frustrations out on Alex.

"Thanks, Alex, for wanting to help. I didn't mean to yell, but it's been a rough day, and it's not over yet. I still have to go back and help the step-Barbie arrange the living room for curtsy class." She gave him a feeble smile. "As you can guess, I'm not exactly looking forward to it. Maybe it'd be different if my mom was—"

Oh, man, why'd I even go there?

Mac clamped her mouth together, lips trembling, unable to finish.

"If she was here, right?" Alex said for her, and Mac nodded, hating how her eyes started to well. When would she ever get over it? *Maybe when two years stops feeling like yesterday,* she thought with a sniff and swiped her hand beneath her nose.

"I've got just the thing to make you feel better." Alex sprang up from the couch and started rummaging through his desk.

Mac half expected the table to crash to the floor one of these days. It held three desktop computers, one with a flat screen and two with "alien-head" monitors (her name for them). It was cluttered high with papers, DVDs, books, and extraneous computer parts whose names Mac couldn't even begin to guess. Coming from a household where everything had its place, Mac had never quite grasped the "save everything" ideology of the Bishops. But if it was part of what had made Alex who he was, then it couldn't be all bad.

"Aha!" he said, raising his arm in victory and returning to the sofa to deposit an oversized coin in her hand. "It's my Kirk-Spock bronze medallion. I used to take it to every Math Olympiad in my back pocket." His face lit up. "I never lost a round."

"You want me to have it?" Mac palmed the coin, the little butterflies in her stomach lifting off and flitting around again.

"Maybe it'll bring you some luck," he said, "like it did for me."

She hardly knew what to say. For the most fleeting moment, it felt like her relationship with Alex had fallen back into place again.

"Alexander Evan Bishop! Time for dinner!"

Mac jumped as Mrs. Bishop screamed up from the bottom of the stairs.

Alex laughed at her wide-eyed expression. "You get used to it," he said, and brushed off his jeans, rising to his feet. "Can I walk you out?"

"Sure." Mac got up, preceding him from the room, careful to watch where she stepped on her way back down.

She said her goodbyes and slipped out the French doors as the Bishops settled around the breakfast room table to eat. For some reason, she paused outside and looked in at them for a minute, a wistfulness passing through her, remembering dinners like that with her parents before her mom had gotten sick and everything had changed.

Mac held the coin tightly as she walked home, afraid to stick it in her pocket for fear of losing it somewhere between the Bishops' house and her own. In fact, she didn't let it out of her sight until she'd reached the privacy of her bedroom and dug her wallet from her purse. She kept one of her favorite letters from Jeanie there, folded up in her coin purse. *I'll be watching you,* it said, *feeling my heart swell, and wishing I could be there beside you to tell you how proud I am of you.*

Mac was about to stick Alex's bronze *Star Trek* medallion

inside the billfold with the note and zip it up when she reconsidered and shoved both in her back pocket.

Who knows? Maybe they'll change my luck. I could use a little help in that department.

"Mah-chelle! Where are you, sugar pie? We could use an extra hand right about now!"

Well, maybe the luck takes a while to start, huh? Mac thought as she trudged back down the stairs and into the living room where Honey stood with her dad. Until Alex's good-luck charm kicked in, Mac figured she'd have to endure being bossed around by the overly made-up blonde busting out of the top of her lacy red Catherine Malandrino camisole. And curtsy practice hadn't even started yet.

Oh, boy.

"C'mon, sweet pea, we need everything pushed to the edges." Honey pointed at the far wall, where a couple of Barcelona chairs and a glass-and-chrome coffee table already rested smack in front of a shabby-chic French armoire. "Just make sure to leave places to sit. Whichever girls aren't practicing need to be watching."

Mac rolled her eyes, earning her a frown from her dad. She couldn't even believe Honey had finagled his help schlepping furniture around. Since Mac's mom had died, he seemed to prefer making himself scarce whenever he was home. Yet here he was with his work clothes still on—blue oxford-cloth shirt, pleated gray pants, and old-fashioned-looking black wingtips—though his cuffs were rolled up and his collar loosened.

Losing Jeanie had given him shadows beneath his eyes that never seemed to go away, but whenever Honey was around, he lit up like a frat boy on a first date. Except for the gray in his hair and the creases that time had worn into his face, Mac thought he looked much the same as he did in the twenty-year-old wedding photograph that she kept in her top dresser drawer. Instead of pleasing her, it made Mac prickle with resentment.

"What's the problem, kiddo?" he asked her, and she realized she'd been staring at him. "You need more muscle?"

"I'm good," she said quickly, and grabbed a teak side table to carry across the room. She even made several more trips with other pieces before a large area in the middle of the floor had been cleared.

"Well, doesn't that look nice?" Honey declared, and hustled over to where Daniel Mackenzie stood beside his daughter. "Good job," she said, and gave Mac a pat on the back. "And here's some sugar for you, my darlin'," she added, and inserted herself between father and daughter, standing on the tiptoes of her red Theory wedges, planting a wet one on Dan's lips.

Ugh! Mac watched in disgust. "Get a room, okay?" Mac finally said so they'd separate without her having to wedge a crowbar between them. "Are we done yet?" Her cheeks heated. Because she'd had enough—in more ways than one.

"Watch your tone, young lady," Daniel started up, but Honey shushed him by patting his chest.

"She's right, honey bun. I've got a million things to do before the girls get here, and it's nearly seven o'clock! So the hanky-panky's gotta wait. Now, let's get that rug out of here," she instructed with a clap, causing Mac to groan since it meant rolling up the large Aubusson rug that was one of the few pieces of decor remaining that Jeanie Mackenzie had picked out.

"What's wrong with practicing curtsies on a rug?" she asked, hearing the whine in her voice and not caring a bit.

"Oh, sweet pea, y'all girls need a smooth surface so you don't trip over anything," Honey told her. "It's gonna take everything you've got just to keep from fallin' down."

"Everyone's going to fall down anyway," Mac muttered, only to get another reprimand from her father.

"If you'd stop grumbling and move it, we'd be done a lot faster," he said, not sounding amused in the least.

Mac stared at him, biting down hard on her bottom lip. She hated when he took Honey's side, which seemed like all the time.

She didn't say another word as they pushed and tugged, rolling up the rug until the crimson and navy pattern could be seen from the inside out, looking a lot like a faded version of itself. Then the three of them threw their arms around it and hauled it through the house and into the garage.

Once they'd finished, Mac's dad bugged out, pleading paperwork he needed to tend to. Mac figured it was more like he didn't want to be anywhere in sight when nine teenage debutantes showed up on his doorstep.

Mac returned to the living room with Honey, hoping to God they were done. She wiped dust from her hands onto her Levi's, which already bore plenty of blue and black ink marks.

"Um, can I be excused now?" Mac asked. "I'd like to be alone for a while before World War Three starts."

Honey's spider-lashed eyes blinked. "World War Three? What're you talkin' about, sweet pea? Ah." A knowing look dawned on her china-doll face. "Laura's not still having problems with Jo Lynn Bidwell, is she?"

Mac thought of what had happened to Laura, and she gritted her teeth. But all she'd say was "Have you ever watched that Animal Planet program on honeybees? How there can't be two queens in a colony, or else they'll fight to the death?"

Honey smiled. "Well, whatever's goin' on between Jo Lynn and Laura, they'll sort it out one of these days. Or else, they won't." She shrugged. "Sometimes you've got to leave it to fate. I had a girl from Atlanta, Teena Stern, who was always doggin' me at pageants. She once put superglue in my tube of eyelash glue, and it's a good thing I loaned that stuff to Miss Louisiana before I used it. Took that girl a week to get her eyes wide open. Instead of setting fire to her hair extensions, I told myself, 'What goes around, comes around, and Teena'll get hers.' Just like that"—Honey snapped her fingers—"Miss Teena developed the worst case of cystic acne I've ever seen. She dropped out of the pageant scene, and I never heard from her since."

Dear God, Mac thought, *help me.*

Another of Honey's beauty pageant tales, and her brain would explode. "Whatever," she said, and headed for the stairs, not even trying to be polite anymore.

"Wait a sec!" Honey called after her. "You're not plannin' on wearing those jeans, are you? And your flip-flops?"

Hello! Mac might have helped the stepmonster move a rug, but she wasn't about to let Honey dress her.

"Mah-chelle?"

Mac didn't turn around. She held tight to the banister and kept going up. If she didn't, she might say something she'd regret—well, something she'd regret once Honey ratted her out to her father. She didn't even breathe until she was safely in her room with the door shut.

The clock on her nightstand showed fifteen minutes before curtsy practice, and Mac planned to use it well. Popping in the earbuds for her iPod, she turned on some Brian Setzer doing swing; then she slipped the bronze medallion and her mother's letter from her pocket. Setting the *Star Trek* coin aside, she smoothed the stationery on her bed and read it for the hundredth time.

> . . . *you can believe I'll be watching you, feeling my heart swell, and wishing I could be there beside you to tell you how proud I am of you.*
>
> *Just keep my love in your heart and hold it close so I'm there whenever you need me. I know it's not the same, and I wish I could be there for your debutante season, holding your hand every step of the way. But you'll have to be strong for me and, most important of all, believe in yourself. Never doubt for a moment that you deserve to be there every bit as much as anyone else.*

Mac wiped at her eyes and sat up, pulling out the earbuds and stowing her iPod away before she carefully folded her mom's letter, wrapping it around her good-luck charm from Alex. She set the bundle on her dresser until she'd changed out of her ink-stained blue jeans—and not because of Honey, but because she knew it was what her mom would've wanted. She donned a pair of tan Capri pants instead, pocketing the note and medallion; then she kicked her flip-flops aside, replacing them with her Sam Edelman ballet flats. She wiped a smudge of dust off her pale blue T-shirt, ran a brush through her hair, and dabbed on some lip gloss.

Sorry, Honey, she thought, *but that's as good as it gets.*

Even shut up in her room, Mac could hear the doorbell ringing once and then again, and when she emerged from her cocoon, the house was filled with the chatter of female voices.

She gritted her teeth and told herself it was now or never. Then she headed down the stairs, catching up with Ginger at the bottom.

"There you are!" Her friend gave her a hug in greeting. "I was about to come upstairs and get you. Honey said you were hiding out." Ginger's red hair was pomaded to death and stuck out in a million directions. She had on cargo pants, a pink SAVE THE ICE CAPS shirt, and bright pink Coach flats.

"Where's Laura?" Mac asked as Ginger linked arms with her and they headed toward the living room. "How's she holding up?"

"She's totally freaked, of course, so I got her a Diet Coke and made her sit down as far away from everyone else as possible. Cindy's keeping her company—"

"Cindy Chow?" Mac croaked the name. *The girl's freaking everywhere.*

Ginger squeezed Mac's hand. "Give her a break, Mac. She's being really sweet when everyone else is treating Laura like a leper. I'm just glad she was here so I didn't have to leave Laura alone when I went to find you. She'd taken some Valium before I picked her up, so she's calm for now. But who knows what'll happen once the Bimbo Cartel shows up. Now, c'mon," Ginger said, giving her a tug.

Mac spotted Cindy across the room, her olive skin glowing and her mouth moving a mile a minute as she chatted with Laura, although Laura didn't seem to be chatting back. Mac thought she looked pretty stoned. "She didn't hear from the GSC, did she?"

"Not so far," Ginger said, sounding relieved. "Just pray we get through tonight without Laura doing anything that'll bring the club down on her before she gets this MySpace mess straightened out," Ginger said under her breath, and Mac realized her friend was truly and certifiably nervous. "Maybe I should ask your stepmom to confiscate cell phones before the lesson—"

"Why?"

"The only thing worse than Internet rumors are humiliating YouTube videos," Ginger explained, though she hesitated as they approached Honey, who cheerfully conversed with several debs in the center of the room. She'd changed into a floor-length sapphire-blue chiffon dress with a beaded belt and matching blue satin shoes. Mac thought the shimmery outfit resembled leftovers from a beauty pageant, but then Honey did seem to like things that sparkled.

"How about you keep an eye on Laura, and I'll watch the evil Bimbos so we prevent anything YouTube-worthy from happening," Mac suggested, offering up a pinkie.

Ginger linked her pinkie with Mac's and said, "Sounds like a good plan, so long as the Bimbos play nice. Do they even *know* what the word 'nice' means?"

"They're late anyway," Mac said, and Ginger realized everyone had arrived but Jo Lynn and her cronies. "Maybe we'll get lucky and they won't even show."

Ginger laughed. "Yeah, right."

As if on cue, the doorbell rang repeatedly, like someone was leaning on the button, and Mac glanced over her shoulder to see the door fly open before Honey could even scramble over to let in the last of her curtsy class.

Jo Lynn Bidwell strode into the foyer with Camie and Trisha in tow, all of them in high heels and floral-print full-skirted dresses, looking like something straight out of *The Stepford Wives.*

Jo Lynn caught her staring and marched straight toward her before Mac could escape. The haughty blonde grinned as she looked Mac up and down. "Hmm, I guess having a new mommy who dresses like a showgirl isn't enough to get you out of your tired Gap getups, is it, Bookworm?"

Trisha and Camie giggled, saying, "Good one, Jo," before the trio sashayed away, settling on the deep-red damask sofa across the room from where Laura sat.

"I could kill her for, oh, so many reasons," Mac hissed, such anger running through her body that she felt the urge to break something—like maybe one of them.

"I'm begging you, *please,* no more drama tonight," Ginger whispered, and dragged her over to Laura and Cindy.

"Hi, Mac" was all Cindy said before Ginger sat down beside her, and they tipped their heads together, chatting like old chums.

Mac swallowed hard as she took a seat next to Laura, who leaned a shoulder hard against her and chirped, "Hey, Mac-adoodle!" just a little too loudly before she resumed sipping her Diet Coke through a straw and smiling goofily.

How much Valium did she take? Mac wondered, figuring it had to have been more than one.

"All right, ladies! It appears that everyone's here," Honey said, clapping hands as she moved around the room in a slow circle. "Yes siree, Bob, all ten of y'all are present and accounted for. So if you'll settle down and look this way, we'll kick off this first curtsy class."

With Laura drugged-up beside her, and Jo Lynn and her evil henchwomen across the room, Mac felt a prickle of apprehension. She just hoped the talisman in her back pocket would provide enough good mojo to keep curtsy practice from blowing up.

An original mind is rarely understood.
—Margaret Fuller

Superficial is easy.
It's real that's complicated.
—Ginger Fore

Twelve

"Have other debs got it easy, doing a simple little curtsy or a court bow after they're introduced? You're darn tootin'. But Texas debs always perform the Dip because it's ours, it's special, and it's bigger than life, just like everything else here in the Lone Star State. Besides it's always fun to one-up those Yankee girls, isn't it?"

As Honey Potts Mackenzie rambled on, Ginger sat on the edge of her seat, keeping one eye on Mac and the other on Laura. Her nerves tingled, and not in a good way. Why did she have the feeling that something bad was going to happen, no matter how vigilant she was?

Sluurrrrp.

Ginger stiffened at the sound of Laura sucking up the last of her Diet Coke through a straw, and apparently she wasn't the only one grossed out by the noise. Honey abruptly stopped talking and glanced in their direction. Ginger swiped the can from Laura's hands and set it out of the way on the floor.

What? Laura mouthed, her blue eyes looking foggy and dilated.

"*Shhh.*" Ginger put a finger to her lips.

Honey picked up where she'd left off, and Ginger tried to listen—really she did—but she had so much on her mind tonight, like Laura and how the GSC would react to the pregnancy rumor, even if it was all a pack of lies, and the ugly stain on her grandmother's ball gown. What would happen if nothing could get it out? Would Rose forgive her? How would she ever find another dress to wear that was even a fraction as perfect?

She felt so rattled that her thigh began to tremble, or at least, she thought it was her thigh. Until she realized the tremor was coming from her purse, which she'd shoved into the chair beside her.

As stealthily as she could, she drew her Razr from her hemp bag and slipped it into her lap. She glanced down, noting that she had a new text message, and it was from Kent Wakefield. It said: Sorry abt everything. Can we start over?

She wasn't exactly sure how he meant to start over with her, but Ginger had to say she was impressed that he'd even offered. After the catastrophe at Rose's last night, she wouldn't have blamed him if he'd never wanted to see her again, much less paint her. Maybe Kent was worthy of a second chance. He might've dissed her artwork in middle school, but he hadn't thrown her to the wolves like Javier had. Yet.

". . . you can put on an old formal or a long bathrobe when you practice at home," Honey was saying, "and stand in front of a mirror so you can watch yourself. You should look like you're sinkin' right into the folds of your skirt, kind of like melting into a puddle. . . ."

"Like the Wicked Witch," Laura murmured before sinking down into the Eames chair and crossing her arms over her chest. Her eyes kept slipping closed, and Ginger elbowed her, making sure she didn't fall asleep.

Laura nudged her back, something Ginger hadn't been expecting, and she nearly toppled out of her seat.

"Are you ladies all right over there?" Honey paused mid-monologue to ask.

Ginger settled back into her chair. "Yes, we're fine, thanks."

"Fine 'n' dandy," Laura mimicked, sounding as loopy as she looked.

Across the way, the Bimbo Cartel snickered.

"Ignore them," Ginger whispered, mostly for Mac's benefit, as she noticed Mac tighten her nail-bitten fingers into fists.

Laura didn't even flinch, and Ginger wondered how long the effects of the Valium would last. She hoped at least until the curtsy session had ended and Jo Lynn and her toadies had taken off. Then the Three Amigas could chillax in Mac's kitchen over pizza and girl-talk. It would give Laura a chance to open up to them. She'd been too quiet all day, ever since she'd run out of the lunchroom and come back with rain-damp hair and a deer-in-the-headlights look. "She's in shock" was how Mac had put it, and Ginger figured that was dead-on.

". . . and that's all I have to say about the history of the Dip. Now it's time for a little practical experience. Let's get everyone up and walking around in a circle," Honey instructed. "I want to see how y'all carry yourselves. I have a feeling we'll have to do some work on that, too."

"We have to practice walking?" Mac groaned, which made Ginger smile, thinking tomboy Mac might very well be one of those who most needed "some work."

"Up, up, up!" Honey prompted, gesturing wildly until each girl in the room was on her feet, though it took some assistance from Mac before Ginger could get Laura up and moving.

They trotted like trained ponies, one after the other, like a strange version of musical chairs, until they all reached their seats and plunked down again.

Honey frowned, tapping a finger against her chin, the other hand on her hip. She hardly looked pleased by the demonstration. A heavy sigh escaped her lips as she told them, "All right, I'm no magician, but I do have a few tricks up my sleeve. Thank goodness you'll all be coming to see me regularly before the Big Night. It's gonna take some doing to make y'all graceful. But let's move on, shall we?"

"Regularly?" Mac said, and gulped. Ginger patted her on the knee.

"Okeydokey, my lovelies, get ready to do the Dip!" Honey squealed, and her frown disappeared, replaced by a toothpaste-ad smile. "For those of y'all who didn't listen to my advice and put on heels"—she stared at Jo Lynn, who stared right back—"feel free to practice first without your shoes on. I don't want anyone hurtin' themselves on the first day. Now, pay careful attention, y'all, while I show you how it should look," she demanded in her Minnie Mouse drawl. "I'm lifting my arms like a swan about to take flight, and then I cross one foot behind the other like so, before I gently lower myself so I'm sitting right about on my heel."

One blue satin shoe slid gracefully behind the other, and she appeared to be drifting slowly down toward the floor. "Now I'm extending my front leg, still keeping it slightly bent as I lean over it, turning my head so my cheek rests on my skirt like it's a pillow."

Ginger stared, not even blinking, and the room was dead silent as Honey performed the maneuver.

"Christ, is the woman a puppet?" Laura muttered, sitting up straighter, the Valium clearly losing its edge. "Who's pulling her strings?"

"Hush," Ginger shushed her, and Laura melodramatically zipped her lips, tossing an imaginary key over her shoulder.

Ginger jerked her chin toward Honey, who was just lifting her head and rising from the floor miraculously. "That's all there is to it," she professed when she stood upright again, lowering her hands to brush at her skirt.

"Brava!" Cindy Chow jumped on her feet and started clapping, like she was at the Houston Metropolitan Opera giving a standing ovation to the lead soprano.

The rest of the girls politely applauded, except for the Bimbo Cartel who, Ginger noticed, merely studied their nails, looking bored.

But Honey seemed not to care. She blushed happily, nodding in Cindy's direction. "Well, thank you kindly for your enthusiasm, Miss Chow, is it? Now how about I show you one more time without this skirt on? Then I'll see what y'all can do." With that, Honey tugged at the beaded belt around her waist until there was a slow *riiiip* of Velcro. The belt flew off as did the skirt attached to it, leaving Honey standing there in blue satin shorts and her sequined high heels.

Ginger had to throw her hand across her mouth to keep from cracking up, though the other girls couldn't hide their nervous giggles.

Mac moaned and buried her face in her hands while Laura crossed her legs and tapped a toe impatiently on the floor, murmuring, "When did this turn into *Dancing with the Stars?*"

"You don't want to jerk your way down." Despite the tittering around her, Honey went right on talking. "Think escalator, not elevator," she said, then proceeded to do the Texas Dip again, only now, without her floor-length skirt, they could watch her feet and legs as they changed positions.

This time when Honey lifted herself like a rising Phoenix, it was she who clapped loudly. "All right, all right, the floor show's over. It's y'all's turn now. Who wants to go first? Let's see what each of you can do, so I'll know how much we've gotta work."

"I'd like to go first." Jo Lynn Bidwell popped out of her chair before anyone else could say a word. She flipped highlighted blond waves off her shoulders and put her nose in the air. "If that's okay with you, Ms. Potts, of course," she added, smoothing her skirt.

"No," Honey said, and Ginger wasn't the only one who released a surprised "Ooooh."

"What did you say?" Jo Lynn bristled, looking like a girl who hadn't heard the word no too often.

"I said, no, it's not 'Ms. Potts.' Please address me as 'Mrs. Mackenzie,'" Honey instructed, the bright smile never leaving her face. "Now, try again."

"May I do the Texas Dip, *Mrs. Mackenzie?*" Jo Lynn ground out, her eyes narrowed on Honey, while the rest of the room snickered behind their hands, except for Camie and Trisha, who scowled.

"Yes, you may." Honey gestured toward the open space in the center of the living room and stepped aside.

Jo Lynn strolled forward a few paces, then turned her back deliberately on Laura—at least, that was how it looked to Ginger.

Laura must've felt the same, as she uttered tightly, "I think I just got dissed." She narrowed her eyes on Jo Lynn's backside, and Ginger put a hand on her shoulder as a reminder to stay put.

"You sure you don't need something to lean on? And I guarantee some of y'all will need a hand from your escorts," Honey said from the sidelines, but Jo Lynn waved her off.

"I was born to Dip," Jo declared, standing posture-perfect with shoulders back and chest out. Trisha and Camie grinned and gave her two thumbs-up.

"Born to Dip? More like Bitsy's made her practice it ever since she turned six . . . with leg weights strapped to her back," Laura whispered, the spark returning to her eyes.

"I hope she eats it," Mac added as she leaned across Laura, and Ginger hushed them both.

"Well, go on then, Miss Jo Lynn. Show us what you've got," Honey urged, and Jo raised her arms and positioned herself with one foot slightly behind the opposite ankle.

The room quiet around her, Jo Lynn executed the deep curtsy perfectly, her body fluidly descending to the floor, her head bowing over the bent knee in front as she turned her cheek toward the floor. Effortlessly, she remained there for several beats before she gracefully came up again without stumbling or hesitating.

The Bimbo Cartel hooted and whistled while the rest of the Rosebuds politely applauded.

"Why, that was certainly nicely done," Honey said, sounding distracted as she looked around her. "How about we get another demonstration?" Her gaze settled squarely on Laura. "What say you, Miss Laura? Are you up to it? Want to give it a shot?"

"*No,*" Ginger begged, clutching at Laura's arm. She was hardly in the best shape to try the killer curtsy, and the last thing Ginger wanted was for her to crash and burn in front of the Bimbos. But Laura shrugged off her hand.

"Sure, I'll do it," she said, and stood up. "Though I think I'll try it barefoot, if that's okay."

"That's all right, sugar," Honey assured her. "Anything you want."

"*Laura's* going to curtsy?" Camie rose from the damask sofa, flipping her dark waves behind her shoulders and pursing her glossy lips with faux concern. "Are you sure that's a good idea, Mrs. Mackenzie? Shouldn't she sit down with her feet up, so her ankles don't swell? Maybe I should take a turn."

"Look, here, sweet pea, interrupting Laura isn't very lady-like. What say you show a little respect for your fellow deb?" Honey chided, and ordered Cam to sit back down.

Laura slipped off her flats and walked slowly toward the center of the room. When she hesitated, Honey nodded, encouraging her. "Go on, baby doll, and take your time. The Dip isn't easy for anyone. . . ."

"What about for any *two?*" Trisha piped up, rearing her strawberry-blond head. "As in, maybe Laura shouldn't be doing the Dip in her condition."

Oh, hell, Ginger thought, her breath catching in her throat, *this is bad. This is very, very bad.*

"What condition?" Honey glanced at Laura, who seemed to have frozen in place. Her cheeks had lost all color. "Are you sick?"

"She's probably just sick in the *mornings*," Cam said, while Trisha giggled behind her. Jo Lynn sat between them, hands in her lap, unnaturally quiet though Ginger could see a self-satisfied smirk on her lips.

Mac slipped into Laura's seat beside Ginger, bending over to hiss, "If they say another word, I'm going over there."

"No, you're not," Ginger insisted, grabbing her hand and holding on.

Laura didn't even turn her head at the insult. In fact, she hadn't moved a muscle.

"What's wrong, Laura? Did you miss taking your folic acid? Or are you having a craving? Something like pickles and ice cream?" Camie egged her on until Mac ground out, *"That's it,"* and jerked out of Ginger's grasp.

Mac strode across the living room, sweeping right past Laura to stand in front of the Bimbo Cartel. "Shut your nasty mouths!"

"Oooh, I'm scared." Camie rose from the settee, hands on hips, and sneered into Mac's face. "What're you gonna do if I don't, Bookworm?"

Mac shoved her hard, and the brunette Bimbo stumbled backward in her high heels and went down fast, her flowered skirt flipping up in the air as she hit the floor with Mac on top of her.

Trisha and Jo Lynn shrieked, cowering together on the sofa just a few feet behind the tangled mess of arms and legs and flying hair.

"Get her off me!" Camie screamed, and Trisha flew to her rescue, floral skirts swaying, as she tried to peel Mac off Camie.

225

"Hey, let her go!" Ginger came out of her seat, rushing over to Mac's aid and getting tangled in flailing arms, like in a vicious game of Twister.

"Stop it! Everybody just stop it right now and return to your seats!" Honey yelled at the top of her lungs, and her voice rose to a pitch high enough to call every dog in the city.

"Here, take my hand," Laura said, and Ginger grabbed eagerly, allowing herself to be pulled onto her feet. Then they took hold of Mac's arms and set her upright as well.

"What's wrong with you?" Ginger said under her breath as she dusted off a disheveled Mac, whose glasses sat cock-eyed on her flushed face. As they walked back to their chairs, Mac kept protesting, "But I had to do it," which made Laura smile and whisper, "Nice tackle, girlfriend."

But Ginger didn't find anything nice about Mac's actions at all, despite her good intentions. She just hoped to God no one had used a camera phone. If one of the debs had taken a shot of the catfight, Mac would get reprimanded by the GSC at the very least, if not banished from the Rosebuds altogether. *What the hell was she thinking?* Ginger wanted to shake her, not thank her as Laura had.

"I can't believe this, I really can't." Honey folded her arms over her chest, glancing at Camie Lindell and then over at Mac. She shook her head, clearly distressed. "If Bootsie Bidwell could see y'all now, I wouldn't have to worry about teaching any of you the Dip. You'd all be out on your fannies by morning. Now, I hope you've gotten that out of your systems so you can start acting like the ladies your mamas would like to think they've raised, instead of a bunch of alley cats with your claws out."

Wedged between a red-faced Trisha and a smug-looking Jo Lynn on the settee, Camie pointed at Mac and whined, "She started it!"

Ginger clamped her hand over Mac's mouth to keep her from shouting back. She'd seen enough drama tonight to carry her through the rest of deb season.

"Oh, so Michelle's to blame, is that it?" Honey barked back, effectively shutting Camie up. "Well, I'd hardly call you innocent, sweet pea, not the way you were mouthing off. So unless you want me telling Miss Bootsie exactly what I saw and heard this evening, we'll just call it a draw. We'll chalk up what transpired to the Dip bein' a nerve-wracking thing to learn. Sometimes girls stumble. Trip-ups happen. Everybody with me on this?" She looked around the room, nodding her blond head when no one gave her any lip. "All right then, let's get on back to practice, shall we? And no more shenanigans!"

They picked up where they'd left off, with Cindy hopping out of her chair to try the Dip next. Laura stayed glued to her seat, and Mac managed to keep her mouth shut. All the while Ginger counted the minutes, thinking it was the longest hour of her life, even worse than when she'd gotten her wisdom teeth pulled.

* * *

"I couldn't help it," Mac said for the tenth time, toying with the piece of Whole Foods tomato basil pizza on the plate in front of her. "Camie *so* asked for it. What else was I supposed to do, just sit there doing nothing while she humiliated Laura?"

"And I, for one, am grateful that one of my BFFs stood up for me," Laura declared, her blue eyes flashing fire. "So what if the GSC hears about it? Mac was only defending me."

"Mac, you should know better! You've been telling Laura to sidestep the Bimbos for ages and then you go and pull a stunt like that." Exasperated, Ginger stared them down from across the round oak table in the Mackenzie's kitchen. "If we don't ignore them, they'll never stop. Don't you get it? They *want* to provoke you into doing something stupid. They *want* y'all to get in trouble."

When neither Mac nor Laura responded except to pick at their pizza, Ginger sighed, frustrated as all hell. She'd hoped that when the three of them had a chance to talk after all the other Rosebuds had left—and Honey had slunk off to her bedroom complaining of a migraine—they'd be calm enough to see how the Bimbos were playing them for fools. Instead, Mac and Laura were treating *her* like she'd done something wrong for wanting to stay on the sidelines.

"You just gave Jo Lynn Bidwell the perfect opportunity to rat you out to Bootsie." Ginger drilled in her point, wondering why they didn't understand. "Destroying people is what she does for fun. She's out to clobber you, Laura, and if it means taking down Mac, too, well"—she threw a hand in the air—"no skin off her surgically refined nose."

"But Honey even said she'd stick up for Mac," Laura reminded her. "Besides, Jo Lynn's toadies started it, right? Everyone was a witness to that."

"Something came over me," Mac grumbled. "I just snapped."

"Well, don't do it again!" Ginger slapped the table, causing all their plates to rattle. "Self-restraint, people," she barked at her friends, her normally soft voice rising. "You have to realize they're masters of manipulation. Think about it. First, Camie mouths off about the rumor, like she wanted to remind everyone in the room about the lie that Laura's pregnant. Who do you think it would benefit if Bootsie knew *that*?" She raised her eyebrows. "If the selection committee hasn't heard about the MySpace dirt already, getting the play-by-play on what happened tonight will only clue them in."

"Thanks for making me lose my appetite entirely," Laura replied, and pushed her plate aside.

"If you're trying to make me feel bad, it's not working." Mac glared at Ginger before tossing her wadded-up paper napkin onto the picked-over pizza on her plate. "I'm not sorry for what I did."

On hearing that, Laura got a satisfied smirk on her face, which ticked Ginger off all the more.

"I don't care if you're sorry or not, Mac. Just remember all that advice you've been dealing out about leaving the Bimbo Cartel alone, and take it." Ginger looked at Mac, then at Laura, then back at Mac again, like she was watching a Ping-Pong tournament. "Can't y'all see that I'm just trying to keep the Three Amigas in this together? Isn't that what you want too? Or am I the only one?"

Though Laura avoided looking at her, Mac set her elbows on the table, her face pinched with guilt. "Okay, okay, I'll promise to behave"—eyes downcast, she gave the bridge of her glasses a push—"if Laura promises to stay away from Dillon. My God, if Jo Lynn gets wind of Laura's plan to train with Big D, it's all over."

"Thanks, Mac," Laura snapped.

"Maybe Jo already knows," Ginger suggested, because it made sense. "Maybe that's what's got the Bimbos riled up tonight."

"But that can't be. . . . It's not possible," Laura sputtered. "The only person in the world who knows about Dillon besides y'all is"—she winced—"Avery."

"You told Avery?" Mac grabbed her dark curls, looking like she wanted to tear them out. "What are you, mental?"

Laura glanced down at her lap, her pale hair falling like curtains on either side of her face. "Sorry, y'all, but it just popped out the other day when I bumped into him at the club. I screwed up, okay?"

God, what else could go wrong, huh?

Ginger covered her face with her hands. This was beyond catastrophic. Not that she was surprised by Mac losing it and taking a crack at Camie Lindell. A huge part of Mac would probably feel relieved if she got dumped from the deb list. But Ginger knew Laura was a different story entirely. The girl had dreamed of becoming a Rosebud since they were kids playing dress-up in Tincy Bell's closet, with Laura striking poses in the three-way mirror with Tincy's tiara on her head. She of all people shouldn't be acting so recklessly and putting her deb status at stake. It made no sense.

What's the matter with you? Ginger wanted to scream. If either of her BFFs forced the GSC's hand, and Ginger had to go through the next eight months until the Ball alone, she would kick them both to the curb for ruining everything.

A flash of anger swept through Ginger's body, and she sat up straight, turning on Laura first. "You need to stop thinking with your heart and start using your brains unless you want to blow your coming out. And you"—she faced Mac next—"need to find a better way to release all that pent-up frustration than taking potshots at foulmouthed Bimbos."

"Hey, none of this is my fault," Mac replied stiffly, glaring at Laura. "She's the one who keeps starting the fires."

"Me?" Laura stared back, openmouthed. "Are you saying I asked for this, is that it? I've had to shut off my BlackBerry because of all the rude calls and e-mails I'm getting. It's like a feeding frenzy." Tears welled in her eyes as she pushed away from the table, her chair scraping against the floor as she stood. "That's it. I've heard enough Laura-bashing in the last twenty-four hours to last me a lifetime." She grabbed her red tote and started for the door, snapping over her shoulder, "I'm out of here."

Ginger made no move to stop her. It wouldn't hurt Laura to stew for a while and consider how she sabotaged herself by striking back at Jo Lynn Bidwell all the time. Sometimes it went beyond frustrating, watching her friend make the same mistakes over and over again. Not that Ginger hadn't made some bad choices, but she'd learned from them, right? Wasn't that the whole purpose of screwing up?

"Um, Ginger?" Mac stood, glancing at the doorway. "Should she be driving when she's so upset like that? No matter what, I don't want her putting the Merc in a ditch."

"Don't worry. She'll be back." Ginger counted to three before she heard Laura's returning footsteps.

"Jesus, Ging, are you coming or not?" Laura said, pouting like a petulant child, before she spun on a heel and disappeared again.

Mac plopped back down. "You drove, didn't you?"

"Uh-huh."

"Hey, would you smack her for me before you drop her off?"

Ginger retrieved her hemp bag from where she'd slung it over the back of her chair, looking Mac squarely in the eyes as she said, "Personally, I'd like to smack you both."

Ginger left Mac staring after her, openmouthed, and braced herself for the cold shoulder she'd doubtless receive the moment she got in the Prius with Laura.

All for one and one for all, huh? she thought with a sigh.

I'm extraordinarily patient
provided I get my own way in the end.
—Margaret Thatcher

The only way to get things done
is to do them yourself.
—Jo Lynn Bidwell

Thirteen

On the Thursday afternoon following a very interesting curtsy practice, Jo Lynn sat between Camie and Trisha on a stone bench in the courtyard at Pine Forest Prep with ten minutes left on their lunch break. The sky above them looked thick with gray clouds, and the air smelled ripe, like rain. The humidity made it feel warmer than it really was, and Jo had rolled up her sleeves as far as they'd go and had unbuttoned her shirt as much as she could without getting called into Dr. Percy's office for a wardrobe malfunction. She had her legs outstretched, her orange velvet Marc Jacobs ballet flats half off her feet, and her face tipped up toward where the sun should have been, as did Cam and Trisha, seated on either side of her.

"I can't believe she showed her face at school this morning," Camie said with a frown. Even though the September sun hid behind the blanket of clouds, her Roberto Cavalli shades were perched on her nose. "She's got to feel like a total outcast. Everyone's talking about her, and she's walking around like a zombie."

"Well, she was a zombie last night, for sure," Trisha

remarked, sliding her Gucci frames low so Jo could glimpse the malicious glint in her eyes. "I think she must've popped some of Mommy's little helpers. Too bad she didn't share them with that Mouse Mackenzie. That girl needed a sedative, for sure. I can't believe she went after you like that, Cam!"

"That loser bruised my elbow," Camie complained, shoving her sleeve up so she could show the purple mark on her arm. "I wish like hell we could blab to the GSC about her attacking me."

"Only, Mouse Mackenzie's obnoxious new mom threatened to squeal on us for trash-talking Laura." Trisha turned to Jo Lynn, who'd been quiet until then. "Can't you just let it slip to Bootsie?"

"Yeah, like, accidentally on purpose?" Camie added, and Trisha giggled.

"No," Jo told them coolly. "I can't."

Her two BFFS glanced at each other, but Jo Lynn didn't explain. Her mother had already warned her once about staying clean during deb season, and she fully intended to do just that, at least on the surface. What she did behind the scenes was a different story entirely.

"You're not letting the Randoms off the hook, are you?" Camie asked, pushing dark hair off her shoulders and fingering a diamond-studded gold hoop dangling from her ear. "I mean, you still want Laura Bell out of the Rosebuds, right?"

"Like, she's going to stay in much longer after all that stuff up on MySpace," Trisha added, pulling her strawberry-blond hair off her face and twisting it into a makeshift ponytail. "If we ever find out who started that one, we owe 'em a big ol' favor." She gave Jo Lynn a look, like, "It was you, wasn't it?"

But Jo didn't bite. She didn't say anything for a while. She just dug deep into her bright orange MJ hobo bag, looking for her lip gloss with the tiny mirror on the side so she could check her teeth for pieces of green from her salad.

"Yes, I still want Laura out of the Rosebuds," she said, ignoring Trish's comment about MySpace altogether. "More than you know." She glanced up at the stubborn gray sky as the wind played in her hair and tugged at the ivy climbing up the school's brick walls. "And I have a really good feeling it'll happen soon. We just have to be careful."

Her heartbeat raced, but she projected a calm she didn't quite feel. Deep inside, she wasn't as confident that Plan C to get Laura ousted was working fast enough, especially with Avery and Dillon complicating the matter.

"But we've got more work to do," she told them. "We're not done yet."

"What kind of work, Jo?" Camie asked as Trisha leaned in to listen. "You saw her last night. Laura's a train wreck. She can't last in the Rosebuds much longer. The GSC must have already heard the talk about the baby. You know they'll be all over her to prove she isn't preggers."

Just having the GSC on Laura's case wasn't enough for Jo anymore. She wanted to take Laura down *all* the way.

"I need to know just what she's up to," Jo Lynn told her friends. "Is she just after Avery, or is she trying to poach Dillon from me?" Even saying the words made Jo's mouth taste sour, like she needed to rinse and spit.

"So what's really going on with you and Big D?" Camie asked, then lowered her voice as a group of younger girls walked past. "I thought you planned to invite him to be your escort to the ball?"

"I still do," Jo replied with an impatient sniff. "But you know how the Glass Slipper Club likes its debs to wait until a few months before the ball to invite peer escorts, just in case."

Cam and Trisha nodded, heads bobbing like pigeons on a power line.

Every deb understood that the GSC didn't even like Rosebuds inviting boyfriends to be their escorts at the ball, because that could end up being, well, messy. *As if my relationship with Dillon isn't messy enough right now,* Jo mused.

She brushed at the tan and black plaid of her skirt, pushing it back down to her knees. She slid her feet back into her flats. "I'm not saying I think Dill would ever cheat on me. Still . . ." She weighed exactly how much to confide, finally forcing herself to just say it. "I didn't tell y'all this before, but I found Laura's number on Dillon's cell phone."

"No way!" Camie's plucked eyebrows shot up.

"Omigod," Trisha breathed.

"And that's not all," Jo went on, making herself forge ahead, because it was time to fess up, whether she wanted to or not. She needed her friends firmly on her side, or else they might not be so willing to stick out their necks for her. She wet her lips. "Dillon called Laura on Labor Day morning, sometime around when y'all saw her at the club."

"What?" both her friends said at once.

"I couldn't ask Dillon about it, or he'd know I'd been snooping in his phone." She stopped, not going into it further. She couldn't. It made her too crazy to think about it, particularly after she'd gotten a text from Dillon this morning, saying: I heard the rumor abt LB. I hope U didn't have anything 2 do with it. All of a sudden he cared what happened with Laura Bell? It was like her nightmare about the Ball coming true, and it positively made her sick!

Jo Lynn took a deep breath to settle down her racing pulse; then she told Camie and Trisha, "You asked what we needed to do next, so here's my idea." She paused for effect before letting it rip. "I think we should follow her, just for a few days. See where she goes, who she hooks up with. I want to catch her in the act, so there's no way she can squirm free this time. Then I'm going to make her sorry she ever messed with me, because she obviously hasn't learned her lesson."

"You want us to tail her? Like on cop shows?" Trisha repeated, gawking. She dangled her sunglasses from her fingers, and her big-lashed eyes kept blinking, like she didn't believe it.

"Yes, just like that," Jo said icily, and started rolling down her sleeves so just the cuffs were turned up.

"And just how're we supposed to do that?" Camie asked. "It's not like we can track her on your GPS."

"No, but she drives a cherry red Mercedes Roadster, and she's like six freaking feet tall, so she's not easy to miss," Jo Lynn snapped, her shoulders so tense it felt like her head was connected to her neck by taut rubber bands. "I figure one of us can follow her when she leaves school and then another one of us can take over, like, a couple hours later."

"Wow." Camie pulled her shades off and squinted at Jo Lynn. "You're totally serious, aren't you?"

"Totally," Jo assured them, surprised she was being second-guessed by her BFFs.

They always went along with all her ideas. It was just the way things worked.

"Tailing Laura Bell. Could we get in trouble for that?"

Trisha asked. "Like, for harassment or stalking or something?"

Jo Lynn looked hard at them both. *Could we get in trouble?* What was up with them? Whatever it was, it was pissing her off.

"Will you do it or not?" she asked, her drawl sounding clipped.

Either they were with her or they were against her, and they knew it. That was the unwritten code. If they abandoned her, she'd pick up two new BFFs who'd follow her blindly.

Camie and Trisha glanced at each other, and one of them mewled, "Jo, I'm just not sure it's—"

The bell rang, and Jo Lynn started at the sound.

The few other girls who'd braved the clouds and cloying air in the courtyard began gathering up their books and purses, tossing their detritus from lunch, and heading back toward the building. Their chatter filled Jo Lynn's ears, fighting for attention with the noisy thoughts in her head. She felt the dull beginnings of a headache.

Jo Lynn rose from the bench, slinging her purse over her shoulder, textbooks clutched to her chest. She raised her chin, refusing to show pain. How many pageants had she entered where it was her against the world? (Well, more like her and Bootsie against the world.) Like, *all* of them. If she had to finish taking Laura down by herself, then she would.

"Forget it," she said to no one in particular, and started to walk. She had cut across the grass toward the stone path that crisscrossed the courtyard when Camie and Trisha caught up with her.

"Hey, Jo-L, wait up!" Trisha said, sounding a little breathless.

"Just tell us one thing, okay?" Camie asked, walking briskly to keep up with Jo's long-legged stride. "Who gets to follow the Swamp Donkey first? Me or Trish?"

* * *

Once classes had ended for the day, Jo Lynn gave Camie last-minute instructions then watched her take off in her blue Lexus coupe, following Laura Bell's red convertible out of the senior lot and away from campus. If Laura didn't lead her anywhere interesting in the next hour, Cam was off the hook and it was Trisha's turn to spy on the Cupcake for a while. On the other hand, if Laura did make a newsworthy pit stop, Camie was to call Jo right away.

Jo Lynn climbed into her Audi moments after Cam's Lexus disappeared down Taylorcrest. She started the car and pulled out her iPhone, calling Dillon to warn him she'd be dropping by on her way home. When she got his voice mail—something that happened *way* too often these days— she said, "To hell with it," and didn't even leave him a message. Instead, she put her Audi in gear and headed for chez Masters.

The Caldwell football coach always cut practice short on the Thursdays before Friday night games, claiming he wanted his boys fresh, not burned out. Jo was hoping to catch Dill alone so she could get something straight between them, namely that she had nothing to do with the gossip about Laura on the Web . . . even if she had to cross her fingers behind her back while she convinced him.

She flew down Taylorcrest and took a right on Bunker Hill, a canopy of thick-leaved branches blotting out most of the dreary-looking sky as she drove. Passing wooden privacy fences and pillared brick mansions set away from the street by wide lawns with curving drives, Jo reached Dillon's cul-de-sac in about five minutes flat. His Mustang wasn't anywhere in sight, but that didn't mean it wasn't safe and sound inside the six-car garage.

Parking the Audi in front, she strode up the sandstone path between the rows of royal palms, the breeze rattling the fronds overhead. She'd barely reached the carved teak doors and pressed the doorbell when she heard a car roll into the drive blasting its horn, and then Big Ray shouting out the opened window. "Well, hell, Jo Lynn, if I'd've known you were dropping by, I would've rolled out the red carpet!"

"Hey, Big Ray!" she called back, waving at him.

"You sure look mighty pretty in your school uniform," he said as he climbed from his pimped-out black Escalade with its tinted windows and flashy rims. "Guess you're here to see my boy."

"Is he home?" she asked. "No one answered the bell."

"Well, let me think." He hitched up belted pants that couldn't seem to get a grip on his hips below the oversized beer belly. He had a bona fide Stetson covering his patchy gray hair, though he swept off the hat as he approached, wiping sweat from his brow with his sleeve. "It's Thursday afternoon, which means Cissy's playing bridge at the Junior League, Juanita's down at Canino's getting fresh produce, and Dillon's probably working out at the club."

"Did he go with his teammates?" Jo asked, afraid that if Avery and Dillon got to talking, Avery might let it slip that

Jo had stopped by on Tuesday night to grill him about whether or not he'd slept with Laura recently. Then he could easily connect the dots linking her to the rumor on MySpace, and she'd be up shit creek without a paddle . . . or a life preserver.

"So far as I know, he goes on his own," Big Ray said as he fumbled with the house key in one hand, his hat in the other. "But even if he's with his friends, he won't be long. So don't worry your sweet little head. He should be here in an hour. You're welcome to come on in and have a Coke if you want to wait."

Jo thought about leaving but ended up nodding. "I'll wait."

"All right, pretty lady." Big Ray gave her a wink. "After you," he said, gesturing with his hat as he unlocked the door and pushed it wide.

A blast of AC set off goose bumps on Jo's arms as she walked into the huge marble foyer.

Big Ray dropped his hat and keys on a glass-topped table beneath a dripping chandelier. "Go on and get settled in the TV room, why don't you," he suggested, "and I'll bring you that Coke."

"Sure thing," Jo said, and wandered through rooms with high-arched doorways with elaborate columns, painted frescoes, carved sculptures perched on marble pedestals, and oversized furniture and fixtures everywhere she looked. Big Ray and Cissy Masters didn't exactly know the meaning of the word "subtle."

Her flats tip-tapping on the marble tiles underfoot, she made her way through a rear hallway lined with photographs of Big Ray in his glory days for the Houston Oilers, and then of Dillon on the football field, throwing touchdown after touchdown, accepting the trophy for Caldwell's MVP, setting the school's passing record, posing with Big Ray at his car dealership, sitting in the shiny black Mustang Big Ray had given him when he'd won state, and on and on until her eyes blurred.

No wonder Big Ray always seemed so worried about Dillon blowing his image. It was obviously one they'd both worked hard to create.

She'd barely reached the terra-cotta-walled TV room and dropped her bag on one of the massive leather sofas when Big Ray appeared with her Coke in his hand.

"I left it in the bottle," he said, " 'cause that's the way Dillon likes to drink it."

"Thanks." She smiled as she took it from him.

He glanced at his diamond-studded Rolex Presidential and winced. "Wish I could keep you company until my boy shows up, but I've got some business to take care of. I've gotta talk to a guy in Tokyo who likes to get cracking at five a.m. . . . his time, not mine." Big Ray laughed and rubbed his sagging jawline. "So I'll be shut up in my office for a while. You can holler if you need me."

Jo Lynn patted his arm. "I'll be fine." She gestured at the giant screen hanging between two stag heads mounted on the wall. "I'll just watch *Oprah* until Dill shows up."

"You do that, sweetheart," he said with a wink; then he was gone.

Jo took a sip of the Coke before setting it down and clicking on the television. She flipped around for thirty seconds before she switched if off again and began pacing the room. She peered out the windows at the magnificent gardens the

Masterses had landscaped around their Mediterranean-inspired patio and pool.

When she checked the clock, not even five minutes had passed. God, she was no good at sitting around, twiddling her thumbs. If only she could put the time to better use, she thought, and hesitated, glancing up at the raised ceiling and realizing that Dillon's room was almost directly overhead, while his dad's office was all the way at the end of the wing. If she just popped upstairs for a bit, no one would be the wiser, would they?

So that was just what Jo did. She left her Coke behind but slipped off her shoes and picked up her bag on her way out. Barefoot, she padded quietly across the tiled floors, returning to the foyer and the curving stairwell with its carved wrought-iron banister. Her shoes in one hand and her purse in the other, she wound her way up and up until she reached the second floor. Dillon's room was first on the right, and she quickly opened the closed door and let herself inside.

Jo went over to the king-sized bed and sat down, dropping her bag and shoes beside her. Impulsively, she leaned back, reclining on the plush brown duvet, stretching her arms overhead and drowning in the scent of Dillon that flooded every breath she took. If she closed her eyes, it was almost like he was there, still asleep with his head on the next pillow, close enough to touch.

They'd had sex here before, when his parents were away, and Jo smiled, a warm sensation spilling through her as she remembered their early days together. When they'd first started dating two years ago, Dillon couldn't get enough of her. He'd called and texted endlessly, had sent her flowers and driven over in the dead of night, enticing her outside to sit beside him in the grass, where they'd stare up at the stars until they couldn't remain even inches apart for another minute. Once, in the wee hours of the morning, he'd climbed onto her balcony and eased through the sliding glass door she'd left unlocked, slipping into bed beside her. She'd awakened to the feel of his mouth on her neck and his hands moving slowly down her body, his fingers sliding gently between her thighs . . .

Jo blushed at the memory, feeling warm in places that had been sadly dormant for a while, thinking that Dillon had been just what she'd needed after the way things had ended with Avery. She couldn't bear it if Dill pulled away from her too.

She slowly sat up, eyes wide as she looked around her, spotting a few framed pictures of them on shelves crowded with trophies and ribbons and plaques. His bedside tables were stacked with men's health magazines, Zone bars, and empty GU packs.

Jo got up and walked straight over to the desk where Dillon's laptop sat, screen open, Sleep button winking at her, daring her to take a seat and peek at Dillon's e-mails, to see if he was keeping any secrets from her. *What's the harm in that?* she decided, and ran her finger over the mouse pad. The computer instantly awakened, flipping to a blue screen that asked for his password.

Dammit.

Jo Lynn looked at the alarm clock on Dillon's nightstand, wondering how much time she had before Dillon got home or Big Ray noticed she was missing from the TV room. She gave herself ten more minutes—fifteen, tops—and then she had to be out of here. OMFG, if Dillon had any idea what she was doing . . .

She pushed the thought from her head and instead pursed her lips and placed her fingers on the keyboard, playing a guessing game, thinking of all the things she knew about Dill, every clue he'd given her as to who he was, and using that, knowing it would just take one lucky turn and she'd be in . . . unless someone caught her first.

When you have no problems,
you're dead.
—Zelda Werner

Problems are like bugs.
The sooner you squash them,
the better you feel.
—Laura Bell

Fourteen

Getting through classes on Thursday was no picnic for Laura. The Pine Forest Prep motto might be *"Via, Veritas, Vita"* "The Way, the Truth, the Life," but this was one instance when the corrupted version, namely "The Lays, the Booze, the Lies," seemed to fit a lot better. Especially the lies. The worst part of it was Laura couldn't prove who'd started the rumor that she was pregnant even though she was sure it was Jo Lynn Bidwell or one of her Bimbos.

She did her best to look cool on the outside, like the nasty buzz on the MySpace page didn't matter and the ugly whispers (*"Who knew she was such a slut?"* . . . *"So who's the baby daddy?"*) weren't getting to her. She couldn't let the Bimbo Cartel think they'd knocked her flat on her ass; she couldn't stand to see them gloat. Though now she understood what it must feel like to be on the receiving end of Simon Cowell's public whippings on *American Idol*, and it sucked.

Except for denying it when directly confronted—*"God, no, I'm not!"*—she forced herself to turn the other cheek, all the while praying the GSC would ignore any whiff of the scandal that wafted in their direction. If Bootsie Bidwell and Company believed it, even for a second, Laura knew she was in for a truly rough ride. And she'd fought way too hard to get onto the Rosebud list to let her dream slip away under such an ugly cloud.

If Laura played Ginger the Eternal Optimist and tried to see anything good at all in this, she figured at least Tincy was getting something she wanted (without even knowing why, since Laura hadn't filled her in yet). Laura was so upset she could barely eat, let alone sleep. If this rumor wasn't cleared up soon, she'd drop a size within a week. While that might make Tincy ecstatic, Laura couldn't imagine a worse way to shrink than the Totally Miserable Diet.

Her appetite wasn't the only thing affected either. Concentrating in class had proved nearly impossible, particularly after Laura had been called into the headmistress's office and Dr. Percy had flapped her jowls for ten minutes flat, grilling her about the rumor on the PFP grapevine that she was "in the family way." When Laura had denied it, she'd been assured that bullying of any kind wasn't tolerated at Pine Forest Prep. Like the Walrus could do a thing about it. Like that zero-tolerance policy made a bit of difference to the parents of the Bimbo Cartel, who wrote the school enormous checks so their daughters could get away with anything, Laura mused. Though her own daddy could buy her way off the hook if he had to, he wouldn't need to, because Laura would never, ever torment someone the way Jo Lynn was tormenting her.

"I think all that hair spray from her pageant days must've made her truly mental," Mac had remarked during a stilted and uncomfortable lunch during which each of the Three

Amigas seemed inordinately quiet, afraid to say something wrong after their argument following curtsy practice. It was one of the first times Laura had been relieved to see the lunch hour end.

Relief flooded her veins when the final bell rang at three o'clock. She bypassed her locker altogether and sprinted out of the ivy-covered buildings, racing to her car only to find someone had written BABY ON BOARD in hot-pink lipstick across the windshield.

Laura shot fluid on the glass and turned the wipers on hyper-speed to blot out the words, smearing arcs of pink that lingered all the way home. She bit her lip, trying not to cry, worrying about what awaited her when she walked through the front door. What if Tincy had heard from Bootsie already? Or what if Bootsie's white Cadillac was parked in the driveway right now, and both Tincy *and* Bootsie were sitting in the living room, listening to the grandfather clock tick as they waited for Laura's arrival so they could double-team her with bad news?

Laura had so convinced herself of that fateful scenario that she was surprised when she turned onto her street and saw Avery's orange 'Vette in the circular driveway.

Oh, shiz, she thought, tempted at first to turn the car around and haul ass in the other direction. But she knew she'd have to face him sooner or later, whether she liked it or not. So she brushed at her damp cheeks, tucked her hair behind her ears, and tried hard to pull herself together.

Even before she'd parked her Roadster, the driver's-side door of the Corvette opened and Avery ambled out. He had on a worn red T-shirt with CALDWELL MUSTANGS emblazoned across the chest, and gray sweats with the number 88 in red on his left thigh. He stood by his car, staring her way, like he could see right through the smudgy windshield, and Laura knew she had no choice.

She pulled her Mercedes in slowly, stopping right behind the Corvette with its GR8HANZ plates. She'd had the AC running on high in the car, but the pits of her shirt were damp when she climbed out and shut the door. She dragged her feet, scuffing the soles of her Mary Jane wedges on the driveway as she approached him. If he'd tried to catch her at a worse time, it wouldn't have been possible. Laura had never felt so rumpled and wrinkled and dispirited as she did at that moment.

She stopped three feet shy of Avery and sighed. "Did my mom make you wait out here, or were you just afraid to be alone with her?"

He barely opened his mouth when Tincy flung open the front door, like she'd been watching for Laura from the window.

"There you are!" she said, motioning Laura inside while giving Avery the evil eye. "Get on inside this instant, missy."

Laura glumly told Avery, "I'll be out in a sec."

He shrugged, as if to say, "I'm not going anywhere."

Tincy grabbed her arm, practically dragging her into the foyer. She started in on Laura as soon as the door had been shut behind them. "What on God's green earth is going on with you? What haven't you been telling me? First, I get a call from Dr. Percy at Pine Forest Prep, and then Bootsie Bidwell requests a private meeting with us in an hour. Would you care to explain, because I'm tired of everyone else dancing around the truth?"

Despite Tincy being half a foot shorter, Laura felt totally

cowed by the tone of her mother's voice and the grave look on her face. "It's . . . it's a rumor, nothing more," Laura stammered, hardly able to meet Tincy's eyes. "Someone wrote something nasty online and now everyone's gossiping about it . . . about me."

"Something nasty?" Tincy's pencil-thin brows arched, though her Botoxed forehead didn't even wrinkle. A thin hand suddenly went to her throat. "Please, don't tell me it's a sex tape."

"It's not a sex tape," Laura said, her eyes filling up with tears again. She swiped at them, explaining in a shaky voice, "Someone's spread the lie that I'm having a baby."

"What?" Tincy teetered on her Blahniks and clutched at the marble edge of the center hall table to steady herself. "A baby?" she repeated, blinking.

Laura swallowed hard and nodded. "But it's not true. I'm not. I swear to God."

But Tincy didn't seem to hear her. "No wonder Bootsie mentioned wanting proof that you hadn't violated any Rosebud rules," she rambled on. "I had no idea what she meant at the time, and she wouldn't get into it, even though I begged her to tell me what she knew. She wanted me to talk to you."

"Well, now you have," Laura said quietly, "and I don't know what kind of proof she expects, unless she wants me to take a pregnancy test."

Tincy stiffened and her gaze fell to Laura's belly. "Are you certain you want to do that?"

What the hell was she implying?

"You think I'm really pregnant?" Laura asked her. "You think I'm lying and trying to hide something like that?"

"I don't know, Laura. Are you?"

Dear God! She wasn't even guilty of anything, and yet *she* had to prove her innocence! It wasn't fair!

She turned away from her mother and caught her reflection in the Venetian glass mirror. So she wasn't thin by any means, and her belly wasn't flat. *Is that it?* She was being punished for her size? Like, if she'd been a twig, no one would've bought the lie for an instant, but since she was curvy to begin with, somehow the lie made sense?

She sniffled back her tears, feeling angrier by the minute. She turned around to face Tincy, this time meeting her eyes. "I guess I have to prove it to you, too, huh? If my own mother won't even believe me, it's no wonder the GSC wants me to pee on a stick. Now if you'll excuse me, I have to talk to Avery." She went over to the door and put her hand on the knob.

Before she could go, Tincy said to her back, "That boy . . . he isn't responsible for this?"

Laura nearly laughed. "No, that boy isn't responsible for anything," she said, glancing at Tincy over her shoulder. "I know precisely who did this to me, Mother, and she's got everyone talking, just like she wanted. But I won't let this ruin my being a Rosebud. I won't."

"Tell me who did this to you, baby. I won't let them get away with it."

Laura told her, "Don't worry, Mother, she won't." Then she opened the door and stepped outside.

Avery still leaned against the hood of his 'Vette, looking just as she left him.

Slowly, she walked over, hoping he didn't notice her red eyes and blotchy cheeks.

"Shouldn't you be at practice?" Laura asked, wishing she didn't sound so out of sorts, but her pulse still raced after her argument with Tincy.

"We had a light practice this afternoon already. Coach doesn't like to work us out hard the day before a Friday night game, though a few of the guys headed over to the cave to pump iron." He folded his arms and leaned against his bumper. "You okay to talk for a minute?"

She glanced toward the front door, knowing that Tincy was probably standing behind it with her ear to the wood. "Yeah, I'm fine," she said. "But let's go around the corner, okay?"

He followed her away from the driveway and toward a secluded spot in the side yard where a carved stone bench sat beneath the umbrella of a weeping willow. Pink Queen Elizabeth roses climbed a trellis alongside the privacy fence, and peppermint crape myrtle lent a sweetness to the air as Laura tucked her skirt beneath her and settled down.

Avery seemed too restless to sit. He stood beneath the willow's dripping branches, the light green leaves nearly touching the top of his head. "I've been trying to reach you all day," he said, every muscle in his body taut as he squatted in front of her, forearms balanced on his thighs. "Is your cell turned off or something?"

She looked him in the eye. "Can you blame me?"

He picked up a berry that was rotting on the ground, tossing it at the fence. "No, I can't blame you a bit." Then he sighed, and his voice softened as he asked her, "It's not true, is it?"

Laura stared at him, her heart sinking into a pit.

Oh, hell, he couldn't really believe it, could he?

It took everything in her not to get up and run away. Despite the fact that she'd done nothing wrong, she felt deeply embarrassed and ashamed.

"What do *you* think, Avery?" The question emerged as a croak, and a warm flush spread through her, inflaming her face. She hated the fact that he'd even had to ask. "You're the only one I've been with like that"—*since the day I met you, God!*—"and we were careful, weren't we?"

He came out of the squat and sat on the bench beside her. "Yeah, we were," he replied, and ran a hand through sandy-brown hair. His handsome face looked so tight, like he was having as much trouble breathing as she.

"I'm still the same old me," she told him, and hugged her belly without even realizing what she was doing. "Nothing's changed."

"So you're *sure*?" he pressed, his drawl anything but slow and lazy. He might slap on his pads and helmet and rush onto Tully field with no fear in his heart. But he was scared now. She could see it in his eyes.

"Bootsie Bidwell called my mother," she told him, all the while wishing she could curl up in a ball and hide. "She wants me to take a pregnancy test to prove it's a lie. Sounds like you'd appreciate that, too. So how about you, me, Tincy, and Bootsie Bidwell hop in my car and take a drive down to Walgreens? I could pee on a stick in the public bathroom while y'all wait outside. How'd that be, Avery? Sure enough for you?"

Her voice trembled as she finished, and she choked back a sob. All she wanted was for him to reach across the mere six inches that separated them, take her in his arms, and say, "It'll be all right, Laura, you'll see. Just hang in there."

Instead, he sat stiffly, his hands on his knees, watching her, and his doubt pricked at her like a million splinters beneath her skin.

Laura's chin began to tremble, and he finally took her hand, smothering it in his. "I'm sorry," he said, and his calloused fingers laced between hers, holding tight. "Whatever you need, I'm here for you."

She eyed him skeptically. "Really?"

"Yes."

Oh, man, how she'd yearned to hear that from him so many times! Only something about it felt wrong, like he was saying it now not because he loved her and wanted to be with her, but because of his guilt.

"I'm on your side, Laura, I am." He let go of her hand, and he gestured helplessly. "I should've come sooner, but everyone was talking and you weren't answering your cell, and I didn't know what to think." He caught his hands behind his head and glanced up at the roof of green above them, the drooping branches rustling in the breeze. "I hope I didn't cause this. . . . I hope my words weren't twisted."

Okay, now he was freaking her out. "Cause this?" she repeated, rubbing at the goose bumps that had risen on her arms. "How do you mean?"

"The other night, after your debutante meeting, Jo Lynn dropped by the house," he said. "I was babysitting, so we just talked for a minute outside in her car. She asked a lot of questions."

"About us?"

"Yeah."

Laura stared at him, feeling like she couldn't breathe. "And you didn't say a word to me?"

"Why would I?" He shrugged dismissively. "She's always in my business, Laura. It's just how she is. I guess I'm used to it. I didn't even wonder about her questions, until—well, until that MySpace page appeared and everyone started talking."

Laura shook her head, thinking surely he didn't, that he couldn't *possibly* have confided something so private to Jo Lynn? "Please, don't say that you spilled about the afternoon you picked me up from the airport? What we did—"

In my bed, she nearly said, but it wouldn't come out. Snippets of those hours flashed through her head: the gentleness of Avery's fingers as they'd traced her lips before he'd kissed her, how he'd teased her nipples with his touch and his tongue until it had nearly driven her crazy, how beautiful he'd said she looked when she undressed in front of him, leaving on only the full-length white deb gloves.

Laura trembled, she felt so betrayed.

"There's no way I'd tell her something like that," he said, reaching out for her again, catching her chin in the palm of his hand, forcing her to look him in the eye. "But it didn't matter. I think she figured it out. Oh, hell"—he winced painfully—"and she might be the one sending you the chocolates, too."

Oh my God!

Laura felt like she'd been sucker punched, even though a part of her had suspected she was being conned. What a fool she'd been, while Jo Lynn had probably been dying of laughter all along.

"Just be careful, okay?" Avery warned as if she needed to hear it.

She tasted bile in her throat, feeling sick to her stomach,

260

suddenly comprehending the depths to which Jo Lynn Bidwell was willing to sink to get back at her, to drag her down so far she could never recover. Jo didn't just want her out of the Rosebuds, did she? She wanted to smash her underfoot like a bug.

"Laura?"

She raised her eyes to him. "She won't leave us alone, will she?"

"She's got . . . issues," he said.

"*Issues?* Now, that's the understatement of the year. The bitch is crazy!" Laura laughed bitterly, then moaned as she covered her face with her hands, wondering just what she'd gotten herself into and how she could possibly pull herself out. "God, this sucks."

Avery drew her toward him, and she leaned against his chest. He tangled his fingers in her hair and pressed her cheek against his shoulder, holding her there. He whispered, "Don't let this beat you down, promise me? Sticks and stones and all that. It'll go away soon enough. Gossip always does."

Did he really believe that? Or was that just what he wanted *her* to believe?

Laura clung to the back of his shirt with her nails, tugging on him. "She played you, you realize that, don't you, Avery? Jo Lynn wanted to start a fire, and you're the one who gave her the gasoline."

He stopped stroking her hair. "You honestly think Jo spread that rumor just to hurt you?"

"Hell yes, that's what I think! Don't you? You know she's got it in for me, Av. She's hated me ever since the day you asked me out."

"I can see her doing a hundred other things to get at you, Laura, but not this." He turned his head and gazed off somewhere over her shoulder. "She just wouldn't. It's too far, even for her."

"Please, don't," Laura told him, completely chilled by his words. "Don't you dare apologize again or defend her. If you can't see what she's up to, then you're completely blind. You say you're on my side, but why does it feel like you always take hers?"

He didn't answer, just blew his cheeks out and said nothing.

"I think we're done here." Though it took every ounce of strength she had, she drew away from him and rose, smoothing her plaid skirt. He had come to her, and that was something. But if she'd hoped for more than that, she didn't get it. She brushed a tear from her cheek, angry at herself for expecting so much from him. "I'm not pregnant, okay? So now you know. If that's the only reason you came, well, you can leave."

For a while, he just sat there, looking up at her dumbly, like he was too confused to move. Finally, he nodded. "If that's how you want it to go down. But you've gotta know that if I could make this go away, I would."

"Well, you can't fix this," Laura said, or maybe it was more like "you won't fix this." That was the whole problem between them, why it never seemed to work out when it should. Avery couldn't or wouldn't see the bad in Jo Lynn Bidwell, even if the bitch were to walk around with slithering snakes on her head in lieu of hair.

But there is someone else who could help, she thought, realizing then that the only guy who could get Jo Lynn off her back wasn't the man standing before her now.

"All right, I'll go, if that's how you feel."

Avery came off the bench and softly moved tear-damp hair from her face, sweeping it behind her ears. Cupping her face, he pressed his mouth against her lips, holding her there until it seemed to Laura that he might never leave her. *Stay, stay, stay,* every one of her heartbeats seemed to cry, until he released her. Then, wordlessly, he walked away, brushing a willow branch aside as he crossed the stepping-stone path to the front drive.

Laura followed behind him, stopping to watch as he opened the door to his Corvette and slid into the driver's seat. With a thwack, the door closed, and he gunned the engine. A second later, he drove off, motor roaring as the 'Vette raced up the street until he was gone.

Laura didn't even wait a full minute before she hurried over to her own car and started it up, thinking of something Avery had said, about the team having a short workout today but some of the guys had gone to the cave to press iron.

Instead of pulling her Roadster around to the garage, she put the Merc in reverse. She knew where she had to go and who she had to talk to: the only person who had any control at all over Jo Lynn Bidwell.

Glancing in the rearview mirror, Laura stared at her pained blue eyes, telling herself, *I am who I am, and I will push back when I'm shoved.*

That settled, she put the car in drive and headed straight to the Villages Country Club, just minutes away. Once there, she slowly wound her way through the parking lot, looking this way and that. It didn't take long before she spotted the black Mustang convertible. She couldn't see much beyond the tinted windows, only the vague shadow of someone's head, or maybe a headrest. But at least she knew Dillon was on the grounds.

Perfect, Laura thought. She'd make this quick and easy.

She parked her Roadster between a Cadillac GTS and a Hummer ironically painted with racing stripes. Without further thought, she got out, slammed the door, and marched over to where the Mustang sat, backed into a spot overhung by an oak tree. Ignoring the anxiety that had her pulse skidding double time, she walked right up to the driver's side and rapped on the window.

With a quiet whir, the glass came sliding down, revealing Dillon Masters's angular face, slick with sweat, and, beyond him, a guy in the passenger's seat. Laura recognized him as the dude who'd been working out with Dillon on Labor Day morning.

"Um, hi, can I talk to you?" she asked, slightly blindsided at not finding Dillon alone.

Dillon hardly looked happy to see her. "Look, we're just on our way out, so if you wanted me to train you—"

"No, it's not about that." She bent over, leaning into the window to look at him eye to eye. She glanced at his friend, who turned his head, ignoring her completely. "What I want," she said quietly, "is for you to call off your bitch of a girlfriend. Tell her to stop harassing me . . . make her retract that lie on MySpace or else you'll be sorry."

"*I'll* be sorry?" Dillon tapped a hand on the steering wheel, and Laura saw his jaw muscle twitch. "You think Jo spread that rumor?" He sighed and shook his head. "She knows I'd be pissed if she had anything to do with that."

"Women," she heard Dillon's workout pal remark with a laugh, though Dillon acted like he hadn't heard.

Laura's spine stiffened. "This isn't a joke," Laura told him, turning shrill, on the verge of totally freaking out. "Get Jo Lynn to back off, or there'll be no private hunting trip with the good ol' boys from UT for you. In fact, I'll have my daddy tell his buddies in the athletic department that you'd make a lousy recruit for the Longhorns and to pass on signing you if they know what's good for them!"

"Whoa, wait a minute. C'mon now," Dillon said, reaching to open his door, and Laura backed up as he got out of the car. He shut the door and stepped toward her, catching her by the wrist and grabbing hold of her hand. "Calm down, all right?" he begged softly before he let her go. He swiped fingers through blond hair slick with sweat. "I'm tired, I've got our first game of the season tomorrow night, and all I want is to get home and take a shower. So let's talk fast, okay?"

Make it fast so he can go home and shower? Well, that sure beats having to go over to Bootsie Bidwell's house in, like thirty minutes to take a pregnancy test, doesn't it? Laura thought, but bit her tongue.

"Just get her to stop," she begged, holding down the fluttering hem of her shirt as the wind began to pick up. Leaves from the oak tree above Dillon's car spiraled down and skittered across her Mary Janes. "Tell Jo Lynn to pull the MySpace page or our deal is *off.* That's all there is to it."

He rubbed his forehead. "You know how Jo is. I can't promise anything. I'm not even sure she's behind it."

But Laura was as sure as she'd ever been about anything in her life.

"That's your problem, not mine," she told him as rain pattered on the asphalt around them. Without another word, she left Dillon standing in the drizzle and ran back to her car.

She flung herself into the driver's seat. The drum of raindrops pelted the car, splattering across the windshield, cleansing away the traces of pink lipstick that remained. As she put the Roadster in reverse and started to back out, a horn blared, and she hit the brakes. Her heart beating a hundred miles a minute, she caught a blur of blue as a sedan flew past.

I don't have a love life.
I have a like life.
—Lorrie Moore

It's hard to kiss and tell
when you haven't really kissed that much.
—Mac Mackenize

Fifteen

Why does doing the right thing—or, at least, what I think is the right thing—always seem to blow up in my face? Why are there so many shades of gray in between black and white? If life is going to come with so many iffy rules, there should be a guidebook you get the day you're born, like the GSC's debutante handbook. Let me know flat out what every action's going to cost me. Then I'll understand what's expected of me, and I won't risk embarrassing myself any more or ticking off my friends.

Mac finished furiously scribbling in her notebook before hooking her pen over the page and closing it up. If her mom had been around, she would've been here to open the door when Mac pulled into the drive after a horrible Thursday at school, asking, "How'd your day go?" and always listening to whatever Mac told her.

Instead, Mac had come home to an empty house. Honey had left a note about getting a massage to rub out the tension caused by last night's debacle at her "Dip-ity Do" class, and Daniel Mackenzie wouldn't be home from work for hours.

Mac had changed out of her school clothes, grabbed an apple from the fridge, and holed up in her room. She reached for the shoe box with her mom's letters just as the rain started coming down, pattering on the windows and making Mac feel lonelier than ever. She pulled out the envelope with the last note her mom had written, reading it once all the way through, though it was the final 'graph that stuck in her head:

> *Live your life, darling girl. Don't be afraid to take chances. Sometimes the best surprises come from standing on your tiptoes and reaching for the stars. I don't want you to miss out on anything because you were scared to try.*

For some reason, Mac didn't think Jeanie Mackenzie had been talking about the Rosebud Ball, not this time. Don't be afraid . . . reach for the stars . . . don't miss out. The phrases struck a chord deep within her, and she realized it was time to take a stand with Alex. She had to go for it or she'd never answer the questions she'd been asking herself, namely, what were they to each other now? Did Mac have real feelings for Alex beyond being his oldest friend? Or was she afraid of losing him to Cindy Chow when he wasn't really hers to lose in the first place?

"Time to face the music, Mackenzie," she told herself, and got up from the bed. She picked up her book bag, retrieved her wallet from inside it, and slipped out the Star Trek coin Alex had given her, which she'd folded in the letter from her mom. After she'd retrieved her cell, she put everything else back. Then she rubbed the coin for luck, stuck it in her back pocket, and used her cell to text Alex a message.

Can U meet me @ the tree house?

Within seconds, his answer: When?

5 min, she wrote him.

Do U know it's raining?

R U scared of getting wet???

Hell no!!! C U Soon

Before Mac left the house, she brushed her hair until she'd gotten all the tangles out. Then she popped an Altoid and used her pink lip gloss from Origins, which tasted like peppermint.

She raced down the stairs, across the foyer, and into the kitchen, stopping only to grab an umbrella before throwing open the rear French doors. Her tennis shoes slapped through damp puddles on the stone patio as she ran across it. Falling rain dappled the pale blue of the pool as she dashed past it, the patter on the water and on branches seeming the only noise around. Mac breathed in the scent of wet grass as she headed toward the hedge border between her house and the Bishops'.

She paused to close the umbrella before using the old path she and Alex had created from slipping between the shrubs so many times through the years. Droplets splashed on her skin as she pushed back tiny branches, and she felt her hair starting to frizz as the drizzle came down on her head.

So much for keeping dry with the umbrella! she thought.

As she walked farther into the Bishops' yard, she had to sidestep Elliott's toys—rubber balls, plastic horseshoes, and a hula hoop—all left out and now rain slick. The closer she got to the old tree house, the more her heart thundered in her chest, and she swallowed hard, willing herself not to be nervous.

It's just Alex, she chastised herself when she reached the midpoint of the yard. She stared up at the small wooden structure built into the crotch of an old oak, nearly twelve feet off the ground. Half the size of her walk-in closet, the house had seemed big once, when she and Alex were kids and had played pirates up there, pretending it was a captured warship filled with ill-gotten treasure. They'd fashioned swords out of sticks and made eye patches out of black construction paper and string.

Why is it so easy to be ten and so much harder to be seventeen?

Maybe part of Mac wanted to recapture that sense of connection with Alex again. It had seemed so simple once.

"Hey, you're getting wet down there," she heard a voice from above, and she glanced up to see Alex sticking his head out the window of the tree house. "It's dry as toast in here. Come on up!"

"Can I take the elevator?" she joked as she approached the wooden ladder permanently attached to the tree house deck. Leaving her umbrella at the base of the tree, she started up, her fingers tightly gripping the damp rungs as she carefully ascended. By the time her head surfaced above the platform, she was out of breath. Sweat dampened her armpits, and she felt a splinter sticking in the palm of her right hand.

"Welcome aboard, matey," Alex said as he reached for her, helping to pull her the rest of the way up.

"Oh, man, this seemed so much easier when we were kids," Mac said, ducking beneath the doorway and into the boxy space. It was dark with the canvas flap lowered over the window and only gloomy light seeping through the cracks between the boards.

The roof was so low Alex had to hunch over to move around.

"Have you been renting out to squirrels?" she asked, and wrinkled her nose at the musty smell.

"Hey, you're the one who wanted to meet here. Besides, it's not that bad." Alex grinned, his pale eyes bright behind his wire rims as he waved her over to the two folding chairs that he'd apparently brushed off. "Take a load off, Cap'n Mac, and tell me what's on your mind."

He settled down with his long legs stretched out in front of him, and she noticed he still had on his tan pants and white shirt, the uniform at Caldwell. There were smudges of dirt at the knees, from crawling around in the tree house, no doubt.

"What's on my mind," Mac repeated, and sank into the chair just a foot away from him. She took her glasses off and rubbed them on the hem of her green Lacoste shirt, wiping off the condensation before she plunked them on again. "I don't know exactly," she said, and sighed.

He pushed lank strands of brown from his face and laughed. "Yeah, right. You always have a reason for everything."

Why? Because she was so practical and reliable, like the Honda Civic Laura had once compared her to? Hey, just because she *drove* one didn't mean she *was* one.

Mac shrugged. "I guess I was feeling nostalgic, going through some of the letters from my mother," she said, picking at the splinter, not looking at him. "I guess I was just

273

missing her." *And missing you,* she wanted to say, but somehow couldn't. "Maybe I just needed to hang out for a while. I don't see you as much as I used to."

"Well, we're both busy with school and all, considering our load of AP courses, and I've got the chess club and computer club, and you've got all your deb stuff now." He hesitated, scratching his jaw. "Speaking of deb stuff, I heard there was some sort of dustup at your house last night." Grinning, he leaned over and poked her. "I heard you knocked Camie Lindell flat on her ass."

"Who told you that?" she said, lifting her head, realizing exactly what he was going to say the minute he uttered, "Cindy."

Cindy Chow. Mac pursed her lips, thinking, *Of course.*

"Did your girlfriend mention that Camie was trying to totally humiliate Laura by making references to that big lie someone posted on MySpace?"

She expected Alex to say, "She's not my girlfriend," but he didn't. Instead, he drew his legs up closer and rested his forearms on his thighs. "Yeah, I heard that, too," he said, and made a face. "Girls can be so vicious. Guys don't fight like that. If we want to have it out with another dude, we do it up front. We don't hide behind words."

"Guys are cavemen," Mac agreed, gnawing on the fleshy part of her palm to get the splinter out. "Girls tend to go for the knife in the back."

"Most girls, maybe," Alex said, sitting up straight. "But not you, Mac."

Mac wiped her hands on her jeans, suddenly wanting to change the subject. "Hey, remember the time we came up here with a bag of candy during Elliott's birthday party," she said, rushing on, "and your dad tied a piñata to the tree? None of the kids could hit the thing worth a darn, so we started tossing the candy down and they thought it was raining packs of Skittles?"

"That was hilarious." He grinned, nodding, and Mac's heart swelled.

"Or when you chased me around the backyard, acting like a zombie, and kept saying—"

"Braaaains," Alex piped up, and fell off the chair, raising his arms in front of him, as Mac watched, giggling and murmuring, "You're crazy!"

"Braaaains," he said again, inching toward her on his knees until he'd bumped right up against her chair and his hands grabbed her shoulders. He pulled her so close that their noses touched, and the lenses of their glasses were just a smidge away from bumping as well.

Mac stopped giggling and swallowed hard instead. He was near enough to kiss, and his eyes seemed to bore right into hers. Her pulse thumped like a drumbeat in her ears, pounding out: *Don't be afraid . . . reach for the stars,* until Mac blurted out, "Will you be my escort for the deb ball?"

Oh, man, where did that come from!

The next few seconds felt like slow motion as he stared at her, a look of pure amazement on his face. He drew back, rising from his knees and bumping his head on the roof of the tree house before he sat down again, looking straight at her.

He moved his mouth, but Mac's ears seemed not to hear him at first. All she could see was his frown, and the disappointment in his face.

She blinked at him, asking, "What?"

"I said, I'm sorry, Mac. I really wish I could." He ran a

hand through his shaggy hair. "But I already said I'd go with someone else."

Mac didn't even bother to ask who. She willed her heart to slow down, willed her chest to stop aching. How she wished she could fling herself from the tree house and fly home and pretend this had never happened!

She tried so hard to be nonchalant, and still her voice cracked as she told him, "I understand."

"I'll see you there though, huh?" Alex said. "We can at least dance or something, right?"

"Sure." She forced a smile despite how twisted she felt on the inside. She knew that if she stuck around another minute, she'd die of shame. Abruptly, she stood up, brushed off her jeans, and lied, "I've got to go. I promised my dad I'd help Honey cook dinner tonight after I finish my homework."

Alex didn't call her on it, though he knew she'd rather eat worms than cook *or* spend time with her stepmonster, much less do both at once. Yet he didn't wisecrack about needing a fire extinguisher to put out her pants.

Instead, he nodded, saying, "I've got stuff to do too."

Mac waited as he descended the slick wooden ladder ahead of her, which gave her a chance to pick the Spock-Kirk coin from her back pocket and leave it on one of the folding chairs. She'd e-mail him later and tell him where she'd left it. But she didn't want it anymore. Its luck definitely didn't seem to have rubbed off on her.

She managed to get down from the tree house without falling and making an even bigger fool of herself. She snatched her umbrella off the ground as she and Alex said their awkward goodbyes. Then she raced for home, unmindful of the rain that fogged her glasses, frizzed her hair, and soaked her clothes.

As she sidled between the bushes and sloshed through the wet grass to her own backyard, she wished she could scream and let it all out, thinking of Alex escorting Cindy Chow to the Rosebud Ball and of Laura possibly not being at the Ball at all if the GSC came down on her because of that nasty rumor.

Mac realized then and there that if she hadn't already assumed being a deb would suck, she knew it now for sure.

She'd never make the same mistake again:
she always made a new mistake instead.
—Wendy Cope

How can you know which risks are worth it
unless you take them?
—Ginger Fore

Sixteen

Ginger spent most of Thursday afternoon sitting at her desk in front of her Mac, where she'd been furiously checking on the MySpace page where the lie about Laura had spread like some obnoxious strain of the flu. She'd posted two comments defending Laura already and was about to post a third when Deena's new housekeeper, Soleil, called up the stairs, "Miss Ginger! There's someone here to see you!"

Maybe Soleil hadn't gotten explicit instructions from Deena, because Ginger technically wasn't supposed to have friends over while she was grounded. So it was a good thing that Deena wasn't home, wasn't it? Having a mother who pimped expensive real estate to her pals—and who actually *liked* to work even though she didn't have to, not with the Dupree family money and the combo of alimony and child support she was getting from Edward Fore—came in handy once in a while.

"Miss Ginger!"

"Coming!" she yelled back as she shut her laptop and sprang up from her chair. She didn't even bother to slip on a pair of shoes, figuring her "guest" had to either be Laura or

Mac, considering all the shit hitting the fan lately. She raced from her turreted room and down the winding stairs that took her past the first-floor landing and down to the cathedral-like foyer.

But as Ginger padded across the polished teak floor and into the living room where Soleil had been trained to deposit visitors, she caught sight of her "guest" well before she'd crossed the threshold to the living room. She came to a dead stop when she realized that it wasn't Laura or Mac at all.

It was Kent Wakefield.

He turned around that very moment, as if sensing the weight of her gaze upon him, and Ginger forced herself to walk toward him, feeling practically naked in shorts and bare feet. If only she'd taken half a second to slip on flip-flops or run a brush through her wild red hair. Too late for that.

"Hey," he said as she neared. He smiled hesitantly, gray eyes crinkling at the corners. He had his dark hair combed back from his clean-shaven face, and a simple white T-shirt hanging loose over a slim pair of black jeans, but kept his arms behind his back, like he was hiding something. "Did you get my message?"

"About starting over?" she asked, thinking of the text he'd sent her last night at curtsy practice, before all hell had broken loose.

"Yeah, that one."

"I got it." She rounded the large leather sofa and took a perch on a scrolled arm, pulling her knees up to her chest.

"So, are we okay?" he asked, walking over and drawing his hand from behind his back. In it, he held a plump bouquet of pink hyacinths wrapped in white paper. He presented them to her, and Ginger lifted them to her nose, inhaling their sweetness.

"Truce?"

"Hyacinth for forgiveness," she said, and he raised his eyebrows, looking surprised that she knew. "My father sent them to my mother a few times when he was cheating on her," she told him bluntly, not embarrassed at all by her family history, though it had taken a while—and a lot of tears—to get to that point. She slid off the scrolled arm and settled onto the sofa itself. "Do you want to sit down?"

He shook his head. "I can't stay long. I just wanted to be sure we were cool about the sixth grade . . . about the dress . . . everything. I really am sorry."

He rocked on his heels, hands jammed in his jeans pockets, looking honestly nervous, and Ginger smiled at him. "Yeah, I'm okay," she said, "about sixth grade and the dress. Everything. My grandmother seems convinced her laundress will have the gown good as new in no time, so maybe we can have a do-over on that first portrait session sometime soon."

"I'd like that."

Ginger surprised herself by telling him, "Me too."

Kent looked around then, at the well-appointed room with the unpainted beamed ceiling, the lead-glass windows, and mostly Arts and Crafts–period antiques. He pointed to an oil that Ginger particularly loved. It hung over the library table where her father used to spread out his paperwork before he'd moved out. "Franz Strahalm," he said, sounding suitably impressed. "He's a master of Southwest landscapes."

"My dad's taste in women might be considered questionable, but he always had great taste in art," Ginger remarked guilelessly, still clutching the hyacinth bouquet in her lap, and Kent's eyes glinted, like he wanted to laugh but wasn't sure it was appropriate.

"Mind if I look around?" he asked.

Ginger shrugged and curled her toes against the soft Persian rug as she smelled the flowers again and wondered what her mother would say if she walked in the door. Deena would probably have a seizure, seeing Ginger in the "parlor" entertaining a young man of whom she actually approved.

Ginger wasn't sure if that was a good thing or a bad thing. She followed Kent with her eyes as he moved about the room, thinking he was certainly taking his time for someone who'd professed he couldn't stay long.

He paused to study a modern-looking canvas filled with heavily brushstroked shapes and splashes of color and vibrant streaks of black.

"Very primitive, but cool," he remarked, tipping his head as he viewed the piece and squinted at the illegible signature in the right-hand corner. "I don't think I know the artist."

"Oh, but you do." Ginger suppressed a giggle as she set the bundle of hyacinths down on the sofa and padded over to stand beside him. She jerked her chin at the canvas.

"I painted that years ago, before someone convinced me my work looked like cat puke."

Kent glanced at her. "You painted that?"

"Guilty as charged."

He scratched his nose, and his neck flushed above his collar. "Hmm. Maybe you shouldn't have listened to the idiot who suggested you didn't have what it takes. He was probably just jealous of your, um, startling originality."

Ginger groaned.

"Too much?" he asked, squinting.

"You had me at the flowers." She wrinkled her freckled nose, and he laughed.

"Okay, okay, I won't overdo it. I said what I came to say, and I won't bother you any more." He glanced at the black-banded TAG Heuer on his wrist and tapped the square face. "I've got another appointment, like, in fifteen minutes. We'll set up a session soon, if that's all right with you? I'll speak to Mrs. Dupree and then give you a call."

"Sounds great," she said, walking him toward the foyer and to the front door.

She saw him out, watching as he dashed down the front steps through the rain. He gave her a quick wave before slipping into the sleek black Ford Explorer (a hybrid, she noticed, which scored even more points than the hyacinths).

His tires splashed through puddles as he drove away from the house, down the private drive toward Piney Point. Ginger stood on the wraparound porch for a while after, breathing in the fresh smell of the rain and running her fingers along the railing as she strolled around the side of the Castle. She felt something close to calm for the first time in days.

Until she caught her mother's raised voice as she rounded the bend toward where the six-car garage hulked, invisible from the front of the house. Ginger hadn't even heard the Jag pull in, but then, she'd been a little preoccupied with Kent.

". . . yes, yes, it's disgraceful if it's true, but no one knows yet if it is, Mother," Deena was yelling into her cell above the noise of the rain, as she carefully crossed the limestone courtyard toward the house, juggling briefcase, phone, and umbrella.

Ginger pressed up close to a columned post, straining to listen.

"Yes, I'm sure they'll deal with her if she's really pregnant. . . . No, of course, there's never been a Rosebud in that condition. . . . Yes, if it's confirmed, she'll be terminated. . . . Now let Bootsie handle it, please. . . . She's Ginger's friend. . . . For God's sake, don't get involved."

Deena didn't even look up as she headed straight for the back door, and probably couldn't have seen Ginger beyond the shield of her enormous umbrella anyhow. But it wouldn't have mattered. Ginger's sense of calm had quickly evaporated, and she ran back toward the front door, flying up the stairs and into her room.

No, no, no, no, no! she thought with every step she took, unsure of how her hopes of debuting with her two best friends could so quickly go up in smoke. The GSC couldn't terminate Laura over a pack of lies, they couldn't! It just felt so freaking wrong.

Out of breath and close to tears, she grabbed up her Razr and called Laura, letting it ring and ring until she got Laura's voice mail.

Damn!

"Call me as soon as you get this," she said frantically before she got up and paced back and forth across her room, her cell in hand, waiting.

Only my dogs will not betray me.
—Maria Callas

I'm not the kind of girl who plays possum.
I'm the kind who runs them over.
—Jo Lynn Bidwell

Seventeen

Jo Lynn was only vaguely aware of the crack of thunder that rattled the windows in Dillon's bedroom, hardly noticing how dark the room had gotten. She'd even lost track of how far along the minute hand of the clock had moved since she'd snuck upstairs after Big Ray had left her in the den with a Coke.

Her fingers kept tapping away on Dillon's keyboard. She was so determined to crack his password and get in. But she'd tried everything she could think of—names, birthdays, anniversaries—and nothing worked. She'd just about given up when she thought of their conversation during the barbecue on Monday, when Big Ray had compared Dillon to some old quarterback named "Broadway Joe," who, Dillon gushed, had passed for four thousand yards before anyone else.

She typed in BroadwayJoe4000, and Dillon's computer let her in.

Oh, God—she rubbed her hands together—*this is it!*

All she had to do was open up his e-mails, and she could see what he'd been up to when she hadn't been looking.

Then something distracted her, and it wasn't another loud rumble of thunder.

She heard music, Fergie's "Glamorous," sounding very muffled, and she realized her cell was going off in her purse.

She grabbed for her bag and popped it open, hauling out her iPhone to see the call was from Camie.

"*What?*" she growled, finally noting the time. She was surprised that Big Ray hadn't come looking for her yet.

"I swear to God, you're not going to believe this," Camie said as breathlessly as if she'd just run a marathon. "I followed Laura Bell to her house from school, and Avery was in her freaking driveway, waiting. They talked for a while before he took off and then she hauled ass over to the country club."

Camie stopped, gulping in a breath, and Jo Lynn urged her on, impatient, "Well, what's next, for Christ's sake?"

"I'm sorry, Jo, but you were right. I saw her with Dillon. She went over to his 'Stang and beat on the window, looking really upset. He got out instantly. I think he was alone in the car, but I can't swear to it. You know how hard it is to see through his tinted windows."

Jo Lynn leaned an elbow on the desk, suddenly light-headed. "What did they do?" she pressed.

"They stood there in the rain, and he . . . he held her hand, like, squeezed it for a minute, before she took off and he got back in his car."

"You're making that up!" Jo snapped, and anger spread through her veins, swelling against her chest until she thought she'd explode.

"I'm not, I swear!" Camie whimpered. "Looks like you were right, Jo. That supersized slut is playing both of us for fools. You think Avery and Dillon both heard the gossip about Laura and freaked out, each of 'em figuring maybe he could be the baby daddy?"

Jo Lynn didn't even comment on that. She couldn't. It was too gut-wrenching to even consider. "Where are you now?" she asked instead.

"I'm driving home. I didn't know what else you wanted me to do."

"Nothing," Jo Lynn told her. Not a damned thing. "You've done enough."

Before Camie had even said goodbye, Jo hung up, gripping her cell so tightly her knuckles blanched. She got up and walked across the room, dropping down on Dillon's bed and doubling over. The idea of Laura with Dillon made her want to puke her guts out.

OhGodohGodohGod! This can't be happening.

She put her head between her knees and rocked herself, this close to hyperventilating.

Was Dillon really cheating on her with the Hostess Cupcake? Had he been lying to Jo all along, covering up his tracks? Had Laura slept with Jo's ex *and* her current man just to strike back? Shit, if that was the case, it was a million times worse than anything Jo Lynn had ever imagined, more horrible than finding Laura's number in Dillon's cell or even her nightmare about Dillon escorting Laura to the Ball.

The fat bitch had obviously gone completely out of control, and it would take more than chocolates and rumors to stop her. It would take something huge and heartbreaking and more destructive than anything Jo Lynn had ever dreamed up.

"Jo Lynn? Where've you gone to, sweetheart?"

Jo's head snapped up at the sound of Big Ray's voice on the other side of the bedroom door. She quickly grabbed her purse, stuffing her cell inside, and then she shut down Dillon's computer, hoping everything was as she'd found it.

Quietly, she popped open the bedroom door and peered out. The coast seemed clear, so she scurried toward the stairwell, glancing over the railing to see Big Ray heading toward the kitchen.

She was just about to slip down the stairs when the front door came open, and she saw Dillon walk in, shaking rain from his hair. Jo backed up the stairs as Big Ray yelled, "Is that you, boy? Did ya see Jo's car out front? If she didn't leave while I was taking a call from Tokyo, she's around here somewhere."

Well, hell. All she needed was for Dillon to find out she'd crept up to his room to snoop without Big Ray even knowing it. She'd rather flee now and answer questions later. *Much* later. She had to take care of Laura Bell first.

So she ran back into Dillon's bedroom, shut the door, and raced over to the sliding glass doors on his balcony. She let herself out, the mist from the drizzle surrounding her as she clutched her bag in one hand and gripped the wrought-iron railing with the other, carefully stepping down the tightly spiraled stairs leading to the back patio.

The rain pelted her, dripping in her face and soaking her shirt to her skin. When she finally got to the bottom, she paused only long enough to push the wet strands of hair from her eyes before she ran like hell around the huge mansion, letting herself out the gate, slipping and sliding on the slick stone path that cut through the royal palms and led right to her car.

She got the Audi rolling as fast as she could, her fingers trembling when she finally dared to pull over beside the ditch off Bunker Hill once she'd completely cleared Dillon's street.

Then she scrambled for her cell phone, speed-dialing Avery Dorman's number, counting every second as she waited for him to pick up, her breathing fast and angry. As soon as she heard his familiar, "Yo," she started in on him, talking so fast he couldn't do much else but listen.

"I've had all I can take of that nasty Laura Bell getting into my business, and it's time you helped me put an end to her sticking her face where it doesn't belong! I have some plans for you and Ms. Humpty Dumpty that'll set her up for a bigger fall than even she can bounce back from."

Dripping rain onto her leather seat, her teeth starting to chatter, she sucked in a breath and rushed on, "And if you don't play it out my way, I *will* tell on you, Avery. I'll tell your parents *everything* that went down between us. Your daddy's so strict and straight that just one word from me and he'll be shipping your ass off to some military school so far away from the football field that every dream you've ever had will go down in flames."

Jo stopped long enough for her heart to slow down, expecting Avery to say something, *anything*. When he didn't, she barked, her hand shaking, "So which is it, huh? Are we on? Or is she worth your risking everything?"

Avery sighed, and Jo Lynn waited for his answer.

ACKNOWLEDGMENTS

Since I was under deadline for this book while planning my wedding, it's amazing that everything fell into place as beautifully as it did! For that, I have to thank Claudia Gabel, my incredibly insightful editor, who pushes me to make every scene as powerful as possible. Also, kudos to Christina Hogrebe and Andrea Cirillo, who put up with my insanity and make every challenge even more fun. My gratitude to all the teen girls I've spoken with and e-mailed with in the past year, who aren't afraid to share pieces of their lives with me so I can get things right. And finally, to my mom (love you!), for all the freedom allowed me in my teen years. It sure makes for a lot of story ideas now!

THE DEBS:
GLOVES OFF

"How completely humiliating!" Laura Delacroix Bell declared as she flushed the toilet, then carefully deposited the plastic dipstick onto a Kleenex spread on the edge of the marbled sink. "I will get Jo Lynn Bidwell for this one day, I swear." She hoped her overly attentive mother, Tincy—currently standing guard outside the door—could hear her every word.

Laura washed her hands and stared at her reflection in the mirror, noting the frustration in her pale eyes and the twin spots of pink on her cheeks.

Did every Rosebud at the first Monday-night meeting in October notice me leaving promptly afterward, escorted out by Bootsie Bidwell and Tincy, like a pair of pearl-wearing pit bulls?

As she'd walked between them, the nasty comments from MySpace had flashed inside her head: Did U hear LB is preggers? OMG, what a skank!

Red-hot anger pulsed through her blood all over again, just as it had the day she'd learned that someone—and she had a good idea who that someone was—had torn her reputation to shreds.

Breathe, she told herself, and closed her eyes momentarily, envisioning herself in her white Vera Wang ball gown, dancing in the arms of her hunky escort—oh, let's say, the love of her life, Avery Dorman—during the deb ball next spring. Within seconds, her frantic heartbeat had slowed, and she reached for the pretty folded linen towels that lay in a basket by the sink, snatching one to dry her hands.

With a sigh, she dropped the crumpled towel and pushed her wheat-blond hair behind her ears, glancing one more time at the minus sign clear as day on the dipstick's belly. When Bootsie Bidwell had initially insisted she take measures to exonerate herself, Laura might've been a little worried; but she had no such uncertainty now. She hadn't even been with her on-again-off-again flame Avery Dorman since mid-August, and it was early October. Maybe Jo Lynn's desperate attempts to keep Laura and Avery apart had really done Laura a favor this time around.

"Take that, Jo-L. I win this round," she said to the mirror, flipping her hair over her shoulder, a fleeting smile touching her lips.

Sticks and stones can break my bones, but names can never hurt me.

What a crock of BS, she thought, swallowing the nasty taste that settled in her mouth.

Names do hurt, and that's the truth, Laura decided, having had epithets slung at her for most of her life, seeing as how her body had never been shaped like a toothpick. The girls she'd grown up with—and most of their mothers—lived by the credo "You can never be too rich or too thin." Well, Laura was plenty rich, thanks to dear old Daddy Harrington Bell, the International King of Porcelain Thrones and Bidets, but she'd *never* been too thin. And she never would be.

Still, she'd been unprepared for the slurs flung at her when the rumor that she'd been sperminated had taken off just after school started. That lie had nearly cost her a spot on the Glass Slipper Club's debutante list alongside her BFFs, Mac Mackenzie and Ginger Fore, and had turned poor Tincy Bell into a groveling mess. Her mother had begged Bootsie and the GSC selection committee to give Laura a chance to prove herself. So they had, and so had she.

This second pregnancy test surely was all the proof they'd need, right? Once they got a look at the latest evidence of her innocence, they'd have to let her off deb probation, wouldn't they?

Laura shook off a fleeting anxiety attack, assuring herself, *They had better.* How could they make her suffer any more than she already had, when she'd done everything to disprove the spiteful gossip? Though she knew the GSC could do whatever it wanted to do. The women who ran it made the rules, and they could change them at will.